THE MARINE

Heroes & Warriors: A Heroes Novel
Volume 1

"Like I'm Gonna Lose You"

By Emily Gray

THE MARINE

Second edition. May 10, 2017.

Copyright © 2017 Emily Gray.

ISBN 978-0-9988684-1-7

Published by Fantastic Optimism Publishing
2017

Cover Design courtesy of Karlie Hyder
karliehyder.wordpress.com

Cover image © 123rf.com

Dedication

For my mom

Thanks for thinking my 8th grade English teacher was a putz.

The Marine

What do you do when everything you've ever known has been taken from you? Family, career, purpose.

Levi Taylor has no family waiting for him after his discharge. He is a broken Marine without a job or direction. The home that has always brought him comfort is the last place he wants to be....until he meets her, a reclusive woman new to his small town.

What do you do when everything you thought you knew is an illusion? Life, love, trust.

Lynn Carter's life is a lie, both the past and the present. She is on her own, just trying to blend in and remain unknown. She discovers it's a difficult task when she becomes the focus of a determined Marine. But can she learn to trust him when everyone she's ever known has deceived her?

When their lives force them to face their pasts and fears, they must decide whether to run and hide or listen to their hearts and fight for the one thing that matters above all else, each other.

Table of Contents

The Marine

1

Him

"Dude, I don't know why I have to wait on you all the time! You take fuckin' forever. You're worse than a woman, D." I razz my friend just as I've done for the last ten years.

"Bite me! And stop your whining, Levi. My job takes patience and finesse. I got skills," he says with a wink.

I snort with laughter. I can't help it. My best friend, Dylan Reed, is so full of himself. But, I have to admit he is correct. His job as Communications Specialist does take finesse and definite skills. He has them, I don't, not that particular kind anyway. I have the muscle. That's why we make a great team. He's the brains. I'm the brawn.

Hating to give him any more reasons to boast, I agree, reluctantly, "Yeah, guess I can't argue with that. But, hurry the hell up, I'm starvin'. And at this rate, Mess will be cleaned out before we even get back."

"I'm almost done," he yells over his shoulder. "I just have to check all the connections to make sure that wicked sand storm we had didn't knock anything else loose on this dish. And, seriously, when aren't you hungry?"

"Hey, I gotta keep up my figure," I boast.

Now, it's his turn to snort in response. "You have no figure. You're just a fucking brick wall."

"Damn straight, and that's how I protect your scrawny ass."

His only response is his favorite finger waved in my direction. Dylan is anything aside from scrawny. Standing at six foot two inches, he's within an inch of my height. But, where he's leaner, tipping the scale at just over two hundred, I've got about forty pounds on him. So, yeah, I'm pretty much a brick wall.

I start gathering up our gear to head back to the MRAP Cougar. I'm ready to get the hell out of, well, hell. Dylan and I have been on this tour for almost a year and I am way past done with the desert. I might be a career solider, but I've spent most of the last ten years in hot, sweltering, disgusting places. I'd like to see some green again. Maybe I just need to take some leave to somewhere relaxing before my next assignment. Home would be the perfect place, but that thought brings an ache to my chest I'd rather ignore. The only positive to my current mission is the company I have with me. Being able to irritate Dylan on a daily basis makes anything tolerable.

I toss everything into the beast that protects us and climb into the driver's seat. "Come on, slow ass!" I bellow over the roar of the engine.

"I'm comin'. Don't get your panties in a wad, princess!" Dylan says. His humor and clear, Southern drawl lace through the words. He stops at the driver's door. "Hey, why the hell are you driving? I'm scheduled today."

Putting some authority in my voice, I say, "Because, asshole, I'd like to get us back to the base on time. I'd rather not get stuck with extra PT for the next month. Besides, the driver's seat was empty. That makes it fair game and my driving's better than yours. Now, get in!"

He smirks, hefting himself in the other seat. "You keep tellin' yourself that, Levi. We both know I'm better at everything."

"You keep thinkin' that buddy. I'm still in charge though." I counter with a glint in my eye. I'm a higher rank than Dylan and I tend to rub it in if given the opportunity, not that it really matters to either of us. Oh, he follows the rules and chain of command, but most of the time, I'm just me to him. He follows my orders and respects my position. I've earned it after all, putting in the extra work to help ensure promotion. But, he also never wanted to be in charge. Another reason we work together so well. He's best left to tinker with his "toys", as he calls them, and is better at it than anyone I know.

Dylan is a pain in my ass. He's the brother I never had. We've been almost inseparable since basic training. He aggravates the shit out of me and has for the last ten years, but I wouldn't have it any other way.

Heading back to our base, we're both ready to call it quits for the day. We're in serious need of showers from being dressed in fatigues and riding through the scorching heat. The desert sun has been especially bright and hot for October. Our patrol has been uneventful, just the way we prefer, although long and stressful like they always are. I can't wait to get back for time to simply relax, or better yet, for this particular tour to be finished. Dylan must be reading my thoughts again because he asks, "You ready to be done with this one?"

Not bothering the deny it, I reply, "Yeah. I need some time to regroup, I think."

"Huh, thought you might be lookin' to get out. We've been in forever, ya know. Maybe it's time to do something else."

Dylan knows where I stand on this particular subject. This is not the first time we've had the conversation. Being a Marine is the only thing I ever wanted to do. I wasn't interested in going through a regular college program. I'm smart, but don't care much for being stuck in a classroom with a book forced into my face. Starting with my earliest memories, I can remember using my hands, building, moving, rearranging. I like to learn by doing rather than sitting. I also like to have a purpose. The military has given me those things. It suits me.

I admit what he already knows. "That's just it, D. I don't know how to do anything else. This is me, who I am. I'm a solider. It's what I've always wanted to do. And, now, it's the only thing I have left."

Understanding crosses his face. "Yeah, I get that."

We settle into a comfortable silence for a while, each with our own thoughts.

The moment I open my mouth to ask Dylan about his plans, our entire world turns into chaos. Suddenly, I feel weightless, and then we're falling. Everything is in slow motion. Sound is erupting from everywhere, a blast, metal tearing apart, and screams, whose I'm not quite sure. We are being tossed through the air like a pinball. There is smoke burning my eyes and a searing, ripping pain in my left leg.

At the same time that our vehicle stops rolling and lands on the passenger's side, everything around me is almost silent. I can only hear a constant ringing. Thankfully, I am still conscious. I look over to find Dylan laying against his door with his head lulled to the side, his eyes shut, his window cracked. I see blood pooling on the glass beneath his head. He is as still as a stone.

"D!!!" I scream, although all I hear is a muffle. I scream his name until my throat is raw. Seeing him there, unresponsive, is my worst nightmare. He is one of the few people I have left in this world.

Time seems to have stopped. I realize I have to get us out of the Cougar, but I'm not in the best position at the moment. I'm kind of hanging in midair. If it weren't for the straps holding me into my seat, I'd have fallen directly on top of Dylan, crushing him. I have no idea how long we've been here or how long we will remain. I try to move my legs, sending agonizing pain shooting through me. Black dots pepper my vision. My left leg is pinned and impossible to maneuver, increasing my panic. I'm a trained solider, but right now, I'm thinking like a brother, one whose whole life is falling apart in front of him. The one thing I do know for certain is we can't stay here like sitting ducks.

I use both my hands to try pulling my leg free and feel tearing along the outside of my knee. The pain I felt before was nothing compared to what it is now. I'm nauseated and my vision is blurry. I can feel myself begin to flow in and out of consciousness. It's pulling at me. I look at Dylan again, noticing the steady rise and fall of his chest, or maybe it's just my mind showing me what I want to see before I have to let go. I tell myself that at least he's breathing.

With the smell of burning fumes still in my nose and a numbness settling in my lower body, I feel myself start to slip away. Before everything goes completely black, I hear the distant sound of heavy metal blades cutting through the air.

2

Eight months later

Him

Coming home always felt the same. It was something I would look forward to every time I returned. I knew exactly what to expect when I rolled into my dusty, country town of Sugar, Kentucky. Nothing changes here, not the atmosphere or the people. The warmth and familiarity would embrace me as soon as I drove into the town limits. I welcomed the small town air. It was crisp and clean. I would breathe deeply, savoring the smell of wildflowers and fresh cut hay. I would remember how good it was to be home and smile.

Smiling now is difficult. My love of this town was irrevocably altered four years ago, which is the last time I traveled these streets. In this moment, I'm not sure I can handle passing through, much less staying for good this time. The reason for my return is definitely less than ideal and a consequence of my own fuck up, which is putting it mildly. Honorably discharged from the Marine Corp, I am a man without a purpose. Everything I learned came from wearing the uniform. A decade of service brought pride and accomplishment. The man I am is the result of being a Marine. Now, it's gone and I have no one to blame except myself.

To make matters worse, I don't know how I'll deal with being where I spent my entire pre-adult life even though I really have no other place to go. The weight of remembering every joyous childhood event is too heavy of a burden. There will be too many questions, looks of sympathy, or worse, just blank stares because no one really knows what to say. I feel like I can't breathe, like I'm suffocating from all the sadness and pain, and

6

anger on top of it, from ultimately feeling like I've been tossed aside. Being in this town surrounded with happy memories might be the hardest place to be, especially knowing that nothing will ever be the same.

I was supposed to come home to sentiments like "Job well done, son!", firm handshakes filled with respect, and gratitude for my service. Instead, it will be words of condolences, pats on the back and hugs radiating sorrow, and tears because my return is purely circumstantial. One event eight months ago has cost me everything I've worked for and left me adrift. I wish I could say I don't remember anything, but I do, every horrible moment. And the aftereffects are even more devastating. I'm an injured Marine without a job, a post to protect, or an objective. And worse yet, I have to come home to no family.

I might be able to figure out how to handle the accident, its aftermath, and my discharge if I knew there was someone waiting for me when I return home. My mother would comfort me and help me put myself back together. My father would put me to work to distract me and let me figure out a new path. Neither would pity me nor accept me feeling sorry for myself. However, they both would allow me the time I needed to adjust, giving me unconditional love and support. But, none of that is possible now because I'm all alone. Everything else is just a memory.

Four years ago, life as I knew it imploded and the wound is still too raw. The two people I loved most in the world are gone, stolen from me in the blink of an eye. All because some drunk jackass was too stupid to stop himself from getting behind the wheel of a car. He survived, of course. My parents did not.

My parents were the example for how relationships are imagined to be. They were everything to each other. They *were* the fairy tale. Friendship, passion, and love rolled altogether. A lot of people think that type of love doesn't exist, but it does. I've witnessed it although I don't imagine I'll ever find it because most people don't. I'm smart enough to know that what my parents had isn't common. It's like trying to find a grenade pin in a barrel of key rings. They were lucky enough to have found it with each other and even luckier that neither had to live without it. That knowledge is the only saving grace that I can find in the whole situation. Neither of my parents had to live one day without the other. I don't think either of them would have survived if they had to try. And now, I'm wondering how I am supposed to make it without them both.

Making my way through town in the light of early morning, the streets are almost bare. Most people will be up by now, but haven't made it into town yet. There is too much work to be done first. Rural living keeps a tight schedule. The steady bustle of Main Street won't happen for a few more hours. I'm relieved I can make my way to the homestead without being noticed. I'm not ready to face the sea of sympathy, no matter how well-intentioned. And the thought of a possible hero's welcome the townsfolk might give me is even less appealing. I am no hero. Heroes are supposed to come home in one piece, whole and larger than life. They don't come home battered, bruised, and missing parts of themselves, especially parts from the inside where they can't be seen. They aren't carrying ten tons of guilt from decisions they can't change. They haven't been told they have to give up the only purpose they've ever known. They are revered. They aren't given a heartfelt

8

'thank you for your service', a quick pat on the back, and sent on their way. They aren't me.

I travel the short distance from the highway, making the few turns, and drive toward my childhood home. Even though the quaint, country Cape Cod stands empty, it's always been inviting. I have always loved this house with its wide wrap-around porch and swing, stone walkway, large windows, and soft, yellow siding. The sight of it brings me some comfort, but a deep ache of despair also burns in my chest. Comfort is exactly what I need now even though there is no one waiting inside to offer it anymore.

I pull into the drive, parking in front of the detached garage and workshop, the place my father loved best besides my mother's kitchen table. I gingerly hop out of my beloved new truck, my one frivolous purchase upon returning to civilian life, and stretch out my aching left leg. Even though I've had a full knee replacement, I still have aches and stiffness because I'm stubborn and only stayed for the minimum required amount of rehabilitation.

Grabbing the duffel bag that contains all of my possessions from the last eleven years, I start up the front steps. I find the entry key hiding in the decorative mailbox where it's been kept for longer than I've been alive. Unlocking the door, a sad smile tugs at my lips as I turn the knob, walking into a flood of memories.

The scene inside the house is just as I left it on my last visit four years earlier. A sucker punch of emotion hits me square in the chest, sadness, grief, and guilt, as I remember laying my parents to rest. At least, I can take comfort in knowing that they are together the way I always remember them being. I just wish I wasn't the one left behind. I roll my shoulders and try to tamp down the melancholy, locking it away. I'm tired of feeling it. It's easier to push it down. And besides, my mother wouldn't want me to wallow. She'd want me to move forward, think of good times, and find my own life. How the hell that's supposed to happen now, I have no idea.

I look around the familiar space. This house was my father's pride and joy. He took great care in making it beautiful and full of warmth for my mother and me. He labored for endless hours and weekends restoring it and then keeping it in pristine shape. The knotty pine floors glow golden from the sunlight and the stone fireplace offers coziness even without being lit. The crown molding gives a feeling of sophistication without seeming out of place in the simple country home. Pine banisters held by twisted wrought iron spokes follow the staircase and are worn smooth from decades of use.

I stand in the living room, taking notice of the furniture covered in sheets awaiting my return. The air in the house is thick, stale, and slightly musty at first, but while I move around the room, I start to smell the familiar lemon cleaner my mother always used. Even though it's been years, the aroma still lingers. There is also a hint of cinnamon though where the smell comes from I have never known. I wouldn't have put it past my mother to hide potpourri in the air vents. One of the many harmless secrets that I'm sure she had.

I drop my duffel bag at the bottom of the stairs, turning my attention to completing the task at hand. There's no better time than the present to start making the house livable, since I'll probably be here for a while, at least until I decide what to do with the place. I push the curtains aside and open the large windows, allowing the sunlight to stream into the space. Then, I move around the room, removing the old, dust coated sheets

10

from the furniture. As the rays brighten the house, a soft spring breeze makes the dust motes dance in the air. Part of me already feels lighter just being in this place, a feeling I didn't expect, but remembering also brings a constant heartache. I remain torn about staying here indefinitely. It might just be too difficult. But, the thought of selling it is almost as crushing as that of living here with the memories.

3

Him

It takes me the better part of the morning to open up the house and get the few rooms I'll initially need usable. My stomach finally reminds me that I've only had a large cup of coffee and a bear claw all day. My appetite isn't what it used to be. Unfortunately, I don't even have to rummage in the kitchen to know there's nothing here to eat. The house has been empty for four years. It is completely devoid of food. I decide I'm at a good stopping point and will have to wander into town for provisions to last the next few days while I make some resolutions.

The prospect of letting everyone know I'm home isn't thrilling. I've known most of the people here my entire life and while I love them dearly, I was hoping for a few days of solitude to prepare myself before being seen. I also wish I could avoid all the apologies about my parents, the questions about my accident and resulting discharge, and especially about my nonexistent plans for the future. I guess I'll have no such luck. More than likely, once I'm seen on the streets of town by one person, everyone will know I'm home. Word passes quickly in a small town. The upside to small town living though is having a refrigerator full of every known casserole and dessert within the next seventy- two hours.

Whether or not there is something to eat won't be a worry. I just wonder if my appetite will return. At least now I can be sure my grocery list will only have to consist of the basic necessities. Realizing my list is minimal lets me make the decision to walk instead of driving the truck, even though my leg could probably use a rest. I was warned to not overdo it since I am still technically in the recovery stage of my knee replacement. But, walking will also help me ease into town and hopefully avoid the possible stampede from the biddies that might occur once my presence is known.

The mile walk to the market is just what I needed after my chores. It clears my mind and eases my heart. The bright sun and clean air rejuvenates me in a way I have long forgotten. The walk has increased my appetite from slight to ravenous, a feeling I haven't had in more than eight months. I realize with a slight chuckle this might not be the best condition to be in when entering a grocery market. I'll likely end up with more than just the necessities I was planning.

I make my way to Miss Sarah's Market, surprisingly still without seeing much activity around town. Of course, it is a weekday and not quite lunchtime yet. Most people are working, either in Rapid City or on their farms, whether big or small. It is Kentucky after all. Farming around here is practically a religion. A person certainly has to dedicate mind, body, and soul to it and do a lot of praying.

Standing in front of the market, I am again flooded with memories. I remember so many things. The feel of sweet, sticky juice running down my chin from the berries displayed for sale; running into the store for my annual Fourth of July rocket popsicle; and the vibrant autumn colors of potted chrysanthemums highlighting the front windows for the Halloween and Thanksgiving seasons. The country market with fresh produce bins running along the entire length of the store is just as it's always been. And Miss Sarah, the sole proprietor, is no doubt inside keeping everything running like a well-oiled machine despite being in her

13

early seventies. She could without question make my previous Sergeant Major quiver, but she has a heart of gold and a soft spot for me.

Smiling to myself, I slip in the door and hear the tinkling bell that announces my arrival. From somewhere near the back, I hear Miss Sarah's voice, sweet and clear, "Welcome to the market. Always a pleasure to have you!"

I quietly search through the aisles and find her taking inventory of the canned goods, glasses slipping down her nose, and a pen tucked behind her ear, engrossed in her spreadsheets. She still does everything by paper and pencil rather than electronically. She avoids technology whenever possible. Both she and the town are forever stuck in the dark ages.

I am suddenly feeling nostalgic, remembering all the times as a child I would jump out and try to scare Miss Sarah I know that I shouldn't provoke her, but can't seem to help myself. I've been away too long and have missed her spunk, even if I'm likely to get an earful if I do scare her. It'll be like old times.

Using my military training along with my ingrained talent for stealth, I sneak up just inches behind her. I take a deep breath and bellow, "Always happy to be seen!"

With reflexes that should belong to someone decades younger than her, Miss Sarah screams, leaping from the stool she's been sitting on and nearly topples over the half dozen boxes of cans she's counting. I am laughing so hard my side aches. I've had to bend over at the waist, clutching my stomach to catch my breath. There are tears streaming down my face. I haven't laughed like this in forever. It feels good.

Once I've regained some control of myself, I peek up to find her scowling at me.

"Levi Taylor! Why you! I ought to bend you over my knee for that! Holy hell! You could have given me a heart attack!"

I snicker and say with a wink, "Not likely, Miss Sarah! You'll out live us all."

Tsking, she replies, "Well, now, you're probably right about that," Her eyes soften and a smile that transforms her graces her face. "Now, since I seem to still be in one piece, don't just stand there. Come give me a hug, young man!"

Feeling a wealth of love for this woman who's been like a second mother to me, I somewhat shyly make my way over to her and stoop to embrace her tightly. She is so slight at not even five feet in height compared to my six foot three inch frame. But I still have no illusions that she couldn't put me over her knee if that was her goal.

I scoop her up and swing her around, loving the little squeal she lets out. She is always so fun and boisterous. It rubs off on whoever is near including me. She can always seem to turn me into an eight year old kid again, looking for the fun in everything. A talent I am certainly in sore need of these days.

As I'm putting her to her feet again, from around the corner of the shelves, I hear hurried words along with scurrying feet and labored breathing.

"Miss Sarah, Miss Sarah!! Are you alright?"

Once I'm sure that Miss Sarah is safely on both feet, I turn and look into the widest hazel eyes I've ever seen. There stands a girl not much bigger than Miss Sarah herself, looking at me with wariness, but also a bit of defiance. That defiance, and the baseball bat in her hands, has me standing up to my full height. I take

15

complete notice of her as my breath catches and my heart rate picks up. I certainly don't fear the bat. I must have a hundred pounds on the girl, and probably more. But, something about her makes me pay attention and keep her in the center of my vision. She is certainly not from around here and the town is not known to have a lot of transplants.

"Oh, my sweet girl. Yes, Lynn, I'm fine," Miss Sarah says on a laugh. "Levi here was just trying to take a few years off my life!"

"Hardly," I counter, never taking my eyes off the girl. "More like keeping you young."

The girl's mouth turns farther down into a frown as she glances between Miss Sarah and me. It's obvious this girl is more than a casual acquaintance to Miss Sarah though she seems out of place in the country store despite her outward appearance. Miss Sarah notices her demeanor instantly and walks over to her, patting her gently on the shoulder, reassuring her. I can see the girl stiffen from the touch and wonder why. I know Miss Sarah to be one of the most loving people to exist. The reaction brings questions to the back of my mind about who she is and why she's here, but more importantly what circumstances she came from that warrant her reaction.

Soothing her gently as if she were a frightened mare, Miss Sarah whispers, "Honestly, Lynn, I'm okay. Levi would never hurt me. I've known him since he was a baby."

Hesitantly after giving me the evil eye again, she says, "Okay, Miss Sarah, if you say so."

The girl, Lynn, doesn't look entirely convinced, but chooses to drop the issue. With one final glare in my direction, she turns on her heel, shoulders square, and walks back around the shelves to the front of the store. The moment she leaves I let out the breath I didn't realize I had been holding and relax my posture. What the heck is that about? It's like I was waiting for her to turn into a tornado and couldn't move from the path of destruction. Apparently, my reaction to the girl doesn't escape the eagle eyes of Miss Sarah. And of course, I'm not surprised. I never could get anything over on her.

"You looked a little shell shocked, my boy." Her gray eyes twinkling as she returns to her stool. Miss Sarah has always been able to see too much.

I grunt.

"Who was that?" I try to ask casually. She snickers at my question.

"That is Lynn Carter. A sweet girl I've hired to help me out. Since it's only spring, I don't have the pick of all the kids home from college and I needed at bit of help around here. She almost literally fell on my doorstep."

That statement immediately has my protective instincts perking up. I will not allow anything to happen to Miss Sarah.

"Oh really? And what exactly do you know about her?" My tone is laced with suspicion.

Clicking her tongue, she turns to me, "Now Levi, don't go getting all bearish on that girl. She's been just wonderful to have around here. She's kind of quiet and does keep to herself. She's staying in the apartment above the store. I have a feeling she's been through a lot. I haven't quite figured her story out yet, but she hasn't given me any reason to question her intentions."

"Sounds to me like she's definitely got a story then and probably not a good one." I mumble to myself, but belatedly remember Miss Sarah has hearing equivalent to an owl.

She rises from her stool with her mouth set in a firm, thin line. I can tell by her determined expression I am about to get a rare, but sound scolding. Using her slender finger, she pokes me in the center of my chest.

With a viper's tongue, Miss Sarah commands, "Look here, Mr. Taylor. You leave that girl alone. She's here for a reason, and while I may not know what that reason is, I can assure you it's a good one. I get the feeling something has her scared, and really badly too. So, if I can provide her with a little bit of security and keep her from feeling alone, then you will most certainly butt out of my business. Do you understand me?"

Grandly admonished and feeling like I'm five years old again, I hang my head. "Yes, ma'am."

More gently, she adds, "Now, I know you mean well, and I love you for it. But, my instincts have never been wrong before when it comes to lost souls. And I can tell you, she most certainly is that."

Feeling slightly guilty at possibly overreacting, I say, "I'm sorry, Miss Sarah. I just can't help wanting to look out for you."

"I know Levi, and your parents would be proud of you for that as am I. All we have is each other anymore." Stepping closer to me, she reaches up, pulling me down to her and kisses my cheek. I inhale her familiar scent of apples and mint. I sigh, ignoring the heaviness in my gut, and try to let go of my worry, knowing she's right. Her instincts are never wrong, not when it comes to how people are, but I know I'll still be on my guard with Lynn until I find out more about her. I cannot let anything happen to this woman. I would be lost without her, possibly more so than without my parents.

Right at that moment, my stomach rumbles loudly, breaking the tension of the situation. We both laugh, our tiff forgotten. Smiling broadly, Miss Sarah takes her best mother hen tone with me.

"Ah, now I know why you came here. Not to see me, but to stock the house, I presume?"

I grin sheepishly. Miss Sarah is rather familiar with how much food I eat or rather what I used to be known to eat.

"Yes, ma'am. Just need a few things though. I figure once I leave here, you'll let Miss Dottie know that I'm home. You two will have me swimming in food by tomorrow."

Laughing as she settles once again on her stool, she says, "Yes, well, that's true enough. All right then, off you go and gather what you need. I've got work to get back to."

I lean down and brush a kiss on her forehead before turning to walk down the aisle.

"Oh, and Levi?" she calls to me.

"Yes, Miss Sarah?"

"Don't forget to take one of the strawberry rhubarb pies that are up front at the register. Dottie brought them in yesterday." Then, looking at me pointedly, she adds, "And mind your manners with Lynn. Please."

Thinking for a moment, I can feel my brows draw together with wariness, but then, I smooth my expression before looking her in the eye.

"Yes, ma'am. I will, on both counts."

She holds my eyes with hers for a moment, then just nods, satisfied she's made her point and turns back to her clipboard and cans, leaving me to find the things I need.

4

Her

I am an idiot of epic proportions. I cannot believe that I just ran, head first into a situation I knew nothing about without even thinking about the consequences. Over the last three months, I've managed to stay hidden. My life has depended on it. But I know better than to think I'm safe. My fight or flight response is constantly working, and mostly set in the flee-very-fast position. So, the fact that I ran straight toward the danger, when I heard Miss Sarah's scream, is more than a little surprising. The reaction is so contradictory to my recent need for self- preservation. Thinking she was in danger, I couldn't help running to her when all of my fighting instincts came to life. I wasn't going to let anything happen to the sweetest and most generous woman I have ever met, even if I hadn't known her that long.

After hearing her scream, I rounded the end of the aisle and almost literally ran into a wall of man. I knew immediately from the scene in front of me that Miss Sarah wasn't in any danger. But, I instantly became aware that I might be for an entirely different reason. The man in front of me was well over six feet with shoulders the width of the Grand Canyon. A tan t-shirt stretched across rippled muscle and dark jeans hung low on narrow hips, molding to one of the most delectable sights a woman can witness. I was certain I had never seen such a specimen of male perfection and this was with his clothes still on. I couldn't begin to imagine the fantasy that lay underneath.

In what seemed like slow motion, he turned to face me and I was completely hypnotized. The moment his crystal blue eyes hit mine, I felt all the breath leave my lungs. Dark blonde hair topped a face carrying chiseled features, high cheekbones, a strong jaw, and a Nordic nose. The angles of his face were sharp, but softened by full lips and long lashes. His hair was longer on top than a normal military cut, but it was obvious the style had been his norm for quite some time. He radiated raw power from every pore. If this man was the example of what the military had to offer, every young adult male would line up around the block to join just to be like him. And every woman under age forty, or maybe even fifty, would be begging to find a man in uniform to take her home.

The tension in the air crackled between us. I knew I was no match for this man even with the well-loved aluminum bat dangling from my fingers. But slight as I was, there was no way I was backing down until I was sure Miss Sarah was completely safe. I stood there board stiff as tall as I could, which was laughable when compared to the behemoth in front of me. I doubted I looked like anything more than a gnat. Gnats, however, are annoying and I could be just that if I wanted to be.

Slowly, noises started to filter back into my ears. I realized Miss Sarah was talking gently, reassuring me that this man, Levi I thought I heard her say, was no danger to her. I found my eyes ping ponging between the two as they affectionately teased each other. The man's disposition was tender and kind with her, but seemed frosty at best when he turned an icy scowl toward me. I realized I'd been staring at him, again, because Miss Sarah was standing directly in front of me, patting my shoulder and I didn't remember her moving in my direction. I had to will myself not to flinch away from her touch. I knew she didn't mean me any harm and that my past and the fear

21

of it finding me wasn't her fault. I've had to become used to not being familiar with anyone anymore. It's too much of a risk.

I focused on her face as I tried to control my sprinting heart rate and breathing. The last thing I needed was to have to explain having a panic attack of epic proportions from a simple affectionate pat. I also didn't want to examine my reaction to the towering brute analyzing me from across the aisle. I had the feeling no secret could be kept hidden around this man. He reminded me of a bloodhound on the hunt. Once he found a scent, he wouldn't let up. That would be a problem. One I didn't need.

Once I had myself together enough that I could walk away without my knees buckling, I threw over one final glare toward the welcoming committee. He certainly didn't seem intimidated in any way. And why would he be? He could probably stuff me in the pocket of his jeans. His really great, nicely filled out jeans. And there go my knees again just like jelly. Mentally smacking myself, I immediately put a halt to that thought process altogether. I did not need to have any of those kinds of thoughts, especially about a stranger, one who could throw a big, complicated wrench in my "remaining unknown" plan.

Having found my resolve, I straightened my spine and went back around the shelves. Thankfully, I didn't have to go far before I was out of view. I didn't make it more than a few steps before I had to reach out and steady myself on a display of sodas. And it's a good thing I was holding onto something when I next heard a masculine rumble from the other aisle. The deep sound of his laugh made my belly quiver. My reaction sent me racing to the front of the store to get as far away as possible from the man that was responsible for the delicious sound. However, I had a feeling that no matter where I went, the source of that sound wasn't going to let me out of his sight for long. Now, I had to argue with myself about whether I was happy with the prospect.

5

Him

I make my way around the store, gathering the things I need. I haven't made a list and know I'll likely forget something although I'm not too worried about it. That's the convenience of living in a small town. People don't have to drive half an hour or more to complete necessary tasks such as grocery shopping. I know I can always come back by the store tomorrow without it being a hassle or disrupting my day.

With the items piled in my arms, I make my way to the register where I see Lynn. She's frowning again, but I'm not entirely sure it's directed at me. She's trying to watch me without being noticed. What she doesn't realize though is that I do notice. I notice everything. I always have, but being a Marine taught me even more about observing. A person doesn't survive a decade in dangerous places without learning to be aware of every minute thing or person, especially about those that don't want to be observed.

I decide in that moment maybe being nice and open with her is the way to gain her trust. Or it will at least help take her guard down as opposed to digging around and asking questions about her. I try to make myself as relaxed as possible to appear casual. But, the closer I get to her, the less relaxed I feel. I have the same reaction to her I had earlier in the canned goods aisle. I feel like I can't get enough air to breathe and my heart rate speeds up. I feel like I'm all tied up in knots. I don't understand my reaction. I have no idea who this girl is and know nothing about her, so why do I feel like she is someone I want to keep close?

I look at her more closely as I approach, now that I don't have the distraction of Miss Sarah's reaction to the girl. I notice though that Lynn is certainly not a girl, but a woman. I'm fairly sure she isn't the same age as I am, but she is older than I originally thought. At first glance, Lynn looks almost ordinary and young, maybe barely twenty, especially with her hair pulled into a braid and laying across her shoulder. I see that she also isn't wearing any makeup, not that she needs it, which lends to a more youthful appearance, especially from a distance. She is in plain clothes of cut-off denim shorts and a t-shirt. They are baggy and hide any hint of shape she might have. I start to wonder what kind of curves she has underneath, bold and almost exaggerated or petite and subtle, but perfectly hourglass. I can feel my body react to the possibility of finding out.

"Are you done staring yet?" she snaps.

Stunned that I have been lost in my head and caught staring, I look everywhere except at her. I berate myself for having such foolish thoughts and give myself a strong mental shake.

I mumble, "Sorry, didn't realize I was. Kind of lost in my own thoughts, got a lot on my mind."

"Humph." The grunt is her only response, but leads me to think that she's doesn't believe me. And, of course, she's right. I was absolutely staring at her, but am not willing to admit why.

I decide this is my chance to lay the groundwork for getting to know her and finding out why she's here. I clear my throat and attempt to defuse the tension in the air.

Searching for words, I try to explain. "Look, I'm sorry for coming off a bit, um...."

"Rude? Offensive? Bearish?" she lashes at me.

25

She is looking at me square in the eye with that tilt of her chin in defiance again. Her reaction catches me slightly off-guard. Man, this girl, woman, has some fire and it's intriguing, especially since there are men I know twice her size that don't stand up to me. I can be rather intimidating. But, I can see she is also trying to mask a fear. Of me? I can't be sure, but seeing it bothers me. I haven't given her a reason to be afraid of me, I don't think, other than my size. The presence of it just conjures more questions about who she is, where she came from, and what exactly could make her so afraid.

I focus on her words and start to chuckle, the corners of my mouth lifting. Her eyes narrow as her hands move to her hips. The gesture allows me to notice a smooth curve showcasing a tiny waist. I imagine my hands could almost encircle her. It reinforces the knowledge of how much smaller she is compared to me. That thought has my protective instincts waking up.

"And what exactly do you find amusing now, Levi?!"

Snapping out of my stupor once again, I notice she's said my name, and relish in the sound of it on her lips even though there is a definite bite in her tone.

I smile broadly. I like the fire. It's sexy as hell.

Playfully, I answer, "I just find your choice of words amusing. Bearish is exactly the description that Miss Sarah would offer for me. Although, she'd tan my hide if I was ever rude or offended someone and she found out about it."

Relaxing a bit, her shoulders lower, as do her hands and eyes. I miss looking into them immediately.

"Oh, well, I suppose anyone could expect the same treatment from her, even me, for what she would consider such atrocious behavior." She smirks a bit and her cheeks stain a faint pink. I can tell she is fond of Miss Sarah.

Seeing her blush stirs long dormant cravings in me. I decide I want, no, I need, to see it again.

Lowering the volume and timber of my voice to barely more than a rumble, I say, "I doubt that she would chastise someone as pretty as you, not severely anyway. She'd probably just offer a click of her tongue."

At my compliment, her eyes instantly find their way back to mine. I can see so much gold in her eyes that they look as though they're shooting sparks. They are full of several emotions, surprise, delight, the wariness of before, and, dare I hope, interest. Her porcelain skin is now covered in a full blush, bringing out the light freckles across her nose. It's a look on her I could get used to seeing and find myself hoping to achieve again. I immediately fantasize about the possibility of seeing it in the comfort of my bed.

The air between us changes again. I realize I haven't schooled my expression. I'm sure my thoughts must be displayed across my face. Lynn quickly looks away, busying herself with ringing up my groceries. I'm not embarrassed by my thoughts, but understand showing them so obviously when we've just met could cause her to put more distance between us. That is the opposite of the goal I am trying to achieve.

Before I can say anything, she switches back to an almost frosty temperament. Her ability to change between cold and hot could give me whiplash. It also piques my interest for finding out how to switch her back to hot.

With a purely business-like tone, she asks, "Did you find everything you needed okay?"

Grinning again, I answer, "Uh, yeah. I've been coming here since before I could walk. I could probably maneuver through here blindfolded and tell you exactly where everything is. I don't think Miss Sarah has changed a thing, ever. Well, that is, until recently."

The pink rises to her cheeks again. She is so reactive and I love it. Hiding anything from me will be impossible where she's concerned.

Somewhat nervously, she says, "Oh, right. Sorry, I'm still getting used to the 'small town, everyone has lived here forever and knows everyone else' way of life. It's a little new to me."

"Oh yeah?" I ask, clearly intrigued.

She shrugs. "Yeah. I'm more of a city gal."

At her words, I give an outright belly laugh. Hearing her use country slang seems borderline ridiculous. I can tell it's not how she usually speaks.

Trying to rein in my laughter, I reply with a smirk, "Well, using terms like gal, no one would doubt that you fit right in here." I can't help the slightly sarcastic, but affectionate, tone in my words.

Her eyes narrow with irritation, but I also notice the spark of fear that passes through them. I hold up my hands in surrender, showing my intention is in no way malicious.

"Easy now. I come in peace," I say with a wink.

She pauses for a second, breathing slowly, then a warm and genuine smile crosses her face. In that moment, she is breathtaking. I suck in a gulp of air, realizing I have never seen a woman look so lovely. And she's not even trying, which makes her all the more potent.

"Sorry. I don't mean to be abrupt. It's rude of me," she whispers.

Finally catching my breath, I tell her gently, "No harm done."

Her reply is a soft thanks, but she follows it with, "I'm hoping I can fit in here," which is barely audible.

I don't think she expected me to hear her, but I do and also notice she's retreated. She's hiding again, although from what I still don't know.

I become aware that she's finished tallying and bagging my items. I hand her the money, just brushing her fingers. There's a shock I feel all the way to my toes. Our eyes collide again and I know she's felt it too.

Stammering, she says, "I... I hope you didn't forget anything."

Emboldened by the electricity between us, I tease, "Oh, I probably did. But, if so, it'll just give me an excuse to see you again tomorrow."

When she ducks her head, I'm pleased to see the becoming-all-too-familiar blush touch her cheeks. I like that my words have such a profound effect on her and wonder how expressive she would be to my touch. I decide immediately that whether I need anything or not, I will most certainly come back tomorrow just to see her.

Grabbing my bags, I head for the door. Turning to push my way out, I call back to her, grinning, "Maybe I'll see you tomorrow."

Lynn looks up at me with too wide eyes like she's prey caught in a hunter's sights, which given my sudden interest in her might be an accurate description.

"Yeah, maybe," she whispers, smiling briefly. However, I can see the fear still lingering. I don't like it. I can definitely tell there is something that has this woman spooked and badly. Right then, I decide to figure out the cause and put an end to it. No one should live in a constant state of fear and worry. That belief is what prompted me to become a Marine, to protect others who couldn't protect themselves. And while I might not still wear the uniform, being a Marine is what I will always be and the job I will always do.

6

Her

My whole body sags against the register counter once Levi leaves the store. I feel as if I've just finished riding the Cyclone at Coney Island, twice in a row. To describe meeting him as a whirlwind of sensation is an understatement. I'm pretty sure my hope of being reclusive and remaining an unknown in this small town has just been shattered into a million pieces. But, right now, part of me really can't find a reason to care. That revelation could prove to be a major complication, one that I don't need.

I've been trying to make every part of my life as simple as possible. I've limited my belongings to what can be packed quickly and only enough that I can carry. I also keep my associations with people to a minimum. I pay everything in cash and never have any identification readily available if I can help it. I don't need anyone knowing who I really am. I can't risk being found. I'm extremely lucky to have made it this long without being discovered.

Two years ago, I never would have thought this could be my life, a life on the run, one of hiding. Newly graduated from a prestigious university, the ink barely dry on my diploma, I had everything right in front of me. I was completely oblivious to any real dangers in the world, at least in regards to how they might impact me. Of course I knew that things like abuse, crime, and violence existed. I'm certainly not stupid. However, I never thought I would experience any of these things personally or from the people I trusted most in my life. I couldn't have been more wrong. I learned about all of these things, including the kind of evil that's responsible for and promotes them.

Growing up in an upper middle class neighborhood, I considered myself safe and protected. I didn't need to worry about problems other people who lived in the city faced regarding their safety, or so I thought. My family's status and name afforded us all the proper security, along with a blissful ignorance. A lot of people would have considered us rich, but that certainly wasn't the case. We were comfortable financially. Unfortunately, that wasn't good enough for my parents. They desired to be in the upper echelon of society, to rub noses with the most important people. That desire would end up costing us everything, including possibly their lives and mine, and certainly my freedom.

Before coming to Sugar, I learned a disturbing life lesson. Most people do things for one reason only, greed. The most common compensations for that greed are either money or power, sometimes both. A major problem, however, is that the greed is like a bottomless pit that can't ever be filled. People are never content with what they have once they get it. It's a drug, a highly addictive one. There always has to be more. And when there isn't, they have to deal with the consequences, go through the withdrawal. In the case of greed, withdrawal for most people turns into either desperation or rage. In the worst cases, they mix together, which creates an extremely volatile combination. I was at the receiving end of both from different people. The desperation came from my parents. The rage, well, that came from the person who I hope never finds me, especially now that he would be in both the desperate and enraged categories since I disappeared.

His name is Richard Whitman. He is, or was, a business associate and friend of my parents. At least that's what I believed. I've known him since my early teens. He watched me grow up. I never thought of him as a stranger, more like family. The thing I learned about thinking of someone as family though is they can fool you most easily. You trust, feeling comfortable with them, and never think of them as the enemy. You never realize they are a wolf in sheep's clothing. Or worse, they could be the monster under the bed. Richard, I discovered too late, is the worst possible nightmare. He is both rolled into one.

While he is older than me by a little more than two decades, I found Richard to be an intriguing and attractive man, at least until recently. He had always been kind when I was younger. As I grew, finishing high school and moving onto college, his demeanor changed showing a subtle, but growing interest. I was euphoric over any attention I received. He made me feel important when most people simply overlooked me, namely my parents. He complimented me often and sought me out on his visits to our home. He always engaged me in conversation and even asked my opinions. Yet, he always kept what could be considered an appropriate distance until my college graduation. He was after all older and a friend of my parents.

While Richard cultivated a friendship of sorts with me, he also pulled me in by offering me a job. He's a well-known and extremely successful businessman in Rapid City. It was a simple assistant-type position, to start, but had a promise of great potential. I would have been a fool to turn it down. And besides, I knew him or I thought I did. To me, this was the best of both worlds. I was in a job I could actually get somewhere with, plus the work wasn't difficult or stressful. It still allowed me to take classes for a graduate program. Also, I was familiar with the boss, so that made it easy.

Richard Whitman didn't get to where he is by being careless, overt, or stupid. He also didn't get there by doing things legally or honorably apparently. As it turns out, all the businesses I was impressed with were fronts for illegal activities. Oh, sure, the legal businesses actually ran, but that's not where Richard made his money. He made his money through underground gambling activities and, worse, loan sharking. He is probably the best there is in Rapid City, a fact I only learned by accident and the reason I took off. When I look back, I can't believe how foolish and naive I was, especially where he was concerned. He was so smooth and calculating. I recognize now he was simply biding his time.

The job I was required to do was simple tasks like making files and copying, that sort of thing. It was also at his house, his very expensive, magnificent house. I didn't think it was at all strange to be working there instead of at one of his offices downtown. I rather liked the idea of working at his home, especially since I was familiar with the place after years of attending holiday parties and dinners there. Plus, I felt working there gave me more of an "in" on moving up professionally because I was the only one allowed in Richard's personal residence, except for his security guys, of course.

There was, however, still one place that no one was allowed to go, ever. This was Richard's private office on the first floor of the house. He always kept it locked, whether he was in or out of it. I didn't consider this odd because I've always known Richard to be a private person. I felt the office represented his status and probably held everything he had ever done to develop his business. So, when I had work to do, it was always left just outside the door on the console table with complete instructions. The only other person I ever saw go in through that door was Duncan, Richard's right-hand man.

For a long time, I didn't really pay attention to the papers I copied. I saw what looked like invoices and receipts, but mostly, I simply did what I was asked. Then, somewhere along the way, I started to notice things change. Included in my stacks, there were now ledger pages. I couldn't figure out why they stood out to me. There wasn't anything on them I recognized, names, places, or descriptions. Still, they seemed more important to me, I suppose because of the fact that I couldn't make sense of anything on them.

After that, I started to get suspicious, which is never a good thing. I paid attention more to everything that was going on around the house. I finally noticed that Duncan was the only one of Richard's employees I ever saw. I also never saw any other friend or acquaintance come by either, despite me remembering dozens of people at his events. And, the number of ledger pages was increasing.

A week before I left, I had stayed at Richard's house a few nights after some extremely late study sessions because his house is much closer to the library than my parents'. My parents had actually been encouraging me to spend time with Richard or at least take him up on his accommodating nature. If I needed anything, whether it was time, money, or convenience, he offered it, and why would I have a reason to say no.

I had come down the stairs, almost reaching the bottom, when I heard voices outside Richard's office door. It was Richard directing Duncan to do something. They were speaking in low tones, so it was difficult to make out everything they said, but what I heard changed everything.

Richard was extremely agitated and saying he was tired of being stonewalled by all the excuses from a client.

He told Duncan to remind them the deal had been made and payment was required.

"They know what is required, Duncan. They have been well aware of it since the beginning of our arrangement. I'm finished playing games. I expect payment in full by close of business today."

"Yes, sir. I will...relay your message." Duncan's voice was filled with a menacing promise.

"See that you do, with a bit of a reminder if necessary. If payment is not made, then the alternate terms of our agreement will be enforced, which I would quite prefer actually. The money means nothing to me. But, the girl...."

Richard trails off, leaving unspoken insinuations hanging in the air. My eyes go wide as a shiver as cold as ice slides down my spine and settles in the pit of my stomach. He's talking about acquiring a person as remittance for a debt.

He continues with even more malice. "I've been kind to them, given them chances. I'm done with that. I don't care that they think we are friends. We have never been friends. This has always been business. And it's time for them to pay what they owe in one form or another."

Even more dread churns in my belly. The pieces are starting to fit together in my head, but I don't want to accept what I'm certain I already know.

"Yes, sir," Duncan responds. Then, I hear the soft beat of footsteps on the marble floor, heading toward the door. Duncan must be leaving to do Richard's bidding.

"Oh, and Duncan," Richard calls with sickening sweet tone, "Please express my gratitude for the Brooks' business. I'll see to it their daughter appreciates their sacrifice."

I can't contain the almost silent gasp that escapes my mouth. I cover my mouth in fear of being heard. The word appreciates drips with diabolical glee. A cold sweat breaks out over my skin as I rush back upstairs like a ghost to the guest room where I've been staying. My mind is swirling trying to put all the pieces of the puzzle together. None of the scenarios I come up with are good. I sink to the floor leaning against the bed, my arms wrapped around my knees.

All this time, my parents haven't been friends of Richard, but clients, and apparently really good ones. Just from the snippet of conversation I heard, I can figure out his type of business. Then, the ledgers flash through my mind, the dozens of entries on each page. I may not have known what they stood for, but I can guess now. People, including my parents, owe Richard money, a lot of it, and he collects.

Suddenly, I remember Richard's comment about my parents' payment. I'm their payment! How could they do that? How despicable does a person have to be to promise their own child as a means of restitution for settling a debt? Or worse, how enormous must the debt be to require that kind of guarantee?

Richard has to know my parents don't have the money probably required to cover the payment. He's counting on it, I'm sure. Like I said, we've been comfortable, but never rich. Clicking into place is the final piece, my college tuition. I graduated from an exclusive, very private, and very expensive college because it made my parents look good. My parents couldn't have afforded it on their own and, once again, appearance is everything. I never questioned it before. Now, I know I should have.

Panic seizes me as I realize I can't stay here any longer, but I have to figure a way out. I can't simply walk out the door. Richard has always been interested in my schedules and commitments. I suddenly understand why. He was keeping tabs on me. I spy my backpack across the room, filled with books from my study session. The library, that's my escape. Richard won't question me going there. I've been there almost every day for the last month.

I recognize I should maintain my usual routine to keep up appearances. I shower quickly, dressing in designer jeans, a cashmere top and suede booties, all gifts from Richard that I can barely stomach putting on now. My hair gets put in its familiar braid over my shoulder. I gather the books to return, although that's not really my intention, stuffing a few necessity items in the bottom of the bag. Now, I only have to get out of the house. I won't be someone else's "solution". My parents will have to clean up their own mess, however that has to happen.

7

Her

I make it halfway to the front door when I hear Richard call from the dining room.

"Ah, Samantha, dear. I didn't realize you were up. Would you care for some coffee or something?" His voice slithers over my skin. I try to stop the rising bile in my throat.

"Oh, no, thank you, Richard. Actually, I need to get going." To me, my voice sounds thin and high-pitched. I try not to cringe.

"Well, we shall just see each other later then." I feel lightheaded at the thought. "Are you feeling alright? You look a little pale."

Quickly, I answer, "Yes, I'm fine. Probably just overworked from studying so late last night. Not enough sleep I'm sure."

His brows pull together in concentration as he studies me. "Hmm, I don't like you working yourself to illness. Where are you headed to today?"

"I have more studying to do. I need to go back to the library. I'll likely be there all day."

In a tone that represents a demand instead of a request, he says, "I do hope today will be the last of that. You are putting too much stress on yourself and I won't stand for it."

As I consider how to answer, Duncan approaches behind me, almost silently. I see an exchange go on between Richard and him with Duncan simply nodding crisply. My throat tightens making it difficult to swallow. I don't want to think about what that nod could mean.

39

Hopefully sounding much calmer than I feel, I manage, "Oh, yes, I'm fairly certain today will be the last day. Now, if you'll excuse me."

Calling to me before I can move away, he says, "Of course, but I insist you take Duncan with you. He can drive you and bring you back once you've finished." Trepidation flows through my veins. I hadn't planned on needing a secondary exit strategy. Trying to remain calm, I remind myself Richard has no idea about what I know. He won't expect me to be plotting anything, which gives me an advantage, but I still need to try and leave the house alone. Giving Duncan the slip will be difficult at best.

"I don't really think that's fair to Duncan, Richard. I honestly have no idea how long I'll be. I'm sure you have other obligations for him." I hope I sound like I'd rather not inconvenience the man and not fearful.

"Don't you worry about that," he counters. "Take all the time you need. Duncan has no problem waiting, I assure you. I want you kept safe." I'm certain he means he wants me kept, safe being an irrelevant word.

Knowing it's pointless to argue, especially if I want to keep suspicions low, I agree a little too brightly. "Oh, okay. Then, I guess I'll be going. 'Bye."

"Farewell, Samantha," he responds with a depraved tone.

I manage to walk to the car without vomiting or screaming hysterically. Sliding in, Duncan closes the door once I'm situated. An idea comes to me as he gets behind the wheel and starts the engine.

"Duncan, I need to go by my parents' first. I know it's out of the way, but I left a couple of books there that I need to return today."

Catching my eye in the rear-view mirror, I give him my best innocent face, smiling slightly.

"Of course, Miss Brooks." Duncan is a man of few words and none of them have a pleasing sound when he speaks. I can almost guarantee most things he does for Richard doesn't require talking. The thought leaves a cold ball of dread in the pit of my stomach. We travel the thirty minutes to my parents' house in silence with me trying not to hyperventilate. Pulling up in the drive, I push open the car door in a rush, not waiting for Duncan. He also exits the car after cutting the motor.

"Oh, Duncan, you can wait here. I'll just be a moment," I say hoping my suggestion is taken.

"No, I'll escort you."

Damn, this is going to be difficult.

I walk into the house to surprised expressions from my parents.

My mother exclaims, "Samantha Lynn! What are you doing here?"

I can tell by her tone something is up. They are both anxious and jittery. I look around the room eyeing a computer bag and briefcase on the coffee table. My gaze also snags the very edge of a luggage bag peeking out from the end of the couch. From the angle, I doubt Duncan sees it. Then, a realization strikes me. They're running! And leaving me to deal with their mess. Bastards. Good thing I have a plan of my own. I can only hope Richard will try to find them before me. I may not want anything to happen to them because they are my parents, but knowing they have such little regard for me changes my sentiments about them being a priority, in a big way. I've become my own priority.

Both my parents pale when they see Duncan. I think I understand his purpose of coming in with me.

41

He wants to make sure I am kept in the dark. It's completely fine by me for everyone to think that way. It gives me more of an advantage and I can use all the help I can get.

Addressing my mother, "I need to get some books. Duncan is running me to the library." Without waiting, I bolt up the stairs.

Once in my room, I dump the books from my backpack and start stuffing in clothes and anything I might need that is easy to carry. I have to be selective because I can't draw attention to myself with an overstuffed bag. I search through my clothes, finding my favorite comfortable pieces, leaving behind all the designer stuff. I also throw in flip flops and an old pair of sneakers. Wherever I'm going, the more inconspicuous I can look, the better. I also grab the stash of cash I have hidden.

I don't know why I kept it. It seemed silly when I never wanted for anything. But, I felt better knowing I had access to some money without always having to ask someone, giving them the control. Now, I'm glad I did it. It's not much by some people's standards. Nevertheless, it'll get me out of the city for a while until I figure something out. Taking a few deep breaths to calm my racing heart, I head back to the front door. My parents and Duncan are still standing right where I left them. Looking at them with a bit of sadness, I wonder what will happen to them. Then, I remember I'm their sacrificial lamb and bitterness washes away my sympathy.

Acting as I would have on any other day, I wave nonchalantly over my shoulder. "See ya!"

Duncan follows me closely, ushering me into the car. While I try not to fidget nervously, he drives me to the library. I walk in, waving to the clerk, and head straight to the second floor for the reference section where I usually occupy a study room. There's a lounge area I indicate to Duncan.

"I guess you can just have a seat there. I'll try to be quick with my work, but first I need to use the restroom." I know I have to keep my backpack with me, so going to the study room first, then claiming to need a bathroom would look stupid. I don't want him questioning why I would keep carrying my pack with me everywhere I go. To minimize any mistakes, I know it's now or never.

I slip into the bathroom under Duncan's watchful gaze. Thankfully, what he doesn't know is that this bathroom has a secondary exit. It's the only one in the library like it.

I breathe with relief when I see no one is in here. Knowing I'm on a time clock, I lock myself in a stall and change my clothes. I tie the sneakers on my feet after pushing the extravagant items to the bottom of the trash can. I creep out of the bathroom and directly across to the stairwell. Flying down the stairs two at a time, I exit the building into an alley. I'm only three blocks from the bus station, running the entire way. My lungs and legs are burning by the time I reach the ticket window. And my heart is exploding, but not only from the exertion.

"What's the next bus leaving?" I wheeze.

The sweet lady behind the counter, smiles, checking the schedule. I'm crawling out of my skin with terror.

Duncan won't wait on that couch much longer without becoming suspicious.

"Oh, well, we have one leaving in four minutes to Sugar. Beautiful little town."

Sugar isn't that far from Rapid City, but I'm hoping it might be one of the last places Richard would

43

look for me. He wouldn't expect me to lie low in a Podunk country town. He thinks money matters to me, and why wouldn't he with how my parents act? I'm hoping he would assume I'm either naive enough or vain enough, maybe both, to want to keep up pretenses like my parents. That's the only chance I have.

Scrambling for my money, I declare, "I'll take a one-way ticket, please."

With my ticket in hand, I climb aboard the bus, finding a seat in the back. I sink down and hide my face. My bag is clutched tightly to my chest as the bus rumbles away from the terminal. I feel tears spill unchecked down my cheeks. I'm alone. How am I supposed to ever trust anyone again?

8

Her

I'm so focused on my memories from the past I don't hear Miss Sarah approach me. As she lays a hand on my arm, I jump out of my skin. If I were a cat, I'd probably be stuck to the ceiling or would have scratched her eyes out. One, possibly two, of my nine lives would certainly be gone.

"Holy crap!!!" The scream erupts from my throat. Then realizing my mistake, I feel horribly guilty. "Oh, ma'am, I am so sorry. I didn't hear you walk up. Please excuse me."

Clutching her shirt, Miss Sarah is chuckling, "Oh dear girl. You're fine, really. I shouldn't have startled you. And there's certainly no better time to use an inappropriate word or two than when you've had the life scared out of you. I've definitely been known to." Her eyes twinkle good-naturedly.

"Well, I really shouldn't. It isn't proper after all. My parents would be appalled." I can feel my lip curl slightly at the hypocrisy of what would make them horrified. "But, thank you for letting it slide, ma'am." I notice she perks up a bit at the mention of my parents, but doesn't ask any question or push the subject. I'm fully aware she won't always do that though. It's a reasonable assumption the longer I stick around the more likely she is to start asking questions, and expecting answers.

Clicking her tongue at me, she says, "Now, you stop with all that ma'am stuff. It's too formal for me, you hear. We may not know a lot about one another, but I'd like to think we've gotten to be friends over these last few months."

Her smile is so warm and genuine. I can't help relaxing around her. Releasing a deep breath, I lean against the old Formica counter.

"Thank you, Miss Sarah. And I agree. I'd like to think we've become friends too." I feel the corners of my mouth turn up at the thought of a friendship with her. I really do like this woman.

"Good, then, you won't mind indulging this old lady a bit with some small talk while we take a little break. We won't likely have many people in until right before the dinner bell," she says, handing me a lemon sweet tea.

Gratefully, I accept the tea and take a big swallow. The day's events have made me shaky and given me quite a thirst.

Just as I'm swallowing another gulp, Miss Sarah's expression turns impish. "What do you think about Levi?"

Sputtering and choking on the tea, I gasp. "Wh-what?" I can feel my face turn pink. Miss Sarah pounds me on the back until I can breathe again.

"Oh, you heard me young lady. I saw the way you looked at him, and he at you. I know spark when I see it." Her eyes are filled with mischief.

I look away and know that I am completely busted, but still can't make myself admit it.

Feigning innocence, badly, I mutter, "I don't know what you mean."

She looks as me shrewdly. "Hmm. Well now. Not many people can fool me, and you certainly aren't going to start by being the first to do it. I know what I saw. However, I'm a decent enough person not to push. I saw the way you flushed when I mentioned his name. Let me just tell you, he was a good boy and he's an even better man. I helped raise him. His mother was my best friend."

Miss Sarah's eyes get misty while she speaks. I can tell she's trying to hold back a great deal of emotion. A knot settles in the pit of my stomach. I'm afraid to ask the question churning in my mind, but I have to know. I feel like the answer will give me some insight into the intriguing Mr. Levi Taylor.

Hesitantly, I ask, "You said she *was* your best friend. Is his mother not alive anymore?"

She sniffles and pats my hand, eyes glistening, but holding mine.

"No, dear. She's not. His father is gone also. Such a tragedy too, for everyone, but especially him. Both of Levi's parents were killed by a drunk driver about four years ago. They were the light of this town and loved him more than it might be possible to love another person. He was their world, along with each other. This is the first time he's been home since the day he buried them."

The sorrow in her voice makes my heart ache for her and especially him. Interested in what brought him home, I ask, "And why is he home now?"

"Well, I'm not sure it's proper for me to say. It's not my story to tell. All I feel comfortable saying is what everyone else already knows anyway." She pauses, seeming to sift through the thoughts in her head. On a deep breath with eyes softening in affection, she continues, "Levi's been a military man since he was eighteen. We all knew he would make a career of it. I think everyone expected it. It seemed to be the perfect fit for him, allowed him to put his protective side to use while giving him

47

direction for his wild side. But, things haven't turned out the way he or the rest of us thought they would. I suppose it means he wasn't in the place he was meant to be. Unfortunately, now I wonder if he's going to allow this to be his place or not."

My head is starting to ache because it seems like Miss Sarah is talking in riddles. I'm really trying to keep up, but she's leaving so many holes in the information she's giving it'd look like Swiss cheese if written on paper. I'm starting to think there is a lot more to Levi Taylor than just swoon-worthy good looks and rippling muscles.

She looks up with eyes shining and adds, sadly, "I've missed him terribly, but I can understand why he's stayed away. I just hope he realizes staying here will help to ease the hurt before he makes a mistake he'll regret and leaves."

My heart breaks at the thought of having to endure such a loss. I'm not sure I can fathom it. I had at one time been the center of my parents' universe too, or so I had thought. I learned differently and that realization was enough to rip me into shreds. Losing them when I still believed we were the perfect family probably would have crushed me. If something happened to them now, however, I'm sure I would be sad simply because they are my parents, but I don't know if it would ruin me. That all changed the day I found out what they did to me.

Shoving the dark thought aside, softly, I whisper, "I can't imagine the hurt he must have."

"Sweetie, I don't think anyone can. I can see it weighing on him. But, even with his strong shoulders he can't bear the burden forever. I wonder what he'll do with the homestead. It was always his favorite place on earth. Used to be, I knew for a fact he would move back to this little town. Now, I'm not so sure he can handle it. There might just be too many memories. He's so lost right now. I think I know how to help him, but he has to be willing to accept it, instead of running away from it."

She looks at me pointedly, which makes me believe she can see everything going on in my head. I'd bet my life that her words have a double meaning and it's directed at me.

"Look, Miss Sarah, I really...."

Holding up her hand to stop me, she interrupts, "Hush, don't start telling me again how you don't know what I'm talking about. I know you do. And it's okay to keep quiet for now. I just want you to know that whatever has brought you to Sugar can be dealt with, too. We can deal with it together. You can't run for the rest of your life young lady. Face your fears and if you don't know how, well, then, find people who can help you. That's what we do here. We help each other."

The concern this woman has shown for me, a virtual stranger, is overwhelming. It's incredible that one person can be so open and accepting. I can feel my eyes tingling from unshed tears and the back of my throat is raw. I clear the lump lodged in my throat with another sip of tea.

Once I'm composed enough to speak again, I say, "Thank you, Miss Sarah. I wish it was that simple. I know you mean well, but I really don't think anyone can help me with this."

I look away because I don't want her to see how truly afraid I am. I'm sure if she did, she wouldn't let me leave the store until every one of my secrets had been unearthed and her questions answered. I don't think I can stomach her view of me changing once she's learned the truth about me.

"We'll see" is all she says as she wraps me in a hug. I am rigid at first, but quickly sink into the embrace. It's been so long since I've had someone in my life who's cared about me with such honesty and without expectation.

9

Him

As I leave the store, thoughts of Lynn consume my mind. Who is she? What brought her to my small town of Sugar? And what exactly is her story? Because I know there is one. I can't deny wanting to find out more about her. Even better, figuring out her story allows me to focus on something else instead of all the things I'd rather forget. I tell myself that my interest is simply because I'm looking out for Miss Sarah. I'd be lost without that woman. However, I can't deny my fingers still tingle from the charge that passed between Lynn and me. I've never had such a reaction to any other woman. Meeting Lynn has definitely started to turn my homecoming from disheartening to intriguing.

Walking the mile home in the Kentucky sun gives me time to think of all the ways I can get to know Lynn. I'm completely distracted with all the possibilities. Thankfully, the military taught me how to put one foot in front of the other by reflex without having to use any concentration whatsoever. I doubt I would have been able to divide my attention if I was driving my truck even though I'd know the way with my eyes closed. Autopilot is an easier concept for my feet rather than when behind the wheel of a vehicle.

I make it home to find the early summer breeze whispering through the house. Although summers here can definitely be warm, my parents never felt the need to install central air throughout the house. The back of the house is surrounded and shaded by mature trees, keeping the temperature down inside. Plus, my mother always wanted the windows open all the time anyway, which moves the air around, along with the ceilings fans. Despite the breeze though, I'm overheated because of the walk and my leg is aching considerably. I probably should have changed from my jeans before venturing into town, but my scar is very noticeable and still looks angry. I'm not anywhere near ready to field questions about my injury or to stomach the pitying expressions. Or even worse, hearing all the comments about heroism and how God's grace brought me home whole. I may have come home, but I'm definitely not whole in any aspect or a hero. The heroes are the guys like my buddy, Dylan, who serve, but have their careers cut too short through no fault of their own. Or, even more so, several of the members of my unit whose lives ended in a scorching desert of hell too far from home.

I walk through the house and into the kitchen, limping considerably as my leg throbs. I need to put away my few purchases and eat something before I do anything else. Not having the energy or desire to cook, I settle on eating a third of Miss Dottie's pie. The strawberries are sticky and sweet, the rhubarb tart. It's the best thing I've had in a long time. Afterwards, I decide a shower is just the thing needed to cool down and hopefully sooth my aching muscles. Making my way up to the bedroom and into the connected bath, I strip down. There aren't any neighbors even remotely close by and I live alone, so modesty isn't an issue, not that it would be anyway. Growing up in the country and a decade of military life have given me a better than average physique and I know it. The only imperfection on the outside is the twelve inch jagged scar running down the outside of my leg and around my knee. The glaring reminder of my time spent serving my country and being tossed aside. I refuse to think about it or acknowledge the guilt eating away at me over the fact that it's my fault.

I step into the beautifully restored claw foot tub original to the house, turn the faucet knobs, and duck under the spray. My father was not as tall as me, but thought ahead, setting the height of the shower nozzle higher than normal, so I don't have to stoop. The cool water slides down my heated skin, refreshing and relaxing me. It helps to work out the aches from overusing my leg. Standing there, I let my mind wander and find it drifting back to Lynn. I remember her smile, the real one that I caught just a glimpse of briefly. It was radiant and gorgeous. The greens and golds in her eyes sparkled as if a light had been turned on behind them. Her skin had warmed and looked luminescent. The way she looked, I could have stared at her endlessly.

Even those few, innocent thoughts have my entire body tightening. I realize I haven't been with anyone for quite a while and I miss the soft warmth of a woman. I'm certainly no monk, but given the most recent years of my military service, especially the last, relationships haven't really been welcomed or even possible. And considering I'm well past my teens and early twenties, one night stands no longer hold much appeal. I'm in no condition to think about a forever relationship, but I would like to find something more than what knowing only first names requires. If I'm being honest, there hasn't really been anyone who's held my attention or motivated me to put in the effort either, until now.

I have no trouble pulling up Lynn's image in my mind. I recall her smooth porcelain skin, sprinkled with light freckles, and imagine how soft her caramel-colored hair might feel tangled around my fingers. Her full, pink lips are a temptation all their own that would make any porn star green with envy. I think back and wonder about the mystery of the body she has hidden beneath the baggy clothes she wore. And then, there was our touch. Brief as it was, that shock, I suspect, is a preview of what a night with her would be like, all heat and electricity. If I concentrate I can still feel it like it went through me when we first touched. I fantasize how magnified that shock would be if we were wrapped up together, skin on skin. Our bodies would vibrate from the waves of it. My own frame reacts from tip to toe, to the thoughts of how she would feel clinging to me and under me, writhing. Even though I don't know exactly how she looks, my assumptions have my length stiff and straining almost instantly. I can't remember ever being so hard and I haven't even seen her, or tasted her. I groan at the thought, at how sweet she must be, even better than Miss Dottie's pie and just as filling.

My hand moves under its own power, griping my steel shaft firmly. I imagine it's her delicate hand on me, stroking me. I wonder if her fingers would be able to grip all the way around me. I doubt it, the theory tapping into my inner caveman. My panting and labored breaths are in time with my movements as my strokes become faster and constricting. I tighten my hold, sensing this will be over quickly. I think about how she might look in the throes of an orgasm and that spectacular image does it. It sends me over the edge. On a ragged breath, I grunt out her name, almost sinking to my knees from the force of my release. Once the spots clear from my vision, I am able to steady myself in the slick tub. I'm thankful Lynn isn't with me to witness my quick performance. The speed at which I reached the finish line reminds me of what it's like being a teenager, all hormones and chaos. That's definitely not how I want things to be with her. Explosive, yes. But,

54

quick? No. If I ever get the chance to experience being with Lynn, I plan to savor every minute, knowing it will likely take all night.

I finish my shower quickly since the water has started to chill. I towel off and make my way to the bed. Sitting on the edge, I stare at the bottles of pills I should probably take for the pain and stress I've put on my leg. I know I have overworked it today, but the thought of the fog that clouds my head when I take them has me deciding against it. I'll endure the discomfort instead. Even in my sleep, the painkillers make everything worse, especially the nightmares. The medicine seems to take away all of my walls, my defense mechanisms, that protect me from remembering and worse, reliving the trauma. I lay down, hoping that my exhaustion and powerful release will send me into a coma-like sleep, and listen to the sounds of crickets and my ticking clock as my eyelids fall shut.

10

Him

I wake with the morning sun. The room is bright and cheery. I am not. I've never been much of a morning person, but growing up as a country kid and then living life in the military, I learned to keep the asinine schedule of getting up with the sun. A habit I definitely intend on breaking just not today, obviously. If I'd had my way, I wouldn't get out of bed before nine. I wish I could have started doing that now, but my body doesn't seem to realize it has the option yet. And unfortunately, once I'm awake, I have to get up. No sense in lying around, plus my body is extremely stiff from the previous day's activities.

I had hoped my usual restless sleep might have been altered considering I crawled into bed in such a relaxed state. I had no such luck though. I remember tossing and turning, never being comfortable, and mostly just on the edge of blissful sleep. At least I didn't greet the pitch black of night in a cold sweat and the sounds of my own screams because of the video of hell running on a loop in my head. The recurring nightmare decided to take the night off. For that I am grateful. Even though my sleep was less than ideal, it was at least still better than what I have been getting.

I scrub my hand down my face. The stubble scrapes across my palm. Out of another habit, I consider shaving, since I didn't last night. My thoughts immediately return to my shower and my blood heats as Lynn's angelic face flashes in my mind. I realize the improved sleep I did get is probably due to my climax from the night before. Or maybe it's simply because of the person who caused the explosive reaction. That activity occurred because of lovely hazel eyes and pale skin dotted with freckles. Even though thoughts of her have my body tensing in the best possible way, they also seem to have a calming effect on my nerves. It looks like a wisp of woman is the reason for better sleep than I've gotten in the previous eight months. I should thank her. A grin pulls at the corners of my mouth as I imagine so many different ways to express my gratitude. The thought of thanking Lynn for anything, especially for this reason in particular, is very appealing. With that in mind, I decide there's nothing wrong with a little scruff and shaving will take entirely too long, so I choose to leave it for the day.

Swinging my legs over the side of the bed, I stand and stretch, releasing a series of pops all through my joints. My leg aches, but not like I expected it might. I thought I had overworked it yesterday and would be in considerable pain today. I guess all the moving around and walking did a lot to work out some of the stress in the muscles surrounding my injury. The physical therapist had told me I was lucky to have regained full movement, but consistent strengthening was needed to maintain it. She wasn't happy when I didn't extend my therapy and only stayed for the minimum time required. But, I had done my time, and done it well. She couldn't argue with that. I never gave her any lip or grumbled too much. She didn't push the issue either when I showed her my discharging papers, just made me swear under the threat of bodily harm that I would continue my exercises so I didn't undo all of my months of hard work.

I appreciated her concern for my physical health, but my mental health just couldn't allow me to stay there any longer. It was impossible for me to be around all the other soldiers, making their way through the veritable minefield of rehabilitation. They weren't the problem though. I was. I couldn't handle it being in my face every day, the daily reminder that we were the ones who made it out alive or the realization that maybe I shouldn't be and it was sheer dumb luck I was.

Making my way down to the kitchen for coffee, I realize being in the house this morning isn't as difficult as it was the day before. The memories are still abundant and even somewhat painful to remember, but the familiarity of home brings with it a welcome comfort too. I know it also helps that other, more interesting, things, namely a certain tempting woman, have been occupying my mind, along with whatever her situation might be. It gives me something much more intriguing to focus on instead of my own crap. I know this is exactly the kind of avoidance behavior all the therapists told me not to indulge in, but I really don't care. It's easier than acknowledging the reason for my nightmares, my guilt.

I round the corner into the kitchen and am practically blinded. I have forgotten how dazzling the kitchen is in the morning sun. My mother's sanctum is exponentially brighter than my bedroom. I have to squint upon entering the room. Being surrounded by almost two full walls of uncovered windows, the sunshine streams in unhindered, blazing and powerful. The solid white quartz countertops and white ash cabinets add to the glistening display, making the room radiant. Catching sight of the flowering fruit trees out the windows makes for a stunning view. The picture created could certainly rival those seen in home magazines. My heart pinches with sadness as I think about the thousands of hours my mother spent in this room fixing my father and me every delicious creation imaginable. I miss the succulent smells, but mostly I miss just watching her tinkering away in her favorite space doing what she loved.

Pushing aside the melancholy, I head straight for the coffeepot. If I am expected to function at all, coffee is in order, and lots of it. I set the machine to brew a strong pot. Then, I spy what's left of Dottie's gooey pie on the counter from the day before. I scoop out a slice with my hand, inhaling it in two bites while standing over the sink. I can hear my mother clicking her tongue at me in mock disapproval. I grin at the image of her silently scolding me with hands on her hips and slight smirk on her lips.

Once I've rinsed my hands, I set to gather what I need for my first mug of morning propellant. Immediately, I discover I failed to buy an important item due to shopping in a distracted state yesterday.

"Shit!" I bellow. I forgot sugar.

My hands ball into fists for a brief second before I remember my comment to Lynn about potentially needing to return to the store. The tension falls out of my hands and my lips turn up into a smile. Now, I have a real excuse to venture to the store instead of a concocted one, which I certainly would have done. My mood brightens considerably, looking forward to the day and seeing her again.

11

Her

I managed to get through the rest of the day yesterday without dying from my own clumsiness or by heart attack, barely. After my potentially life-altering and enticing encounter with Levi Taylor, distraction became my middle name. Before the close of business, my injury count totaled four. Miss Sarah almost scared the life right out of me. I dropped a box of canned soups on my foot, twice. And, I successfully sliced my finger with a pair of scissors while trying to open another box of inventory. I feel lucky to have made it into bed in one piece without any further incidents.

My focus has been completely disrupted, but I know I can't let it happen again. I tell myself my reaction to Levi is a one-time thing, a fluke. There's no way the kind of connection I felt around him is a lasting thing and surely won't be as strong a second time. I also doubt he feels the same thing.

This morning I'm busy rearranging and stocking the low shelves at the front of the store with all the scrumptious baked goods Miss Sarah's sister, Dottie, sends in every few days. I swear if I stay here, I'll gain ten pounds before the end of summer. The thought sends a pinching pain to my heart. It certainly wasn't my intention to stay anywhere for long given my need to hide from Richard. However, this place has given me a taste of what comfort is like, of what it might be like to be settled. And, honestly, those feelings have even more to do with Miss Sarah. She has been so caring and wonderful. She's also let me see that a simple life might be best. It can be so full and never lacks in the things that are important, like laughter and love.

Lost in my thoughts and arranging pies, I vaguely hear the store's bell over the door tinkling. "Good morning!" I say automatically, without turning around to see who I'm addressing.

"Well, good morning!" I hear in a distinctive rumble. There's humor in his voice as well as a sort of strained groan.

Realizing I've been bending over from the waist with my butt in the air, I whip around. My movement sends the blackberry tart in my hand splattering to the floor. My gaze locks on Levi standing there, looking even more delicious than I remember. His frame fills the doorway. He looks relaxed, but not completely rested. Although his eyes are a sparkling, brilliant blue, I see faint shadows under them. He hasn't shaved, leaving a scruff on his face. I am frozen in place because he is mouth-watering.

With a chuckle, he asks, pointing to the dessert, "Um, I hope you weren't aiming that at me?"

Confused, I look around and stammer, "Wh-What?" I see a pile of gooey mess about halfway between us. "Oh, crud. That was the last blackberry one."

"So, you weren't aiming for me then," he says, a grin splitting his lips.

Understanding his question, I laugh, "No, certainly not. I was actually planning on eating that one." Then, with a bit of sass and my hand on my hip, I add, "I wouldn't waste such decadence."

Levi's face splits into a full-blown, megawatt smile.

Feeling more confident than ever before, I continue with a pout, "But now, it's met a fate worse than my belly."

I see a flash in Levi's eyes and his expression changes as he stares at my bottom lip sticking out. I shouldn't be trying to draw his attention, but I definitely have it. I can feel the usual heat climb up my cheeks. His eyes dilate and the corner of his mouth twitches. I immediately want to diffuse the electricity in the air between us. It's more than I can handle right now. Remembering I need to clean up the mess, I reach behind the checkout counter for the roll of paper towels and cleaner. I focus on cleaning up the sticky mess.

Levi strides toward me and squats slowly. He reaches out to take the paper towels and brushes my hand. The charge that travels up my arm from his touch has me gasping and my eyes flying wide. We are both completely still and looking into each other's eyes. I can tell from his expression he's as surprised by our connection as I am.

Clearing his throat, "Um, I was just going to help."

Feeling a bit nervous, I rush to say, "Oh, no, that's alright. I've got this. It was my mistake."

He pauses for a moment and then in a sincere tone, he answers, "Well, I'd say I'm partially responsible since I startled you. I'll just gather up the tart and you can wipe down the floor."

"Okay," I say, relaxing.

I watch as his huge hands scoop up the tart disaster in one motion. Compared to his, my hands look minuscule. It probably would have taken me three times to gather up all the mess. I try to focus on the task in front of me instead of ogling over him as I spray cleaner on the sticky syrup. Nevertheless though, questions about

62

how big he is everywhere else come to mind after thinking about his hands. I feel the heat creeping up my face.

Suddenly, it hits me that he's actually here. I realize he's come to the store again today. Tilting my head, I tease, "Um, I take it you forgot something yesterday?"

Grinning, he replies, "I told you I probably would. I forgot sugar for my coffee."

I gasp with genuine dismay. "Oh, dear. That is a tragedy! How can you walk around without having had any coffee?"

"A tragedy of the worst kind!" he wholeheartedly agrees. "And, honestly, I'm not sure how I'm even functioning at the moment. I think I was only able to get myself out the door because I know I can swipe a cup from the pot Miss Sarah always has made before heading back home."

Laughing, I say, "I think that woman would mainline coffee if she could. I need my morning coffee, but I'm nothing like her. I don't know how she does it. I'm not going to try and convince her to change her habits though. Given her age and energy, it seems to be working for her."

Levi shakes his head, an affectionate smile on his lips. "I'd have an easier time getting my previous commander to change his mind than her."

Intrigued to find out more about Levi, I ask, "Military? Huh, probably a stupid question. I guess it's pretty obvious that you serve."

A shadow passes over his face. He looks so lost for a brief second. If I hadn't been paying attention, I probably would have missed it. His demeanor changes instantly and the pitch of his voice is strained.

"Served, past tense. I've been discharged."

I start to ask about it, but he abruptly stands and throws all the used paper towels in the trashcan. The air he is giving off is one of absolute frustration and despair. I can't imagine what circumstances could have happened to make this solid mountain of a man feel so sad. I don't know the reasons behind him being home, but I suddenly want to find them out. I shouldn't because I know I can't stay here. Yet, all I can feel is the pull of Levi. He makes me want to know him and soothe his burdens.

With a detached tone, he says over his shoulder, "I'm going to go in the back and get that coffee." Then, he walks off in a hurry, leaving me stunned and confused.

12

Him

I am a complete jackass. I'm running away from a woman who is likely half my size as if she's holding a live grenade. All because of one statement that could have required me to give explanations for things I don't want to think about. And because the grief and uncertainty I feel is weighing me down like lead boots. I've never run from anything in my life. I'm a goddamn Marine, but here I am, hiding and running, like a coward. Hiding because I don't want others to see my struggle. Running because I don't want to face it myself. How does a man, a leader, ask for help? I don't know how.

Instead, I practically sprint across the store to find a cup of coffee that holds no answers. I walk away from a real connection with the first woman that's ever captured my attention beyond the physical.

I walk into the back lounge with my head hung low. Miss Sarah is sitting at the small dinette table. She immediately rises and rushes to me, cupping my face with her small, soft hands. Concern is etched in her expression.

"Oh, Levi, my sweet boy. What is the matter? Where is my favorite smile?"

I release a shuddering breath as my shoulders sag a bit more. Miss Sarah directs me to a chair, pushing me slightly to sit, not that I give any resistance. In her mother hen fashion, she pours me a cup of coffee, fixing it how I prefer, and slides it onto the table. My hands grip the cup, feeling the heat that is almost painful. I give her a small smile.

"Thanks."

Touching my arm gently, she asks, "You want to tell me what's going on? I'm never seen you look so glum. Well, except for once, of course."

At her statement, my eyes meet hers. She thinks she knows the problem instantly, or at least part of it.

With her eyes shining with unshed tears, she whispers, "Dear boy, I miss them horribly too. Every day. I knew it might be hard once you came home, but you aren't alone. You must know that."

I shrug. "I do. I guess. But, it's more than that. I just don't know what to do with myself. The military was my life. I have no purpose anymore and no one to guide me."

"You're wrong. You do have a purpose. You just have to find it. And as far as needing someone to guide you, you don't. You never did." Her voice is full of strength and conviction.

Countering, I argue, "Yes, I did. I always looked to Dad. He made sure I was doing what I needed to do."

"No, Levi," she says more softly, "Your dad never told you what to do. He never would have. He knew how strong your will was. When you set your mind to do something, you do it. He just made sure that you went about things the right way and could handle any consequences. Your guide has always been your heart and your gut. They've never steered you wrong."

I hang my head. Admitting the fear I have been holding inside, I tell her, "I don't know if I can trust them anymore. My biggest mistake cost me my career along with Dylan's. It almost cost me my best friend's life. How can I trust that the decisions I make won't cause worse situations especially for those I care about?"

She grips my hand and waits until I'm looking up at her again. "Levi, honey. That wasn't your fault. It wasn't a mistake you made. What happened was the result of war and an insane person putting a bomb on the side of the road. You wouldn't have chosen for you and Dylan to have the accident. And I'm sure he doesn't blame you. You have to stop blaming yourself."

My words are barely a mumble. "I don't know if I can. I don't know how to get past it."

"You start living again, my boy. Simple as that. Your parents wouldn't want anything less for you." She makes it sound so easy.

"How?"

"Well, you start by taking hold of the opportunities right in front of you. Don't let them pass you by," she says, her eyes twinkling. "I know a young girl who herself is in need of a little living."

I shake my head in disbelief. "Miss Sarah, I am in no way ready for matchmaking."

"Oh, posh. Who said anything about matchmaking? I'm simply trying to get two people I hold dear to spend a little time having some fun." Then, she lifts her shoulder innocently, saying, "And, well, whatever comes of it, comes of it. I can tell you like her."

Flabbergasted, I say, "I hardly know her." I barely contain the admission I'd like to change the fact.

Completely, unfazed, Miss Sarah continues, "Nonsense. You don't have to know someone's life story to know you feel something. I'm just saying it won't do you any harm to get to know her."

"I suppose you're right," I agree, then duck my head in shame, confessing, "I think I owe her an apology actually."

Behind me, I hear the soft shuffling of feet coming into the doorway.

Miss Sarah gets up from her chair, comes over to my side, and puts her arms around my shoulders. She leans in kissing my temple and whispers, "Looks like you may have that chance."

I look up to meet Lynn's gaze. I can tell she is uncertain about whether she's intruding. Miss Sarah excuses herself, lightly squeezing Lynn's hand on the way out.

In a singsong voice, she gives her parting advice, "Opportunities, Levi."

I hang my head feeling embarrassed, but chuckle. Miss Sarah has never been known for being subtle.

Rising from my chair, I clear my throat and find a little courage. "I'm sorry for before, the way I acted. I kind of took off on you without an explanation."

"Um, yeah, well, it's okay," she says shyly.

Intently, I tell her, "No, Lynn, it's not. You didn't do anything wrong."

"Can I ask what happened?" She's hesitant, although clearly curious and concerned.

"I'm just kind of going through some stuff right now. Can't say that I'm ready to talk about it yet." I see her face deflate, so I rush on. "But, I will be, once I figure out myself what's going on."

She ponders my words. "Okay. I can understand that." Next, she says, "I know we don't know each other well, but I'm here if you need anything."

First, she accepts my explanation without more questions or prying. Then, she offers me her consideration.

I'm blown away. "Thanks" is the only response I can give her.

Maybe Miss Sarah is correct. Maybe I simply have to pay attention to the opportunities right in front of me to start living again, one step at a time.

13

Her

My heart breaks from the look of despair etched on Levi's face when I entered the room. How does a man whose presence fills any space, who seems so solid, a man with such bearing seem so lost? From what I've felt, he's the kind of man who fights with everything he has through all obstacles. I can't imagine what it is that has him doubting his ability to do just that. Seeing him like this almost breaks me, has me thinking only of him and not about how I shouldn't get involved.

In all honesty, I should stay far away from Levi. But, I can't. I have a thousand reasons not to be involved with him and none of them have anything to do with him. Really though, I'm a fool to think that I'm not already in too deep. Even from only the short time I've known him, I don't want to think about never getting to know him better or seeing him again. It brings an ache to my belly and a pain to my heart. As a result of that, I decide to soak in any time I can get with him even if it means shattering my heart later. I just hope it won't shatter his too.

Trying to lighten the air between us, I tease, "Hey, did you get your coffee yet?"

The corner of his lip turns up in a small smile. "Oh, well, yeah. Miss Sarah poured me a cup, but I don't actually remember drinking it even though it's gone."

"I guess that means you're heading out then?" I can't help the disappointment ringing through my words.

He hesitates and looks at me. "I suppose, but I don't really have any plans for the day. Not quite sure what I'll do with myself."

Not wanting him to leave and encouraged by his uncertainty, I trip over my tongue and suggest, "Um, you could hang out here, with me. I mean, if you want to. There's a bunch of stocking and inventory I'm trying to get done to keep Miss Sarah from having to do it. I know that woman is a workhorse, but she seriously needs to take a break!"

He chuckles at my accurate description of Miss Sarah and says, "She has no clue how. If you were able to get it all done, she would just find something else to do."

Even in the short time I've known Miss Sarah, I can guarantee Levi is right, so I agree with him. "True, but at least none of it would involve heavy lifting and her climbing to reach the top shelves. I can deal with her doing other stuff. I just would rather her not end up in a heap on the floor."

"You and me both darlin'." His use of endearments makes me feel giddy. He smiles at me as I feel my cheeks turn pink.

I ask, shyly, "So, you might be inspired to stay?"

With his eyes twinkling, he says, "Hmm, well now, that might depend on my work environment for the day and the benefits of the job."

Straight-faced, I explain, "Your work environment obviously is here. And as far as benefits of the job, it's a one day job. What kind of benefits are you expecting?"

Clearly struggling to keep up with a mock business tone, Levi points out, "Yes, my work environment is here. But, will I be expected to work on my own or with a partner?"

"Oh, uh, well, which ever you prefer, I guess." I can't hide the smile on my face.

"Good, then I choose to be with you the entire day." All pretense of professionalism is gone as he continues. "Now, about my benefits."

"I don't really have anything to offer you for benefits." I know the moment the words leave my mouth they're a lie. There are a lot of things I might offer him if he wanted them.

His eyes flash with desire as he scans me from head to toe. "Darlin', I beg to disagree, completely. But, as much as I would appreciate anything you willing offered, I was thinking about something a little simpler and less complicated for right now."

I can't help the goosebumps that erupt over my skin. I'm a little disappointed at his ability to control his wants so well, but appreciate his choice to takes things slowly.

"Okay. What do you have in mind then?"

"How about one of Miss Dottie's life-altering goodies?" Playfully, he adds, "I'd be willing to share."

Smiling, I say, "I think that could definitely be arranged."

Nodding crisply, he concludes our negotiations. "Good, then we have established the terms of my temporary employment." He raises his arm to usher us out of the room. "Now, Boss, lead the way. I am under your command."

Leading Levi through the aisles, I gather a pen and the clipboard with all the inventory lists attached. We spend the next few hours counting and cataloging each item, from boxes of animal crackers to zesty Italian dressing. We joke and tease, laughing almost continuously. A common source for material is my diminutive size and his mammoth body structure. It's fun and lighthearted, just what I think both of us need. Miss Sarah has made herself scarce, the sneak, although I could hug her right now for her cunning ways.

Levi and I decide to take a lunch break when the noise from both of our stomachs is heard. I'm only slightly embarrassed since his rumbles considerably louder than mine. As promised, I grab one of Miss Dottie's gooey concoctions to share. Sitting at the little table in the back, I slide it between us.

Levi licks his lips reverently.

"Ooo, the peach cobbler. Sooo good." He's practically drooling already.

"I haven't tasted this one," I tell him excitedly. His eyes are like saucers from his surprise.

"Oh, dear lord. You are missin' out! Here, you get the first spoonful." Using his own, he scoops out a heaping taste and has it hovering right in front of my mouth. "Come on, open up. You won't be disappointed."

Tentatively, I open my mouth, watching him. He carefully slides the spoon into my mouth, intently focused on his task. I'm in a state of shock because he's feeding me. It's such an intimate act. Then, my eyes go wide as the tart and sweet flavors burst in my mouth.

"Oh my god," I moan, my eyelids growing heavy. When I finish chewing and look at Levi again, his face is awash with desire.

I feel myself flush, but am feeling a little bold. I pick up my spoon and scoop up a massive bite for him. As I stretch it toward him, he opens his mouth automatically. His eyes are still on me the entire time. However, I can tell he's having a hard time not closing them to savor his treat in ecstasy. We continue our nourishing dance until the entire cobbler is gone. We've barely spoken any words, but the tension in the room is a living thing.

Knowing we should get back to the inventory, I stand with difficulty and clean up the mess. As I'm about to suggest we get back to our task, Levi rises slowly, like he's afraid one of us will spook. He's probably right. He carefully crosses to me and puts his hands on my shoulders. I don't flinch, but my entire body is rigid. I am literally frozen in place, waiting to see what it is he's doing. He leans in, his gaze never leaving mine. Finally, when he's only a whisper away, his eyes dart to the corner of my mouth. He very softly presses his lips there. I can feel his tongue swipe gently along part of my bottom lip. I can't help the whimper that escapes me. I feel Levi's grip tighten slightly in response as my knees turn to jelly. Then, with the same slowness, he backs away and loosens his hold, dropping his hands to his sides.

Clearing his throat and looking unsure of my response, he murmurs, "I'm sorry. I didn't really plan to do that. Just couldn't help myself. You had the smallest drop of peach syrup at the corner of your mouth."

Still locked in place, I answer, "Oh, well, then, thank you?"

My face flames at the absurdity of my response. I look directly in his eyes, seeing the same bewilderment I feel churning in my stomach. I realize we are both completely terrified. It feels like we are navigating a slippery slope, but knowing it's not only me puts me slightly at ease. I give him the littlest smile, showing him everything is okay. In that moment, all the awkwardness falls away and we burst out laughing.

As he exhales deeply to regain his composure, he chuckles, "I'm not sure I've ever heard thanks given in the form of a question. But, I suppose it's better than you using that baseball bat you carried with you the first day we met."

Sheepishly, I dip my head. "Yeah, sorry about that. I'm not usually so aggressive."

"Well, that's unfortunate," he comments suggestively.

I lift my face to see him watching me closely. He holds my gaze a moment more before extending his hand out to me. "Come on, we should get back to work."

I easily put my hand in his and say, "Okay. I would like to get this done today."

"Then, let's get back to it," he replies.

The rest of the afternoon goes by quickly as we work at a steady pace. I'm excited we've made it down to the final few boxes.

Pointing to the top shelves that hold a surplus of soup boxes, I tell Levi, "Okay, so we just have to count those extra ones and we'll be done. Let me just get a small ladder, so I can reach them."

"Darlin', I'm still not sure you could reach," he snickers. "There's no need for that anyway. I'll just use the stool we have and hand the boxes down to you."

With my hands on my hips, I glare at him. "Fine." Then, with a twitch of my lips, "Smart ass."

Grinning from ear to ear, he climbs to retrieve the first box. Unfortunately, the box must be badly packed. As he turns to hand it to me, his whole body shifts to a slant. He drops the box and starts to step from the stool in order to regain his balance. His movement is quick and his body is positioned at an odd angle. It's obvious he won't land well. His left foot hits the floor with a thud, taking the full force of his weight. I expect his leg to buckle underneath him, but he remains upright with a thundering groan. Jaw locked in place, he is stock-still. I can see sweat beading at his temples. He is obviously in a tremendous amount of pain.

Panicked, I rush to him. "Oh, Levi! Are you alright? What can I do?"

"Nothing!" he barks.

Needing something to do, but unsure about what that should be, I say, "Let me go get Miss Sarah."

"No! I'm fine." His tone is laced with such menace it takes everything I have not to run and hide from him. I'm never heard him sound so violent and lethal. I can't do anything, except stand there. He's made it clear he wants no help from me. I don't want to make the situation worse.

Exhaling through his nose and looking like an enraged bull, he snarls, "I need to leave." Without a goodbye or backward glance to me, he turns and departs, leaving me confused and hurt. Watching him, I see he is limping badly.

Upon hearing his truck squealing away from the store, Miss Sarah finds me in exactly the same spot before Levi left.

"Lynn, dear, what happened? Did Levi just leave?" she questions.

Not knowing what else to say, I answer, simply, "Um, yeah. He did."

Sounding as confused as I feel, she asks with concern, "What on earth made him tear out of here like that? Is everything alright?"

I can't stop the tears from forming in my eyes. I look at her, hiccupping, "I don't really know, Miss Sarah. Levi was helping me with the inventory. We were just finishing up when he lost his balance on the stool. He didn't fall, but landed on his leg. He seemed to be in a lot of pain. Then, he practically exploded, snapping at me, and stormed out of here."

She looks toward the front window with her fingers pressed to her lips. "Oh dear."

Wanting to know how I can help him, I beg, "What, Miss Sarah? Tell me what happened please."

"Well, it's not really my story to tell, Lynn, as I said before. You should hear it from Levi, but I will tell you that he's home because of an injury from the service. It's his leg. His left leg."

I gasp, feeling my knees give out beneath me and fall to the stool.

"Oh no. That's the leg he landed on."

"I was wondering how he might handle things if something happened," she says almost to herself. Then, trying to explain, she continues, "He's always been pretty easy-going. Driven, but never harsh. He's different now since coming home. A lot of things have changed for him. He's not as light-hearted as he once was."

Hopefully, I ask, "Miss Sarah, what can I do?"

With sadness filling her eyes, she tells me, "Right now, nothing really. Just give him some time."

Miss Sarah walks away solemnly to return to her work. Even though I should do the same, I linger on the stool between the shelves of canned goods, thinking the connection Levi and I made today might have just been reduced to ashes.

14

Him

The banging on the front door won't stop. I try to ignore it by pulling the pillow over my head to block out the sound, but it doesn't work. The noise just increases, becoming more insistent. It sounds like whoever is down there will eventually break down the door. I can only think of one person who has the nerve to be knocking on my door like that.

"Come on Levi!! Dude, I know you're in there! Open the fucking door!" The last words are punctuated with several forceful blows.

Dylan Reed, one of my former unit members, my best friend, and the closest thing I have to a real brother. Dylan and I have been through everything and then some together. If there is somewhere to go past hell, then we've been there, and survived, mostly. We entered boot camp at the same time and have had each other's back since then. Every assignment, mission, and re-stationing that we were able to have together made us into an incredible team. Our commanding officers noticed and eventually we became a package deal no matter where we went.

We've always had a silent communication between us, an extreme understanding of each other. I think it's what made us so close from the very beginning. We are opposites in a lot of ways, complementing one another, but have a similarity in being country boys and only children to older parents. We share a bond in being star athletes in school who could have played professionally, but that felt a need to do something more in our lives. We are also both quick with a line and relish in soft, pretty women. But, the thing that makes our connection the strongest is our intolerance of each other's bullshit excuses. I might be able to pull something over on someone else, including Miss Sarah, but not with Dylan, nor him with me. And both of us have too much respect for the other to even try.

We were a phenomenal team and then the accident happened. I'm the reason he's banging on my front door right now, instead of still serving his country.

He continues to pound on the entrance, his impatience increasing. I'm surprised he doesn't just open it to let himself in considering he knows it's unlocked. Probably the only reason he doesn't is because of his southern, Georgia manners, the ones his mother drilled into him from birth.

I groan and roll myself off the bed. My leg is painfully stiff and protests any movement. The floor is cool against my feet, but I barely notice. I run my hand through my hair and down my face. I can tell my hair is sticking out in all directions. I haven't shaved in days or even showered for that matter. I don't even bother looking in the mirror. I'm sure the sight is disgusting. My mother would be appalled.

I shuffle down the stairs wearing the same gym shorts I've been in for the better part of a week and open the door. I have to shield my eyes from the light. It's blinding. I'm not sure exactly what time it is, but the sun is shining high overhead so it must be some time around midday. I squint into a face that's furious and almost as familiar as my own. I feel equal parts of relief and aggravation at seeing him. Because of both emotions, I just want to punch him.

"Man, you look like horse shit." His serious look hides most of his concern.

"Fuck you." I grumble as I step aside to let him in.

79

His expression turning smug, he says, "Damn, ya smell like it too." Now, I want to punch him twice as hard.

I know there's no point in trying to convince him to go away because he won't. He's as annoying as a yellow jacket with a soda can. He never gives up. It's the best quality about him and what makes him extremely good at his job, when he had it.

He ambles into the house, dropping his gear at the foot of the stairs. I guess he's staying a while. I don't question him about how long. His answer would be indefinitely if I asked him, which I won't, but I also know I don't have to either.

He proceeds to open all the windows, letting in the sweet smelling breeze I've missed blowing through the house. The house is so stuffy and dank, worse than when I returned.

"How can you breathe in here?" he asks with disgust in his voice.

I sink onto the couch. "Wasn't really thinking about it much. What are you doing here, D?"

He pins me with an ice cold stare. "Obviously saving your sorry ass from wallowing in your own filth."

I cringe at his words because I am in fact completely pathetic, but hardly worth saving.

He continues, "I've been calling for a couple of weeks without an answer. I knew it would take a while before you finished your rehab, but I figured you had to be home by now. I knew you wouldn't want to stay there any longer than absolutely necessary. Wanted to check in with you, but obviously you couldn't just answer the damn phone. So, instead of having my fill of some soft, southern women, I had to drag myself here to help you pull your very large, very hard head out of your ass."

I take a deep, shuddering breath. Dylan sits on the coffee table in front of me, leaning on his knees. His shoulders are bunched with tension and his eyes look as tired as I feel. I can see the aggravation plainly on his face, but also the concern and unwavering affection we have for one another as brothers.

"I had no idea it was this bad. Dude, what happened?"

I straighten my shoulders some and look him squarely in the eye. I'll always give him my respect and honesty even if it paints me in an unflattering light. He deserves nothing less from me. While Dylan will understand me having a hard time of it, he won't appreciate me being a pansy. We aren't built that way.

"I had a setback," I tell him.

He snorts. "A setback? Brother, this isn't just a setback. This is the end if you let this continue." Then more softly, "And I won't allow that to happen."

His words are like a punch in the gut, one I surely need. I know I need to get out of this dark hole I'm in before I can't climb out again. I think about the fact that he's here with me, watching my back, like he always has. I can feel my chest loosening and some weight being lifted from me. I can count on Dylan, no matter what. He might let me fall on my face to teach me a lesson, but he'll at least put a pillow there before I hit to soften the blow. And he'll never make me face anything alone.

It's time for honesty, at least mostly. "I was doin' okay, then I twisted the shit out of my knee. I had to take those damn pills because the pain was so bad."

I can see all the questions in his eyes, but he doesn't ask them, even though I know he needs the answers. "And?"

81

Sighing heavily, I tell him, "And I was a jerk, a grade A, first-class one to someone who didn't deserve it."

"Well, I know it wasn't Miss Sarah because that woman would string you up by your balls while smiling sweetly." His description of Miss Sarah is absolutely accurate.

"Yeah, no, it wasn't her."

Intrigued, he asks, "But, someone important?"

Even though I probably shouldn't be pursuing anything with Lynn, I can't seem to help myself. And the thought of losing the chance because of my own stupidity depresses me further.

In a sullen voice, I admit, "Maybe. I probably won't be able to find out now."

"Not smelling and looking like this, you won't," he smirks, then seriously, he says, "I have a feeling you might get another chance as long as you weren't a complete jerk every time she saw you."

Quietly, I tell him, "I tried not to be."

"Then, you *might* have a chance. Of course, now that I'm here, your odds have gotten worse." I can always count on Dylan and his lack of humility.

Rolling my eyes, I snort, "Whatever, jackass."

"Hey, is that any way to treat me after having traveled six hundred miles just to tell you take a shower?" His insulted tone is purely an act. I don't think I've ever seen him offended.

I firmly remind him, "Hey, I didn't ask you to come here."

"But, you've got me, so deal with it. You good?" It's a loaded question, of course.

"Yeah, okay. I'm good." I look at his face and see his eyebrow arch to his hairline, showing his skepticism. I heave another breath, forcing myself to be completely honest, "Or at least I will be," I say, "Thanks D. Thanks for coming."

I see some of the tension leave his frame as well and realize that maybe I'm not the only one who needs a little help dealing with our past. He stares at me for a moment with an unreadable expression. If I was more with it, I would probably question him about it, but then it's gone just as quickly as it appeared and he reverts back to his need to irritate me.

"Now," he snickers with a slap of his knees, "where the hell are the gasoline and the pressure washer? Because we need to burn those shorts and hose you down. You could give pigs a run for their money. You reek something awful!"

My lip pulls up just slightly at his humor. I know if he's commenting on any aroma I'm giving off, it must be really bad because we've spent too many days together out in the blazing desert heat in full gear without access to a shower. But, I still can't give him any satisfaction.

"Funny, smart ass."

"Hey, I just tell it like it is, buddy." Dylan winks, his casual, laid-back nature returning even though I can still see the concern clearly swirling in his eyes.

I can already breathe easier knowing he's here. He'll help me find the strength I need to get my head straight again. Dylan won't let me give up on myself. He's not made that way. And maybe somehow along the way I can deal with my guilt over costing him his career.

15

Him

Once our initial squaring off ends, Dylan and I go back to our usual companionable ease with each other. He manages to throw together a simple late lunch while I practically drown myself in the shower, removing layers of grime and filth. Now, I sit in the same spot on the couch watching him play solitaire quietly. I know he's simply waiting, waiting for me to take things at my own pace, which is fine with me. He doesn't push. But, I also know that if I don't make a continuous effort to snap out of this funk, he'll take matters into his own hands. The form it would take is probably the same size and shape as a two by four. At least I appear clean shaven and human again. I also managed to eat something. I suppose that's enough progress for him at the moment.

As Dylan gathers up the cards, there's a soft, but firm knock on the front door. Before I can even start to rise from sitting, he is striding across the room to answer it. He swings the door wide to reveal an owl-eyed Lynn.

From my vantage point, I can see her eyes are the size of saucers and knuckles have gone white from tightly clasping the foil-covered container she has in her hands. She is obviously surprised and nervous. I'm just not sure whether it's because she didn't expect the door to open or because of the fact that it wasn't me who answered it.

Exaggerating his Southern accent a bit, Dylan calls to me. "Levi, my brother, you have been holding out on me. I knew the views up here were gorgeous, but you failed to mention that they were delivered directly to your front door."

Lynn is the picture of country comfort in worn denim cut-offs, woven sandals, a clingy, light pink tank top, and the end of her long braid falling over her shoulder. The sight of her is delectable. I can tell Dylan agrees. He is getting quite his fill of looking at her.

I can see dueling reactions cross Lynn's face. Her guard is up immediately from the straightening of her spine, but there is also a light blush forming across her cheeks I think because of Dylan's obvious visual appreciation. She, like so many women, is affected by Dylan's charm. I don't like it.

I've decided I no longer need a best friend and have plenty of land to bury his body. Lumbering to my feet and growling possessively, I snap at him, "Can it, D."

"Just enjoying the scenery, my friend," he responds with another casual glance at Lynn.

His low chuckle meets my ear as I somewhat forcefully push him out of the way so I am the only thing in her line of sight. I see the tension in Lynn's shoulders ease once her eyes meet mine. A soft smile curls on her lips. My body automatically starts to heat up from the sweet expression. God, how I've missed simply looking at her. It seems like an eternity rather than just days since I last saw her.

"Hi," she whispers softly.

"Hey you. What are you doing here?" I will have to begrudgingly thank my pain in the ass friend later for showing up and getting me to focus enough to shower. If Lynn had seen how I looked three hours ago, I have no doubt she'd be running for the hills.

"I was starting to worry after the way you left the store. Since you haven't been in, I wanted to check on you." She suddenly looks uncertain. "Is that okay?"

I can feel my face split into a stupid grin and a fluttering in my chest at her concern.

"Hell yeah, that's okay." I'm elated she didn't seem to take my asinine behavior personally.

She lets out a surprised laugh at my candor and color stains her face. There's the blush I love so much. Maybe I should be more aloof or keep my distance, but I don't want to. I've spent too many days trapped in a dark hole, trying to find a way out, trying to find a light. She is that light, one I need to help pull myself up. And, this is exactly what I have wanted from the moment I met her, for her to lose the timid cloud that has surrounded her. I wanted her to show the strong, sassy woman I have seen in small glimpses. The fact that she has sought me out is a huge step. However, just as quickly as her anxiousness abated, it returns.

"Okay, well, seems like you're good," she rushes quickly. "So, I'll just go." She turns to step off the porch.

"No, wait!" I panic. I don't want her to leave. "Um, I mean, you don't have to go."

Turning back toward me, she hesitates, "Well, I don't want to intrude and I can see you have company."

I throw my thumb over my shoulder at Dylan, who's disappeared into the kitchen, "Oh, him? He's nobody."

"I heard that. Love you too buddy," he calls. I know the only reason he heard me is because he's eavesdropping.

A smirk tugs at her lips. I silently thank him for already putting her at ease. I look beyond her shoulder to the direction she would be heading if she left and realize there isn't another vehicle parked in the driveway. I frown.

"Lynn? How did you get here?" I ask, already knowing I won't like the answer.

86

Reluctantly and a little too brightly, she tells me, "Oh, I walked. It's no big deal. It was nice."

Oh, hell no. It is a big deal. While I have walked to and from town a thousand times since I turned a double digit age, there is no way I am comfortable with her, or any woman for that matter, walking the same road, especially alone, even if this town is the safest place I know. I feel the urge to roar at her blasé statement to make my point, but am sure it wouldn't be received with the concern with which I intend it.

So, I instead tamp down my frustration and calmly, but sternly say, "It is a big deal, darlin'. You shouldn't have walked alone." More softly, I add, "But, I guess you wouldn't have had to if it wasn't for me storming out on you the other day. The blame is on me for that. I am sorry. I was horrible and you didn't deserve it."

Her face softens. "Uh, it's okay. I know you didn't mean it."

It's clear she isn't accustomed to other people apologizing for their actions. That realization makes me wonder more about what is going on with her. How could this beautiful, sweet woman not know she deserves to be respected? She deserves for someone to willingly give her an apology for their bad behavior, even if it was unintentional.

I move aside from the doorway, giving a silent indication I'd like her to stay, saying, "Well, now I guess we have established that I was a jerk and you might consider staying for a while?" She needs to be the one to make this decision. I don't want her to feel cornered or pushed. If she doesn't want to stay, I won't make her, but I'm hoping like hell that she does.

Lynn takes a deep breath, letting it out slowly, and walks over the threshold. I let out the breath I have been holding, relieved.

"Great, because I can't quite manage walking you back to town right now with my leg. The only other option is riding back in the truck with that guy," I say, pointing at Dylan. "And there's no way I'm leaving you alone with the likes of him."

Sauntering back into the living room, he replies, "Hey, she'd be in good hands, my friend."

"That's exactly why I won't allow it," I growl, closing the door. I can see a little blush return to Lynn's face, but not as much as before. I wonder if it's caused by Dylan's statement or mine. I notice though that she didn't move any farther into the room without me. That action leaves me hopeful. Maybe she isn't as affected by Mr. Suave as much as I thought. I'm relieved my friend gets to keep all his teeth tonight.

Crossing the room toward us, Dylan has a gleam in his eye. I know this look. I sigh inwardly. He might just lose a tooth or ten, after all.

"Since my lunkhead of a best friend seems to have no intention of introducing me to you, let me do the honors. I'm Dylan Reed, the better." He extends his hand to Lynn for a handshake.

Distracted by his seemingly unfinished sentence, she lifts her hand to him, saying curiously, "The better what?"

Belatedly, I remember that Dylan never shakes a lady's hand. With a wink and a Cheshire cat size grin, he turns her knuckles up and brushes his lips across them, saying, "The better at, well, everything, ma'am."

I stomp forward and push him in the chest, hard, disconnecting him from Lynn and sending him staggering backward several steps.

"Dude, you are beggin' for an ass beating tonight!" I roar.

He is laughing uncontrollably, apparently intentionally provoking my reaction. Damn him. At least this is better than him using a two by four on my head.

I look at Lynn. She is simply standing there, staring at Dylan, confusion plain on her face. Apparently, she doesn't know what to make of him. Most days admittedly, neither do I and I've known him for more than a decade.

Shaking my head, I tell her through clenched teeth, "Don't mind him. He's an idiot."

I love Dylan, would walk through hell's fire for him, and have more than once, but I will hurt him if he touches her again. A point I intend on making clearly known to him later.

She looks up at me and her eyes widen slightly. I see her pupils expand and a flush brightens her skin. She glances away quickly as her color deepens. Whatever she saw when she looked at me, she liked. I feel like puffing out my chest and flicking my buddy the bird.

Clearing her throat, Lynn speaks up, "Nice to meet you. I guess." She nervously peeks sideways at me. Then, says, "I'm Lynn."

He just snickers. "It's nice to meet you, Lynn. You'll have to excuse the grumpy bear over there. It's feeding time here at the zoo and he getting a little riled up."

With mischief in her eye, she says almost too softly to hear, "I kind of like him riled up."

And just like that the irritation at my best friend's earlier antics evaporates while all the blood in my head rushes south. Thankfully, he is moving back to the kitchen and doesn't hear her.

Trying to keep control on any caveman tendencies, I search for something to distract me. My eye snags on the bowl she's carrying. I point to it. "Um, is that for me?"

Shyly, she says, "Yeah, I brought you Miss Dottie's peach cobbler."

Our eyes clash together. Clearly, we are both remembering the best part of our last day at the store. It doesn't register that Lynn and I are still standing in the entryway, staring at each other, until Dylan returns carrying a tray piled with food.

Oblivious to the electricity in the air, he tells her, "So, Lynn, we were just going to hang, maybe watch a movie, and eat. Nothing spectacular, just frozen pizza, some chips with dip, a few cold beers, if you'd like to join us."

"Um." I can see she's uncertain, but am not sure why.

"Please?" I ask softly. This is my chance to make up for my behavior. I can't let it slip away.

She searches my face and finally gives me a sweet smile. Her eyes dart between mine and my lips. "Sure, sounds nice," she answers. "But, do you have some soda instead though?"

Relaxing with a grin, I say, "Yeah, no problem. Make yourself at home while I go get it."

I take the bowl of cobbler from her and move to the kitchen, trying not to limp too much along the way. I know it's macho crap, yet I don't want Lynn to see any weakness. My leg is better, but is still stiff and extremely

90

sore, especially since I stopped taking the prescription pain medication. I am done with that shit.

16

Him

I rummage around the kitchen grabbing two glasses with ice and three sodas. When I return to the living room, Lynn has moved from the entryway, however she isn't sitting down. She seems unsure about where to sit between the choices of the recliner, the two wing back chairs, or the couch. Dylan is busy perusing the movie cabinet for something to watch. I'm certain he has already made a decision. He is simply being polite, waiting for her and me to sit where we want first. I'm grateful he's figured out not pushing her is how to make her relax.

I can tell she's thinking things through and is hesitant. Normally, I would place my hand lightly on her back to steer her where I would like her to be, but I can't do that with my hands full of our drinks. I realize maybe it's better that I don't have the opportunity anyway. I want her as comfortable as possible and somehow I know that means she has to be in control of the decisions right now.

I pass in front of her, setting the sodas and glasses on the big ottoman. I sit on the farthest side from her on the couch, making sure if she did sit with me it wouldn't be on my injured side. A moment later, I can see she's made her choice. Slowly, she settles on the couch with me, although maintaining a distance so we aren't touching. At least she's not glued to the other arm away from me.

Turning to me, tentatively, she asks, "How's your leg?"

Figures she would get right to the point. Even when she has been her most reserved, she's still direct with me. "It's good," I exaggerate.

She looks at me pointedly, but doesn't mention the limp, which now I'm positive she noticed.

Reluctantly, I admit, "Okay, so it's not great, but it is getting better. Just really sore mostly and stiff. I just need to keep up with my exercises for strengthening it. It'll be in good working order sometime soon."

She reaches out and lightly strokes her thumb under my eye, along my cheekbone. Electricity flows through me at her touch. She drops her hand and I miss the contact immediately.

"You look tired," she says.

My posture deflates instantly. I can't lie to her. I won't. Even though I hardly know her, I do know that telling her anything untrue, intentionally, will be the death of us. Whatever us is.

"I am," I admit. "I haven't been sleeping well." I pour the drinks into our glasses, watching the bubbles fizz. I can feel her eyes on me. She's waiting for more patiently.

Sighing, I realize I will never get her to trust me with her secrets if I don't trust her with mine. I decide to reveal some of my weakness.

I look into her eyes to find the strength I need and begin, "I was injured overseas, an accident that hurt my knee. I had to have a complete replacement done. I was put on prescription medicine for the pain. I was on the pills for months. They make me feel horrible, disconnected. I hate taking them. I eventually only took them when I absolutely couldn't stand the pain anymore and hid the rest from the doctors. But, lately, I think I've been pushing myself, my leg, too much. So, when I twisted it last week, I was in a lot of pain, enough to need the pills."

I can see her thinking about everything, trying to understand. "So, they don't help you sleep?"

"No, actually, they give me nightmares, so, I purposely don't sleep when I take them." I can't handle telling her yet that they aren't truly nightmares. They are memories that become twisted because of the medicine. The realities I saw on missions were gruesome and unimaginable. They are bad enough on their own, but what happens in my head to the scenes when I take the pills would make anyone go completely insane. So, when I have to take the medication, I can either take a temporary trip to crazy town by not sleeping or go ahead and make a standing reservation for a padded room. I like my freedom a little too much to be confined permanently.

Looking at me with sympathy, she says, "That doesn't sound healthy."

I shrug, not knowing what else to do. "It's not. That's why I haven't been around this week. Wasn't really fit to be around people. Had to get my head back on straight first."

"Hmm," is her only response.

Worried, I ask, "What?" I don't like it when there's something going on in her head that she's not expressing. Dropping her eyes, she wrings her hands together. "Well, maybe I shouldn't stay then."

Gently laying my hand over hers, I plead, "No, please. Stay. I'm doin' better. Dylan here came by at the right time. And having you here, well, it helps."

"I came by to kick his ass for not returning my calls. He's always got to be looked after and I drew the short straw," he interjects. I think he's tired of being left out of the conversation.

"Dude, bite me. You can leave," I tell him with more venom than I actually mean.

Completely unperturbed by my ire, he says, "Nah, think I'll stick around for a bit. Lots to become familiar with around here." He's wearing his happier-than-a-pig-in-slop grin as he glances at Lynn.

I'm about to come off the couch and remove it from his smug face when Lynn's hand softly lands on my arm. The small gesture has my entire body frozen in place. It's amazing how one little touch from her can stop me in my tracks and defuse my whirlwind emotions.

She smiles sweetly and then directs her attention to Dylan. "As amusing as you two are to watch, I didn't come here to see blood be spilled. So, what'd you pick for us to watch?"

"A classic, of course. One about two grumpy old men," he announces, holding up the movie.

Positively delighted, she beams. "Oh, I haven't seen that one." Dylan is back on my good side for picking a comedy, which we all need.

Appalled, Dylan stares at her. "You have got to be kidding me!?"

She leans slightly back into the couch, shyly saying, "No, I haven't really had a lot of time in my life for movie watching."

I can tell that Lynn is trying to keep the conversation light, but I hear the tension in her voice when she says anything about her past, no matter how trivial the statement. Now is no different.

Overlooking her slight change in tone, Dylan hoots, "Well, Lynn, you are in for some laughs! I love these two old codgers."

We all settle in to watch the movie with Lynn and me on the couch and Dylan in the recliner. The pizza and sodas have been polished off before the movie is halfway finished. I get up to clear the plates and go make some popcorn for us to enjoy. I can hear my best friend and the girl I want laughing with ease. It brings a smile to my face. I could get used to this.

I join them back in the living room, carrying two heaping bowls of buttered popcorn, handing one to Dylan.

I have no doubt he'll consume the entire thing on his own. He's a popcorn hog.

I settle back on the couch with Lynn, looking at her and ask, "I was thinking we could just share a bowl?"

She smiles. "Sure."

She kicks off her shoes and curls her legs beneath her, scooting closer to me. Her knee is pressed into my thigh. I feel the usual hum that crosses my skin whenever we have any contact with one another. I hand her the bowl to hold and put my arm across the back of the couch in a relaxed position even though I am anything except that. I long to put my arm around her and pull her close, knowing she'll fit perfectly.

After a while, I get lucky and my wish is granted. We've finished most of the popcorn and Lynn places it on the ottoman in front of the couch. When she leans back against the couch, she snuggles closer to me into the nook of my shoulder. She pushes up, causing my arm to drape around her, my hand landing gently on her denim clad hip.

I spend the next few hours completely unaware of anything, other than every move and breath Lynn makes. I breathe in her scent and relish in the warmth of her body next to mine.

17

Him

The second movie Dylan put in is over and Lynn has fallen asleep against me. She is making soft murmuring noises. I couldn't ask for a more perfect moment, but I know we can't stay like this. I wouldn't be able to move in the morning and Lynn would surely have a horrible crick in her neck.

Dylan rises from the recliner and gathers everything to take into the kitchen. "You gonna wake her," he asks.

I'm torn. I know it might be upsetting waking up in a strange place, but she's sleeping so calmly. I don't have the heart to wake her to take her home.

"Nah, I think I'll just put her in my room. I hope she doesn't freak out though."

He looks at her carefully and then says, "With the way she's sleeping right now, I think she might not open her eyes until the sun comes up. She looked pretty beat when she got here."

I look down at her. I realize he's right when I see her lashes fanned across the dark circles under her eyes.

Apparently, I'm not the only one who hasn't been sleeping.

"Need any help? I'd be happy to put her to bed," he winks.

Growling lowly, I respond, "No, I got it, asshole. You keep your hands to yourself where she's concerned." Maneuvering the stairs while carrying her will take some finesse, however, there's no way I'll allow Dylan to put his hands anywhere on her body.

He just chuckles as he strolls out of the room.

Hoping not to wake her, I gently secure my arm around her back while the other slides beneath her knees. I move her to my lap in one fluid motion. She snuggles deeper into me, sighing contentedly. She feels incredible against me. I'm a goner if things ever go any further than this for us.

I know standing will be difficult although not because of her weight. I would barely know she's in my arms if not for her scent surrounding me and the feel of her in my hands. The problem is my leg won't want to cooperate because I have been sitting for so long.

I stand using my good leg and my upper body to keep her steady while I work on flexing the rehabilitated muscles to get them limber. When I feel like I can trust my movements, I head toward the stairs. Even though I know she would protest at me giving up my own space, I plan to put Lynn in my room and I'll return to the couch. I don't want to frighten her by lying down next to her.

After maneuvering up the stairs without much trouble, I cross the room to my bed. Laying her gently in the center, I cover her with my favorite blanket. For a moment, all I can do is simply stare at her. She looks so perfect, curled up in my bed, like she's belonged there all along. It takes every ounce of will I have not to crawl in next to her.

Reluctantly, I make my way back to the living room, shutting off lights along the way. I strip off my shirt, immediately missing the scent she left on my shoulder. I settle on the couch, leaving my shorts on, aware that at any moment Lynn could appear. There's no use in trying to find a comfortable position though, not when the woman I want is where I want her and I'm not beside her. I watch the moon filter in the window and torture myself thinking about what it would be like to lie beside her.

To my surprise, I must have dozed off because I awaken sometime later to the sound of shuffling feet. I watch as Lynn tiptoes down the stairs, entering the living room. She moves silently to stand at the end of the couch. With the blanket and moonlight wrapped around her, she looks like an angel. I sit up slowly careful not to startle her.

"Lynn? You okay?" I whisper, but my voice sounds loud in the dead of night.

I barely see her nervously biting on her bottom lip.

"Uh, yeah. I just woke up and panicked a bit. Kind of didn't remember where I was." I can hear the trepidation in her voice.

Hating that my prediction was correct, I hurry to try to put her at ease and explain. "I'm sorry. You were sleeping so peacefully, I didn't want to wake you. I thought you'd be uncomfortable staying here on the couch and figured my bed would be better."

I can just make out the small, sweet smile she gives me. "That's very thoughtful of you. Thank you. It was more comfortable there. Sort of."

"Sort of?" I hedge, hopeful.

Hesitantly, she answers, "Well, I woke up alone."

Hope blooms in my chest at what she could be saying.

"I didn't want to overstep any boundaries. I felt like lying with you might seem a bit, um, forward and I didn't want that. I want you to be comfortable in every way."

She looks me straight in the eye and says, "I am. With you, that is. Even though I'm still not certain why. I mean I've only known you for such a short time, but that doesn't seem to matter. When I'm with you, I feel safe." She pauses. I see her debate over an idea for just a moment, then, "Can I stay with you, down here?"

I want to pound on my chest for her saying I make her feel secure. My macho side is eating it up. But, my rational side is questioning her words. While I do want her to feel safe, I want more than that too. I don't just want to be a place for her to hide. I realize now I want to be everything. I want to be the place she wants to be and the person she wants to be with, not because it's an easy option, only because it's right. I'll have to figure out later if she'll let me be all of those things or just a safe haven. For now, I decide to just put it aside. I don't want to waste the time I have with her while she is standing right in front of me.

I stand slowly, hoping that I won't suddenly discover this is all a dream even though it's the best one I can remember having in forever. Extending my hand, I reach for her. She places her hand in mine and steps forward around the couch. I take the blanket from around her shoulders and she shivers. The air in the house is cool and crisp. Looking up at me, she removes the band securing the end of her braid. Her fingers move gracefully, undoing the woven strands. The light scent of vanilla immediately hits me. Now, a shiver runs across my skin. On their own, it seems, my hands move. My fingers thread through her thick, honeyed hair, sliding to the ends. It's softer than silk. I watch as her golden eyes search my face. After a moment, she closes her eyes and a soft exhale escapes her lips. Every muscle in my body has locked in place. I desperately try to keep my touch

100

light as my hands run down her arms. Goosebumps have broken out over her skin. It takes every ounce of control I have not to press my body to hers and claim her mouth.

I whisper, "Come on, let's lie down. You'll get chilled standing here much longer."

I turn and push the over-sized ottoman next to the couch to give my back some added support behind me. The couch is wide, but I don't want to feel like I'm going to fall on the floor at any moment or flatten Lynn into the cushions trying to make room for myself.

She lies down on her left side and I am on my right, facing each other. My arm is a pillow for her head, which fits just under my chin. I don't press against her too much. I want her to decide how close she wants to be. To my surprise and pleasure, she fits us together, twining her legs with mine and crushing her fantastic little body to me. I pull my hips away just slightly to try and keep my sanity, reminding my rock hard cock he's not getting any action tonight. She apparently is not happy with our position and has other ideas. She scoots her hips closer and plasters herself against me. I'm pretty sure my brain short-circuits as I wrap my other arm around her hips and lower back tightly, possessively. I hear her sigh contentedly and feel all the tension drain out of her body.

Despite the demands of my body, I say softly, "Go to sleep, darlin'," kissing the top of her head.

I'm pretty sure she's already more than halfway there because a soft murmur is the only response I hear.

18

Her

My eyes open to the sunlight streaming in brightly through Levi's living room windows. Sadly, I'm alone on the couch. Levi's blanket is tucked tightly around me, showing me that he has once again taken care of me without demanding anything in return. I have wondered how I can trust him so easily given the people in my past, but this shows me the reason. He is giving and considerate. He goes out of his way to see to my needs before his own. And there is never any pressure from him regarding anything. He also has a way of putting me at ease with a simple gesture or word.

With thoughts of him swirling in my head, I can't keep from burying my nose into the folds and breathe in the scent of him. Even just the smell I have come to know as his has my body waking up like a live wire. I can feel myself blush as I recall the night before. It was wonderful lying wrapped in his arms, however, I find myself craving more from him every minute we spend together.

I woke up in his bed, chilled and disappointed from being alone. I remember feeling like I was floating with the warmth and solidness of him against me, but then found him absent when my eyes opened in the middle of the night. He must have carried me upstairs and retreated, giving up his space to me. I couldn't help the affection I felt at the gesture, even though I would have preferred feeling him next to me.

After tossing and turning for several minutes, I finally gave up and silently made my way downstairs, hoping not to wake him. Although praying at the same time he wouldn't be asleep. As I hit the bottom of the stairs, I saw my prayer was granted, along with so much more. My mouth went dry at the sight of him stretched out on the couch, shirtless. My fingers ache to run over the muscled plane of his chest and stomach. He was temptation solidified. I didn't want to go back to his bed alone. However, I also wasn't sure I had enough restraint to keep me from giving into my craving for him if we were behind a closed door. I decided staying on the couch might help me control myself, especially knowing Dylan was in the house.

As he ran his fingers through my hair, a slow ache started low in my belly. All my nerves tingled from the contact. His touch was so slow and gentle, disciplined even, like he was handling a skittish animal. I suppose that's exactly what I'm like, a scared and wary creature just waiting for the reality I think I know to turn into a cloud of deception.

I gazed up into his handsome face, looking for any of the same cunning and deceit I should have seen with my parents and Richard so long ago, but there was none of that. The only things I saw were concern, hopefulness, and desire, all of which I'm sure he could have hidden from me if he chose. The fact that he didn't was another small piece of proof showing me I could trust him.

As his hands moved down my hair and arms, I let all my thoughts disappear, relishing in his touch. Everything around me faded into nothing. It was only a fog of sensation. His voice guided me to the couch. I laid down, wedged between the back cushions and Levi's muscled body. I could tell he was trying to give me some space or maybe just keeping himself at a distance. Whatever the case, I wasn't letting it happen. Lying next to him was the sweetest torture. If that contact was all I could allow for now, I was definitely making sure it was from head to toe. Feeling his arm securing me against him was the final thing I needed to let go of my tension. Surrounded by Levi's scent and body, I could feel myself sink into a cocoon of warmth and drifted off into the deepest sleep I'd had in a long time.

Smiling from the memory, I stretch like a well-rested cat and catch the low, deep rumble of male voices coming from the kitchen. Wrapping the blanket around me, I walk across the cool wooden floor, stopping just outside the doorway. My intention isn't to eavesdrop, but all my movement stops when I hear Levi and Dylan's conversation.

"I don't know, D. I'm positive something big is going on with Lynn. I want to help her, if she'll let me, but I don't know how to convince her she can trust me." I can hear the concern and frustration battling in Levi's voice.

Dylan answers with his usual amused annoyance. "Levi, dude, as usual, you are pretty dense. From what I can see, she already does trust you."

Sounding hopeful, he asks, "Ya think so, man?"

"She's here, isn't she?" Dylan counters. "I don't see Lynn as a woman who wants to stay in a place where she doesn't feel safe. Besides, she came to you, remember?"

There's a pause. I can tell Levi is considering Dylan's words. I'm a little shocked to learn these two men are so perceptive. Neither has known me for very long, but they have both figured out several of my issues and how to combat them. It's no wonder they're best friends and have a solid bond.

Finally agreeing, Levi says, "Yeah, I guess you're right. I just want her to know that I'll protect her with everything I've got, if it comes to that."

"Just keep doin' what you're doing. You're the most dependable and loyal guy I know. Seems to me the best way for her to learn that is just by you showing her."

Dylan's description of Levi gives me a warm feeling all over while a smile grows on my lips.

"Thanks, man. That means a lot."

Their words sink in, making me feel truly safe for the first time in months. It's a luxury I really can't afford though. I realize with absolute clarity that me being here in town and with them could also put them in danger. Richard will stop at nothing to find me and he won't care who gets in his way. He is ruthless and powerful. He'll use all of his resources to get what he wants. And right now, it's quite possible he wants revenge against me for not dutifully doing what he wants. I wrap the blanket more tightly around my shoulders as the thought leaves me feeling bitterly cold and angry. I have to figure out how to deal with him once and for all to reclaim my life. I refuse to have anyone else getting hurt because of my parents' mistakes.

The smell of coffee has me deciding it's time to stop hovering outside the doorway, I run my fingers through my hair to try and appear somewhat presentable. Thank goodness I don't have a mirror. I'm sure I would be mortified at the reflection.

Stepping into the kitchen, I do my best to mask my thoughts and the emotions I am not ready to explain. Levi's gaze seeks me out the moment I pass over the threshold even though my feet haven't made a sound. For a second, I can see him looking for something, answers probably, but as usual, he doesn't pry. Then, a wide smile spreads across his face.

"Good morning, darlin'."

I can feel my cheeks flush at his attention. I'm not usually a morning person. However, the thought of seeing that smile in the morning could possibly turn me into one. I smile in return.

"Morning," I say softly, then, "Is that coffee I smell?" Both men laugh as Levi reaches for a mug to fill.

Humor weaves through his words as he says, "I'll warn you, it's high octane. Milk or sugar? Afraid I don't have any flavored stuff to spruce it up for you."

I shrug. "That's okay. I like it strong. The stronger, the better. And I don't use any of that frilly stuff. Just some sugar please."

They stare at me, clearly surprised. Apparently that wasn't the response they expected. I take some satisfaction in keeping them guessing.

"What? I'd mainline coffee if I could first thing in the morning," I blurt out. Chuckles and smiles from both men follow my statement.

Levi crosses the kitchen, steaming mug in hand. He passes it to me and kisses me lightly on the cheek. I duck my head feeling myself blush once again. I can't seem to control that particular reaction when he's around me. He just grins as he steps away. It's clear the coloring of my cheeks is a source of amusement for him.

"Levi, I think I like her more than I did last night," Dylan gloats. I had forgotten he was even in the room.

Levi's eyes snap to his friend. "Dude, don't you have somewhere else to be?"

With his eyes twinkling, he leans back against the counter top, casually, saying, "Nope. I'm good right here."

Levi snarls as Dylan just shrugs his shoulders unaffected by his best friend's fabricated temper. It's obvious both take a lot of pleasure in aggravating one another.

I take a seat on a stool at the extended counter, letting my hands soak in the warmth from the mug. I watch in fascination the scene before me. It seems an unspoken conversation is going on between the men. After a minute, Dylan simply nods his head once and drains his coffee cup.

"Okay, as much as I've love to hang around here with you two, I'm going to head into town to see Miss Sarah. Figure I'll help in the store for a bit. You kids have fun!"

Levi and I watch as Dylan gives a little salute and saunters out the back door, leaving us alone.

Levi's attention shifts back to me, "So, you don't have to be into work today?" He barely covers the eagerness in his voice.

Smiling, I tell him, "No. I told Miss Sarah I was coming to check on you. She said not to bother with coming in, that she'd manage. She worries about you."

Levi ducks his head, looking regretful. "Yeah, I know. She's like a second mother to me. She was mom's best friend. After they died, I'm not sure what it would have been like without her around."

My heart aches for him. "I'm so sorry, Levi. I can't imagine losing someone so important."

And, honestly, I couldn't. While at one time I thought I was close to my parents, it's clear I never had the relationship with my parents that Levi did with his. I envy him. Even knowing what I do about my parents and how they had lied to me, losing them is still difficult. But, only because I lost the possibility of what could have been. For Levi, I'm sure the loss is gut-wrenching. He lost the reality.

"Well, I don't want to spend the day being all mopey, not when I have you all to myself," he grins. Just like that he changes the heavy mood in the air to lightness and fills it with innuendo.

I find my heart rate kicking up at thinking about spending time away from everyone, having him all to myself. I'm not sure I can control the desires I have building for this man. Keeping my distance emotionally and physically from Levi is proving to be a challenge, and one I'm more than willing to lose.

"Okay, so, finish up your coffee. I'm sure you want to freshen up. There's an extra toothbrush in the cabinet in my bathroom. You're welcome to it. I've got to get a few things together for the plans I have in mind for the day. Meet me back here in the kitchen in about twenty." With that, he brushes his lips over my forehead and exits the room. I'm giddy at the prospect of a frivolous day. I haven't had one in longer than I can remember.

19

Her

Swallowing the last of my coffee, I dash upstairs to brush my teeth and put some order to my hair. Taking a glance in the mirror, I cringe at the sight I see. It's a wonder Levi didn't push me out the door with a bag over my head.

I decide the only way to tame my wild tresses is to wet them. Since I feel disgusting after walking here yesterday and falling asleep with all that grime on my skin, I figure a fast shower will help me feel presentable. I lather up my hair and body quickly, relishing in the smells that remind me of Levi. Stepping out of the shower, I towel dry and wring out my hair. Looking at my clothes from the day before, I sneer. The thought of putting them back on isn't all that appealing, however I don't have anything else. I shake out the tank and shorts, seeing they don't look as bad as I thought, but I can't stomach the idea of putting on the same panties again. I'll have to go without and immediately wonder what Levi's reaction might be if he knew. The thought makes me feel bold and brazen. Wanting to hurry back to the kitchen where Levi is no doubt already waiting, I swirl my damp hair into a bun and bound down the stairs.

Practically skipping into the room, I skid to a halt at the sight of him, damp haired and gorgeous leaning against the counter, the picture of ease. He looks up and my breath catches as it always does when he looks at me.

"I thought we might have a picnic. There's the perfect spot here on the property," he suggests, elbowing the basket behind him.

Giddy with excitement, I answer, "That sounds lovely."

"Great!" he says enthusiastically.

Levi picks up the loaded picnic basket up from the table and takes my hand in his. He pushes his way out the back screen door, leaving the main door wide open.

Hesitantly, I ask, "Do you want me to close that?"

"Nah, no one's around to bother the place," he says casually. "Plus, D should be back from town sometime later. Besides, that's one of the joys of living in a small town. You don't have to worry about silly things like closing and locking doors all the time."

I don't consider keeping doors closed and locked a silly thing. For me they are a necessity for survival, but I keep my opinion to myself. I figure voicing it would bring up too many questions, ones I'm not ready to answer just yet, so I quickly change the subject.

"Are we walking to your perfect spot?" I'm curious about our plans for the day.

While we move away from the house, Levi clasps my hand gently in his. The feeling is so natural and comfortable. It seems like such an ordinary gesture although to me it's intimate and meaningful. A small smile tugs at my lips.

Answering my question, Levi explains, "No, just out to the garage. While it *is* the perfect spot, walking to it might be a bit of a trek. We'll need something that moves a little faster and will let us move over the terrain of the property easily."

My feet come to a complete stop. I'm suddenly not sure I'll like his choice of transportation. When my feet halt, he's still walking and the opposing movement jerks our hands from one another. He stops and turns to me with a questioning look. I'm certain my feelings are showing all over my face. Immediately, he comes to my side.

Clearly concerned, he assures me, "Lynn, there's nothing to worry about. I promise. I won't let anything happen to you."

The sincerity and truth of his statement shines brightly in his eyes. It's obvious he means it, which allows me to breathe a little easier. With my chin up, I take a deep breath, grabbing his hand again as I exhale and step toward the garage. I hear the light rumble of laughter deep in his chest. I'm not sure what I've done to amuse him, but his lack of irritation about my nerves eases them even more. With anyone else I would automatically be on the defensive.

We stroll out to the garage, hand in hand. It's as if we had been doing this sort of thing for years. There was no awkwardness or hesitation on Levi's part. No questioning or indecision. It seemed this was just the way Levi wanted it, so it was. Part of me is certain he'll make it easy to fall for him. The other part is still terrified of the exact same thing.

On the way across the yard, I look in every direction. The sun is brilliant and warm, showcasing the property. His land is so beautiful, lush and green, covered with a multitude of trees and rolling hills. And the house in the middle of it all reminds me of the scenes in Currier and Ives' lithographs. It really is the perfect day for a picnic.

He stops me outside the garage, placing the basket at my feet. Smirking slightly, he says, "You wait here while I get our chariot."

His expression is, dare I say, gleeful? It is certainly mischievous. I can feel the beginning of unease forming in the bottom of my belly. Just then, I hear the rumble of a motor and my stomach drops to my knees. He rides out of the garage on a death trap!

I balk at him, "You have got to be kidding!"

Levi's face is lit up like the fireworks on the Fourth of July. He looks so youthful in this moment, grinning from ear to ear. His expression is just like a ten year old boy who is about to pull the best prank of his young life. There is a certain giddiness about him I haven't seen before. At any other time, I would welcome this joyfulness from him. But, right now, I am not amused. The obvious enjoyment he is having in this situation does not take priority over me risking my life on some mechanical contraption.

He drives over to me and sits idling. "Hop on!" he shouts.

I eye him sitting atop of the four-wheeler with trepidation. I'm not sure which emotion is stronger. Nervousness at riding on the machine itself or exhilaration at sitting with my body pressed up against Levi. When he looks at me over his shoulder with a knowing grin, I'm sure it's the latter. Gathering my courage, I take a deep breath and walk the few steps over to the side of the death cart. He takes the basket from my hands, strapping it to the back. Then, he extends his hand to help me up and smiles.

"Come on. It'll be fun," he promises.

I know my face is the picture of doubt as I bite my bottom lip. He turns on the sit toward me. Gently, he brushes a stray hair away from my face and cups my cheek. I find myself leaning into his touch. His thumb strokes my skin lightly, sending shivers through my body. Looking me with softening eyes, his expression becomes honest and sincere.

112

"I won't let anything happen to you. You're safe with me."

He has no idea what those words mean to me. They mean so much more than he could possibly realize.

Earnestly, he watches like he's almost expecting me to laugh in his face or afraid I'll simply walk away.

Putting my hand in his, I see him release a breath, smiling. I step up on the foot rest and swing my leg over the seat. I sit down behind him. There are still several inches between us, but I can feel the heat radiating from his body. Before I understand what he's doing, Levi reaches back, grabbing my hips on both sides and pulls me flush against him. I gasp at the contact. My legs are straddled around his hips, cradling him, and my chest is smashed into his back. My body warms all over, instantly. There is no space, not even a paper's width, separating us now. I guess he had a problem with it when there was. I can't say that I am opposed to our current position either.

Levi looks back over his shoulder and I see his blue topaz eyes swirling with desire. He doesn't try to mask it. He reaches back one more time taking both my hands until they are wrapped around the front of him. I grab handfuls of his shirt. The only thing I am aware of in that moment is the feeling of rippling abs under his clothing and the luscious fervor spreading through my lower body. A sound something between a sigh and a moan escapes me. I stiffen slightly hoping he didn't hear it.

He drapes one of his arms across both of my hands and grips my right forearm, squeezing gently. I can feel him take a deep breath. Once he releases it, his whole body relaxes.

He lightly rubs my arm as he says, almost to himself, "Now, this is better."

He glances back at me with a grin kicked up on one side of his mouth. I instantly know I'm in trouble.

However, before I can change my mind, he warns, "I'm gonna need you to hold on *really* tight."

As the last syllable leaves his lips, he guns the four-wheeler, taking off as if the devil himself is chasing us. I squeal, trying to plaster my body more snugly against him, sinking claws into his concrete stomach, and burying my face in between his shoulder blades. I squeeze my eyes shut, too scared to see the world go by in a blur. I find myself praying it will be over soon or at least that I don't die. And I am so not a religious person. I can feel his laughter rumbling in his chest against my cheek like a miniature earthquake. He is thoroughly amused and I vow to have him singing soprano before the day's over.

20

Her

After the violent take-off, our ride becomes smooth and settled. I loosen my death grip hold just a little and peek through my eyelids. All I see is sprawling green pastures edged with trees swaying in the breeze. The landscape is incredible.

I take a calming breath to loosen my tense muscles. The familiar scent of Levi surrounds me and he smells really good, rustic and inherently male. The scent reminds me of an early spring day right after winter thaws and newly cut wood. It's subtle and pleasing. I breath in more deeply, uncurling my fists, and splay my hands across Levi's abdomen. He quickly rubs my hand before returning it to the handle grips. The touch is tender and sweet.

Since the fear of bodily injury is no longer an enormous concern, I am suddenly aware of the intimacy our proximity to each other creates. It reminds me of the night before. I can feel a full blush rise to my cheeks. I'm glad he can't see me. I'm sure he would be laughing in my face. I shift on the seat, making it seem like I'm trying to get comfortable instead of doing what I'm actually doing, which is putting a little distance between us, just as he tried to do. Part of me instantly regrets it because I've lost some of the warmth from being so close to Levi. I hear a sound that can only be identified as a growl. Without turning his head, saying a word, or slowing the four-wheeler, he reaches behind and cups his hand behind my left knee. He gives a good hard tug, pulling me flush against him again, caresses my kneecap, and then resumes his previous position with both hands

115

on the handle bars. Okay, I guess that gesture tells me his opinion on the matter. I decide it might be better to concentrate on the passing scenery instead of the growing need I have for him.

We travel for what seems like another ten minutes over flat fields and rolling hills. Just ahead I can see the approaching tree line. As we near it, I see a path, partially overgrown, yet still well defined from decades of obvious use I'm sure. Levi slows his speed to maneuver through the trees and brush. He has to duck his head a few times to avoid some wayward saplings smacking him in the face.

We emerge from the woods into a small clearing, showcasing a glistening pool. Levi parks the four-wheeler off to the side near the trees and shuts off the engine. The musical noise from the forest canopy takes over along with the soothing sound of trickling water. I slip off the back and walk closer to the water's edge. The small lagoon is flanked on several sides by a few large rocks, perfect for diving into the reflective surface. The area is surrounded by tall evergreens and a bed of fragrant needles, creating a soft pad for walking. I catch sight of a thick, knotted rope hanging from one of the largest pines. A smile curves my lips as I imagine a younger Levi swinging wildly and plunging into the center of the swimming hole.

"The view here is perfect," I say.

He doesn't respond immediately and I turn to look at him over my shoulder. He is staring directly at me. My gaze collides with his. His eyes smolder with barely restrained desire. My entire body erupts with goosebumps as a shiver races down my spine.

His timbre is low and deep as he rumbles, "I couldn't agree more."

The need I feel for him from only one look is powerful, but also terrifying. Shyly lowering my head, I nibble on my bottom lip nervously. I hear Levi get off the ATV and walk purposefully toward me. With the curve of his finger, he tips up my chin to look at me. His expression has changed. The passion I saw before is still there, however less intense because of the genuine affection that accompanies it. He brushes a light kiss across my cheek and leans his forehead against mine, gathering his control once again.

Leaning back, he says, "So, are you hungry or should we swim first to work up an appetite?" He smirks devilishly because I imagine there are other ways he is thinking of to work up his appetite.

I decide to steer clear of dangerous topics, instead answering, "Swimming? Won't the water be too cold? And more importantly, swim in what exactly?"

His eyebrow arches and a mischievous grin flashes as his eyes take a wandering glance down my body. "Well...you could swim in what you have on or..." He leaves the unfinished sentence hanging in the air.

Becoming mildly uncomfortable, I take a step away from him and quickly reply, "I'll just stay in this. It could use a wash anyway."

Levi laughs, reaching for my arm.

Gently, he apologizes, "Lynn, darlin', it's okay. I'm just teasing. I honestly had no intention of us swimming without our clothes. I didn't mean to make you feel uneasy."

I blow out a big breath, smiling shyly. "Oh, okay."

Fully focused on me again, he says, "Now, make no mistake. I do very much want to see you without your clothes, but not unless you decide that's the direction

117

we're going. And definitely not until you're ready." And then, more softly, "I can wait, Lynn. And I will, somewhat patiently." There's a sparkle in his eye at the last words, which makes me giggle.

I smile up at him. He is so sincere. I can tell that holding back his desire is difficult. I hope it's as difficult as it is for me. I'm learning he does it because he believes what I need is more important. Once again, my inner voice tells me how easy it would be to fall head over heels for him.

Slipping off my shoes, I tug on his hand. I'm ready to enjoy our day. "Come on. Show me your little watering hole."

His boyish smile returns as he pulls his shirt over his head. I marvel at the stunning physique in front of me and just for a moment rethink the swimming with no clothes option. Before I can throw caution to the wind, he grabs my hand, jogging to the edge of the pool. In one fluid motion, he scoops me up and tosses me through the air. I'm on a downward decent by the time my brain catches up with what he's done. I scream bloody murder, cursing his name all the way down, kicking and flailing my limbs until I hit the water. I come up sputtering and ready to give him a tongue lashing the likes of which he has never seen. The water is freezing! But, before I can get the first word out, I am doused with a wave as a boulder the size of Levi's body plummets into the water beside me.

I'm wiping my face clean of streaming drops as I hear Levi break the surface laughing uncontrollably. It's a wonder he doesn't swallow half the pond. Looking at his expression, I can't help laughing, too. He is so thoroughly amused it's hard to be angry. He is completely carefree in this moment. Every worry line and dark shadow I've seen on his face since the first day we met has disappeared and

118

he is magnificent. Even yesterday, when I showed up after days of him secluding himself and saw him at the worst I ever have, he was handsome. Yet now, he is absolutely transformed. I can't imagine the things that must weigh on him to cause such a change in him. I vow to myself to make today the break that he deserves.

We spend the next hour or so paddling around in the water. At one point, we revert into a couple of children by having a water fight and are both laughing all over again. Levi, of course, wins because his hands are at least twice the size of mine, allowing him to send an entire wave over my head. If I wasn't already in the water, I would be soaked to the bone. By the time the sun is high in the sky, we are simply enjoying the quiet together. Somehow, Levi finds some reserve energy and laps around me in the small pool while I float lazily in the middle.

I straighten up in the water and am about to mention the picnic basket when something bumps into my foot causing me to squeal. Levi is instantly alert and his entire body rigid.

As he moves closer to me, I see him scanning the area, "What? What is it?"

The moment he is in within an arm's reach, I open my mouth to tell him when my foot is bumped a second time. I scream again, catapulting myself into his arms. I wrap my legs around his hips and my arms around his neck. I know he can't touch the bottom here, but my fear is overriding my common sense. He instinctively catches me, keeping us both afloat.

Alarmed, he asks, "Lynn, what is it?"

Somehow I find my voice and stammer, "I...I don't know. Something bumped my foot."

119

Immediately, I feel a funny vibration all over my body. I wonder what could be in the water causing it, then realization dawns. It's Levi shaking with quiet laughter. I scowl at him.

"Oh, darlin', it's probably just a catfish or maybe a turtle." He pinches his lips together, trying not to laugh, failing spectacularly.

I swat him on the shoulder as I loosen my death grip on him and burying my face into the crook of his neck. I'm sure my cheeks are on fire from embarrassment now. He must think I'm such an idiot.

"Oh..." is the only sound I can manage through my mortification.

Finally getting himself under control, Levi rubs my back, soothingly.

"I'm sorry. I probably should have told you," he apologizes. "Honestly, it just didn't occur to me. I've been coming here to swim since I was a kid. Guess I'm just used to them being here and don't notice them anymore."

Still buried in his shoulder, I mumble, "It's fine, really. I shouldn't be so surprised. I didn't think of it either although for an entirely different reason."

"Oh yeah, and what reason is that?" he asks as he lifts my chin to look at him.

Nervous that he'll laugh at *me* this time, I say, "Well, I've never been swimming in anything other than an actual pool. Not a whole lot of live animals in those."

He looks at me, clearly surprised. "Really?"

I decide it's probably time to open up at little and stop hiding, at least from Levi. It's still hard to look at him though.

Taking a deep breath, I start, "Yes, well, my parents wouldn't have allowed this sort of thing. They would have frowned upon what might be considered

120

frolicking in the outdoors." I even use air quotes at the end of my sentence and can't help the snicker that follows behind my words. "They're kind of snobby."

He looks at me for a moment, I guess mulling over my description.

"Thank goodness you don't take after them then," he finally responds with seriousness. I peer at him up through my lashes and smile, saying softly, "No, I guess I don't."

He chuckles. "No, you definitely don't."

I suddenly realize that this whole time Levi has been treading water. He's kept us from sinking with me glued to him like a dead weight. I start to untangle myself. Immediately, his hands land on my hips to stop and hold me in place.

His voice is husky as he asks, "And where exactly do you think you're going?"

I nibble on my lip, suddenly shy. "Well...I figure it might be better to let go, so that we both don't drown. I'm sure it can't be easy staying afloat having my added pounds to hold."

Pinning me with a stare, he growls lightly. "Uh, no, that's a shit answer. You weigh nothing. Besides, I rather like you clinging to me." And just like that, the electricity between us sparks to life again.

Vaguely, I'm aware we've moved from the center of the pool. We are now closer to the side where we entered and no longer bobbing up and down. Levi has carried us to where he can reach the bottom.

Levi's eyes become heavy lidded and his fingers grip a little tighter on the outside of my thighs. His intense gaze moves to my lips. I instantly remember he doesn't have a shirt on and my hands can roam freely over his bare skin. His eyes collide with mine as my fingers start to move. They glide over his shoulders and up his neck to clutch his jaw. I slowly lower my mouth to him as his lips part, keeping my eyes locked with his. I can see his pupils dilate. I don't think either one of us is breathing. Part of me can't believe I'm making the first move, but it's impossible to wait any longer.

I sweep my lips softly across, then settle them firmly against his. As I wrap my arms around his shoulders again, I let the tip of my tongue glide over his bottom lip. That simple gesture breaks his haze. All at once, he moves. His hand grasps my bottom, clamping me against him, while his other travels up my back and anchors my head making me immobile, not that I had any plans to go anywhere. Once he has me flattened against him, he nibbles at my lip, seeking permission for more. I grant it by giving him my own little nip. Without wasting anymore time, he seals our lips together, plunging his tongue into my mouth. Everything else falls away. The only thing I can think of right now is Levi. I can't recall my name, or where we are, or what we talked about five minutes ago. It's just him.

His hand on my backside grips tighter, forcing me even closer. I feel every inch of his desire. My own need turns into an inferno, making me lock my ankles behind him. The water of the lagoon is no longer cold. All I feel is the heat between us, the heat we are making.

As our kiss starts to slow, Levi cups my cheek with his hand. He leaves several sweet kisses on my lips before pulling back slightly. His face is tinged with a little bit of sorrow.

Before I can ask him what's wrong, he says, "As much as I would love to stay right where we are, I think we should move up onto the bank." Then smirking, "I'm not sure I can concentrate on keeping us from falling into the water if you continue to kiss me like that."

Feeling the blush spread across my face, all I can manage to say is, "Oh."

Giving him one last chaste kiss, I unwrap my legs, sliding down his body. A groan rumbles from Levi's chest from the full body contact. I begin to pull away when his fingers dig into my sides. He helps me move close to the edge since I still can't touch my feet to the bottom. There's an immediate feeling of loss once we've separated. Apparently, Levi feels it, too, because he finds my hand and twines our fingers together when I've reached a place where I can walk.

We make our way out of the water and closer to the trees. Brushing a kiss across my knuckles, Levi crosses to the four-wheeler, grabbing the basket. He also snags a small towel I hadn't noticed before, handing it to me. I smile, accepting it, and begin wiping myself off. Most of the water dripping into my face is coming from my hair, so I take down what's left of the bun to wring it out.

Finding an area where the sun breaks through the canopy, Levi pulls a blanket out and spreads it over the fragrant pine needles. While he sets up a little spot for our lunch, I watch him. I think about all that he has done for me since first meeting him. He's been so kind and gentle with me, never pushing me beyond my comfort zone. I know he has questions, yet has never pressured for answers. I think it's time I give him some. He deserves to know the truth, even if it means he might walk away from me. I have to stop running and that begins with telling Levi who I really am.

21

Him

I move around our little site, setting up the picnic we brought. I couldn't keep the smile off my face if I tried.

Today has gone better than I could have hoped. I feel like Lynn is finally letting me in, taking some of the walls down or at least opening a door.

Dripping wet, she tries to control the water running off her. She uses the towel to pat her legs and arms dry. She squeezes out the excess by scrunching up her shirt, exposing an expanse of her soft skin. I can't help gawking. She unwinds her hair, letting the heavy locks fall. She's so beautiful. I can't believe I ever thought her to be ordinary.

As I watch her, Lynn starts to chew on the corner of her lip. Her eyes stare off into space. I can see indecision play over her face. She is wrestling with something big. I know the moment her mind is made up. She straightens her spine and anxiety settles in the pit of my stomach. Maybe she's decided she won't let me in after all. The thought is more than disappointing.

"Lynn? Lynn, what is it?" I question.

She doesn't respond the first time I say her name. This isn't the only occasion it's happened. It's as if she doesn't hear me or recognize her own name. Then, finally, she's surprised out of her fog, looking at me with those wide hazel eyes. Right now, they are more green than gold, a sign I've learned that she's fearful. Now, my worry multiplies. I'm the last person she needs to be afraid of in the world. Maybe I've pushed her too much even though I've tried to give her plenty of space.

She clasps her hands, pinching her fingers tightly together. When she glances at me, all I see is worry. She looks away and walks back to the edge of the pool, leaving her back to me.

Careful to keep my voice low and my tone soothing, I ask, "What's wrong?"

I put the items in my hand on the blanket and walk behind her, placing my hands on her shoulders. She heaves a huge sigh like the weight of the world has settled on her.

My worry increases. "Talk to me, darlin'. Let me help you."

Turning her slowly to face me, I see a few silent tears flowing down her cheeks.

Her voice wavers. "I.....I have something to tell you, something I should have told you a while ago."

My arms fall away from her and hang at my sides. My stomach plummets to the ground. She's going to leave me and walk away. I can't take losing someone else. Even though we haven't known each other long, Lynn has become incredibly important to me, more than I'm probably willing to admit at this point.

I can see her physically preparing herself before she begins.

"My life is, well,....a disaster," she chuckles, without any humor. "I'm not from here."

I can't help snickering. "Um, I kind of figured that out, considering I've lived here my entire life."

Her eyes cut to me, but there's no heat behind her frustration. If anything, my sarcastic comment has lessened her discomfort. "Okay, smart ass."

"Sorry," I mumble, trying to contain my amusement. "Please continue." She starts to wander as she talks.

125

"I grew up in Rapid City. My parents are, or were....well, I don't know. They're prominent people. Their name holds some weight, apparently not enough though. They've made some mistakes, really serious ones from what I've figured out. The problem is I don't know a lot of what is going on. I just know who they associate with and that he's not a nice man. The fact that they have had dealings with him has pretty much ruined my life. I came here to get away from all of it."

Worried she'll close up on me, I don't want to interrupt her. However, the more Lynn says, the more confused I get. She's rambling and it's difficult to keep up.

"Lynn.." I say softly.

"Please don't call me that," she begs.

Now, I'm even more confused. "But, it's your name."

"No, it's not. Not exactly."

I'm stunned. Although I'm not sure I should be completely surprised. On more than one occasion, I have called to her without her answering me right away. This revelation certainly explains why.

Her shoulders lose their stiffness as she breathes deeply. Her voice is shaky and unsure.

"My middle name is Lynn. It's not what I go by though, never has been. My first name is Samantha, but only *one* person has ever called me that. My parents call me by both names, Samantha Lynn. I hate it. They think it makes them sound like they come from old Southern money, which we don't. To them, everything is about appearance. And my last name isn't Carter. That's my grandmother's maiden name. My real last name is Brooks." She stops her pacing. Facing me, she crosses her arms over her middle as if guarding herself.

126

I can't stand the space or the wall she's trying to build between us. Closing the distance in three strides, I'm directly in front of her, standing toe to toe. She has to crane her neck to look up at me. Her eyes are tinged with remorse. It's clear she regrets her deception, but some of her wariness is still present, too. I'm struck by the thought that she's worried I will be on the one to walk away because she lied. The truth is quite the opposite. Finding out that she has been living in hiding only makes me want to keep her close and safe. I give her a small smile, trying to ease her worry.

"So, you've told me what everyone else calls you, but what about me? I can just keep using darlin' if you like, but an actual name would be nice too."

It's obvious she didn't expect this reaction from me. After a moment, she says, "Everyone who knows me, the real me, calls me Sam." Then, hesitantly, "You're not angry?"

"No, not with you." I can see the question in her eyes. "Obviously, I don't know everything that's going on...yet. But, I can understand reasons for you not being completely truthful about who you are. If your goal was to keep your parents away, you were simply trying to protect yourself. I get that. I am angry that they put you in this position though. It's not right you felt it was necessary to go to such an extreme."

She braces herself as she continues, "Well, there's more to it and none of it's good."

All I want to do is calm her fears. "We'll get to that, but not right now. One step at a time, okay?" She's taken a huge step in trusting me. However, I know if I don't proceed carefully she could close up on me again.

Lowering her arms, she relaxes. "Okay." Then, her eyes glisten as she wonders, "What about Miss

Sarah? Do you think she'll forgive me? She's been so wonderful to me."

Confidently, I tell her, "Oh, I doubt you have to worry about her. I have a feeling she's known a lot more than she's let on all along. Nothing gets by that woman."

"There's so much more you don't know," she whispers as her head droops.

"I'm certain there is, but we don't have to deal with it this very second." I lift her chin with my finger and remind her, "I'm not going anywhere. Not unless you want me to?"

Shyly, she smiles. "No. I like you with me."

Relieved we agree on that, I respond, "Good, me too. Whatever is going on, we'll deal with it together. Now, we still have our basket waiting and personally, I'm starving."

Giggling at me, she agrees, "Yeah, I could eat." Then after a moment, she whispers, "Thank you."

"For what?"

"For not walking away. I was so scared you'd want nothing to do with me anymore," she admits.

"Sam," I say, liking the sound of her name, "I'm a Marine. I can't leave someone behind. It's not in me." I see her expression turning to disappointment as she considers my answer. I quickly continue, "But, with you it's more than that. Whatever is between us, I can't let go of it. I don't want to. I care about you."

Her eyes shine brightly. The sparks of gold I like so much are returning. "I care about you, too. It terrifies me, but I do."

Trying to put her at ease, I confess, "Well, just so you know, it terrifies the shit out of me. Glad to know we're on the same page."

She laughs, all of the tension draining out of her. I reach for her and she steps willing into my embrace. Gathering her up, I hold her against me, savoring the feel of her. I thread my fingers through her damp hair. I tilt her face up. Before I close my mouth over hers, I tell her, "Thank you for trusting me." Then, I claim her mouth for a languid, sweet kiss that makes both of us press together more tightly.

Before things get deliciously out of hand, I separate us and lead her up to the blanket. We spend the rest of our time at the pool enjoying ourselves. We eat our picnic while I tell her stories about helping my father in the garage and skipping rocks together in the lower part of the creek after a storm. I tell her about peeling potatoes for dinner and shining the wood floors with cloths on our feet with my mother. I remember all the good times. The comfort they bring me chinks away some more of my despair. Sugar might just be where I need to stay to become whole again.

I pull out the dessert she brought me and Sam smiles. Peach cobbler has now become my all-time favorite thing. After stuffing ourselves and putting the leftovers back in the basket, I stretch out. She settles herself against me, laying her head on my shoulder. It doesn't take long until her breathing becomes soft and even. She's fallen asleep. It's understandable after everything that's happened today.

I take advantage of my circumstances and enjoy the feel of her next to me. Her hair has dried in soft waves and smells like the water and my shampoo. It reminds me that she's slept in my bed and washed in my shower. I also vividly recall our time spent on the couch. All of it has my body heating up again.

129

My mind replays the memories until I feel Sam move. Opening my eyes, I realize I must have dozed off as well. The sun isn't as bright and is starting to sink behind the trees.

We sit up and I turn her toward me. "Hey, I had a great time today."

"Oh, yeah, me too. It's been really nice." She looks disappointed.

"Sam...I'm not saying that I want it to end, but I do think we should head to the house. With the sun setting, the mosquitoes will be out very soon. I'd rather not be eaten alive."

Laughing lightly, she grins. "Yeah, I think I'll pass on that too."

She looks so relieved I can't help leaning over to give her another kiss. She bows into me turning it into more than a simple little peck.

Struggling to pull myself away, "Oh, boy, we need to put that on hold." I take a deep breath to control my building need for her. Finally, I manage to stand and extend a hand to help her up. Tugging gently, I say, "Come on, let's pack up and head back."

Smiling with a flush on her cheeks, Sam helps me fold the blanket and closes up the basket. When it's all secure, she climbs onto the four-wheeler. This time she presses herself tightly against me without any reservation. She wraps her arms around me, spreading one hand across my belly and the other over my chest. I feel her lay her cheek in the middle of my back and sigh contentedly.

I start up the engine and find the path heading back through the trees. With the sun setting, the air has cooled. Parts of our clothes are not completely dry which prompts me to go slower for the return trip. I don't want

Sam to become chilled. Even with my body to block the wind, I feel her snuggle as near to me as she can, trying to stay warm. Having her close is almost the best thing I can imagine.

22

Her

We park in the garage and walk back to the house, hand in hand. I am hoping Dylan has decided to make himself scarce. I don't want my time with Levi to end.

Levi holds the door as I slip into the kitchen before him. Feeling his eyes glued to me, I heighten the movements of my hair and hips, swaying both together. His hand gently catches my arm and turns me toward him. Framing my face with his hands, he presses his lips to mine. The kiss is soft and sweet, the opposite of everything I'm feeling. I wrap my arms around his neck, pulling myself to my toes. I trace the seam of his mouth with my tongue. He groans, wrapping his arm around my back, picking me up. My feet dangle in the air. I giggle, pressing my face into his neck. It didn't take much convincing to put us on the same page.

For a moment, I worrying about him lifting my weight, then realize I shouldn't. He carries me effortlessly up the stairs to his bedroom like he's a man on a mission, which I'm sure he is. Levi closes the door with his foot, walking to the bed. He slides me down his body until my feet are safely on the floor again. I pull him to me for another kiss because he's just increased my need for him by ten. Our kiss becomes insistent. I'm desperate for more.

"Sam," Levi pleads.

I love hearing his voice say my name, my real name.

His voice wavers. "I want you so much. It's all I can think about. Tell me what you want."

I can only answer him honestly. "You, Levi. Just you."

He sits on the bed and pulls me onto his lap. His warm and strong, slightly callused fingers are like butterflies on my skin. They whisper everywhere, my arms, legs, and face. The skin where they touch erupts in a trail of goosebumps. Tentative at first, his hands move constantly. Then, they become bolder. His eyes smolder with his need. He never breaks his gaze on my face while his hands do their exploring. I want him to move faster, yet relish in the lingering of his touch. I can't get enough even though I've already had more than I should.

His fingers creep to the hem of my shirt, slowly pushing it aside. His thumb brushes my stomach, sending quivers through my middle. His palm moves to the side of my rib cage, then around me. His hand is splayed between my shoulder blades, almost completely covering my back. I am so small next to him. It's like his body can swallow me up. It's such a delicious thought.

The pressure of his palm is constant and increases gently, bringing me toward him. My mind is in a fog of desire. Everything slows while my pulse quickens. My breath becomes ragged and uneven. I pull only the smallest wisps of air into my lungs. I am dizzy with anticipation. Then, his lips connect with mine and I'm lost.

He lifts me up allowing me to wrap my legs around his hips. My hands move to his head, holding him in place as our tongues duel. He angles my head slightly to plunge deeper and I can't hold back a moan from escaping. He crushes my body to him. Suddenly, I have to feel him against me, skin on skin. I grab at his shirt, desperate to have it gone. One handed, he pulls it over his head. My hands wander over his magnificent

133

chest. He's perfect as if sculpted from marble, but so warm to my touch.

He holds the sides of my shirt, looking at me and the question clear in his eyes. I finish the job for him in answer and pull it off. A strangled groan comes from him as he just stares at me. I reach behind me to unclasp my bra, letting it fall to the floor.

"My god." The words are strangled. The expression on Levi's face can only be described as reverence. I have never seen such passion before now. I didn't know it existed.

He's kissing me everywhere in the next moment, my lips, jaw, and neck. He moves with purpose down to my breast and immediately sucks it into the warmth of his mouth. I gasp at the pull that's sent directly to my core. His tongue swirls over my nipple, then sucks again, making it strain for more. My body is a flash of heat as he repeats the same treatment on the other side. I bow into him, my hands trying to pull him closer still, begging him not to stop. His face is smashed into my chest as he licks and nips while his fingers dig into my back. I can't hold back the soft, strangled whines coming from me. I can feel him trying to control his need. It's a fight I want him to lose.

He turns and lays me on the bed, his knees under my thighs. He pulls at the button of my shorts, then stops and looks at me.

Heaving a breath, he whispers, "We don't have to go all the way, or do anything else if you don't want. But, please, I just need to see you, all of you, if you'll let me."

In this moment, there is no way my voice will work. The only answer I can give him is to shimmy out of my shorts. I see his eyes widen when he realizes I didn't have any panties on under them. His hands bunch into fists on his thighs as his eyes travel deliberately over every inch of me.

His voice is like gravel when he speaks. "Woman, if I had known nothing lay underneath, we wouldn't have made it out to the swimming hole."

I feel like I might combust from the heat of his gaze. Moaning, I plead, "Levi."

His hands slowly smooth up my legs to my hips. He's savoring this moment like he's not sure it's really happening. Then, with a serious expression, he looks at me. Worry cuts through my haze.

"I want you to know, no matter how far we go tonight or any other night, I'm clean. I was tested at every health evaluation during my time in the military and was never with anyone without protection."

Feeling relieved he's not stopping us and overwhelmed by his sense of responsibility, I answer, "Thank you for thinking of taking care of us, of me. I'm clean, too, and on the pill. I have been since college."

His response is so sincere. "That's all I want to do, Sam. I want to take care of you."

I twine my fingers with his, pulling him on top of me. The weight of him over me is heavenly. We kiss until both of us are panting.

Tugging at the waistband of his shorts, I tell him, "Let me see you, Levi."

He pushes off the bed, standing beside it. I sit up while he toes off his shoes and drops his shorts. Levi is breath-taking. I let my gaze eat him up from his broad shoulders and rippled torso to his trim waist and lean hips. My eyes travel down his leg, lingering on his scar. It's white and pulled tight. It's a stark contrast compared to his tanned skin. Levi's body is coiled tightly under my visual examination. I can feel him waiting. I reach out lightly floating my fingers over the entire scar, even circling his knee. He shivers at the contact, but never says a word. I can only feel pride and admiration for him. The scar represents his sacrifice, his honor, and most of all, his strength. Leaning in, I follow down the scar with several kisses. Meeting his eyes, I can feel tears pool on my lids. I won't let them fall. They are not about feeling sorry for him. They are about showing him acceptance and gratitude for being the person he is.

When I've finished showing him my admiration, I continue my visual parade. My eyes land on my prize. He's thick and beautiful. He is so hard the skin is stretched taut. I shiver at the image of my mouth fitting around him. I lick my lips in anticipation. I hear a low growl come from him, but he doesn't move.

I remember his sentiment about taking care of me. That's what I want, too. I want to take care of him, to make him feel adored, show him he's important. I roll to my knees and crawl to him. I reach out my hand to stroke him. I swear he stops breathing. As I wrap my hand around him, he hisses through his teeth. I don't usually do this, but I can't seem to stop myself with Levi. The thought of learning how he tastes has me clamping my thighs together as everything aches with desperate need.

Using a tortured voice, Levi says, "Sam, you don't have to do this."

Levi has no idea how wrong he is. In this moment, there is nothing else I should be doing. Determination filling my words, I tell him, "Oh, but I do."

With that, I suck the head of his cock into my mouth. I close my eyes and moan as my tongue swirls over the crown. I find the ridge on the underside and run the tip of my tongue along it. Levi groans in blissful agony. His hand grips my shoulder as he rests his knees against the bed for stability. He tunnels the fingers of his other hand into my hair. He doesn't put any pressure there though, letting me know I'm the one in control. That gives me more confidence. Placing my hands on his hips, I lick around him once more then take him into my mouth as far as I can. I stroke him in and out in a steady rhythm, flattening my tongue on the way out. When I feel his grip tighten and hear his breath heaving, I know he's close. I wrap one of my hands around the base of his cock, squeezing lightly, and start to suck as I continue my movements. I feel his body coil, shaking slightly. His balls draw up. Suddenly, he pulls out of my mouth at the last second, shouting my name. We both watch in fascination as he spills himself all over my breasts. The only sound in the room is our identical panting.

Watching me with a smoldering gaze, he declares, "That was the sexist thing I've ever seen. Thank you." His gratitude has me blushing, but I'm not hiding from him like I used to when we first met.

"You're welcome. It was my pleasure," I whisper huskily. Levi growls as fire ignites in his eyes again.

"Sam, I'll show you my pleasure in a minute. Let me get a towel to clean you up first."

As he walks across to bathroom, I'm touched by his thoughtfulness. I hear the faucet turn on and a moment later he is striding back to me, comfortable with his nudity. Focused on his task, he reverently and carefully wipes my breasts and stomach with the warm washcloth. Once he's finished, he places the towel on the nightstand and turns. There is a calculating glint in his eye.

"Now, my turn, or should I say, your turn."

He stalks toward me, making me feel like his prey in the most decadent way. A shiver races down my spine.

137

Levi sees it and a wicked gleam lights in his eyes while a smirk curls his lip. He's lethal to my sense of self-preservation, not that I want to save myself from him.

Placing his hands on the outside of my knees, he leans into me, pushing me back with his body. I lie back as he once again crawls over me. He seals his lips with mine. His kiss is thorough and intense. My entire body is overloaded with lust.

Levi pays attention to every part of me. He kisses along my jaw then sucks lightly on my ear lobe. Next, he nips at the tendon in my neck sending a riot of goosebumps over my arms. I can feel my nipples tightening against his chest and so does he. He rocks slightly rubbing his chest against mine. I gasp at the contact, arching my back for more. My breasts are aching for him. Prolonging my torture, Levi trails his tongue down between them and across my belly. I squirm, trying to let him know what I need. Unfazed by my wanton distress, he wraps his hands around my ribs, holding me steady as he continues to trace the underside of each breast with his tongue. I let out a strangled noise of agony and bliss. I hear a soft chuckle. He is enjoying my torment, which is also evident from his hard length against my thigh. I resolve if he stops now I'll kill him in his sleep.

I feel him grow even larger and decide that maybe he is contributing to his own suffering as well. I hope it means he will move things along before I die from longing. He must read my thoughts because he moves his hands, cupping both my breasts, and suckles them both one at a time deeply. It sends heat rushing to my core. My back arches off the bed as I run my leg up the outside of his hip. He moves his hand down my side pushing my leg flat and skims across to the apex of my thighs. I whimper

138

in anticipation. He strokes his fingers through my folds and back up. I moan. I'm wet and ready for him.

Groaning, he says, "Oh, Sam, I can feel how much you need this."

"Please," I strangle out.

"Shh, I'll make it all better. Just stay with me a little longer." With that, he slowly pushes one finger into me.

I practically sob it feels so good. I can hardly catch my breath.

He strokes in and out a few times, then takes one of my breasts into his mouth again. From the pull on my nipple, I feel my body coat Levi's fingers even more. As he sucks again, he pushes in another finger, stretching me. I bite my lip to keep from screaming out.

Levi is paying attention to everything I do. He tells me, "Oh, no, darlin'. I want to hear you. I want to know how good I make you feel."

His hand resumes the slide into me and I groan, throwing my hands above my head. Now, he doubles his efforts, working his mouth and fingers together, leaving me gasping. My head is slowly rocking back and forth as I feel myself spiraling out of control.

Levi knows I'm close. He encourages me. "That's it, Sam. I want to see it. I want to hear you say my name. Come for me."

He returns to my nipple and sucks on it while his fingers pump faster. Then, he presses his thumb on my clit, rubbing in circles. The combination is my undoing. I fall apart, screaming his name.

"Levi!"

He continues until I am wrung out completely. My whole body is deliciously limp and sated. Levi climbs over me, turning my head and claims my mouth in a fevered kiss.

"That was beautiful. *You* are beautiful."

"Mmmm." I'm so relaxed I can't even speak.

I feel the bed shift as Levi gets up and folds down the covers. He, then, picks me up and places me in the center. I whimper because I think he's leaving, but he climbs in next to me, pulling me close.

Speaking low, he murmurs, "Shh, sleep now, darlin'. I've got you."

With my head cradled in his arm and tucked under his chin, I lay my cheek against his chest. The rest of my body is as close as I can get it. I feel his arms tighten while he kisses my forehead. I am in a cocoon of warmth. Sighing contentedly, I drift off to sleep, thinking about how easy it would be to just stay right here.

23

Her

Opening my eyes this morning, I wish for a rewind button. I want to go back, never having to move forward from last night. I had thought about how easy it would be to stay here. However, in the bright morning light, I know it's not. I can't stay here with my past hanging over me. I just don't know how to fix the problem. Richard is not someone I can simply walk away from without repercussions. He demands everyone pay the price owed to him, some higher than others. Unfortunately, I'm not sure what my cost will be. That uncertainty is what has made me stay hidden. I do know if I want any kind of life, especially one with Levi, I have to face Richard. This means I also have to leave Levi, which after what happened between us has me thinking I'd rather lose a limb. Both my head and heart start to ache. I can't handle thinking about these things this early in the morning, especially not before any coffee.

Pushing the negative aside for now, I stretch like a cat and practically purr. I'm alone in the bed, but Levi's side is still warm. He couldn't have left too long ago. I want to go downstairs to look for him, yet I can't go prancing around naked with Dylan in the house. And I definitely do not want to put on my disgusting clothes that I showed up in two days ago. I decide I'll have to borrow one of Levi's t-shirts. He's so big it will cover me to my knees anyway. Rummaging through his drawers, I find the tan shirt he wore when we first met and it smells wholly of him. Perfect. I slip into the bathroom to rinse my face, brush my teeth, and run my fingers through my hair, trying to put some order to it.

When I feel mostly presentable, I pad lightly on bare feet to the kitchen. No one is around, even though I notice it's already late morning. The inner back door is open indicating someone left to go out that way. Normally, I would close and lock the door, but remember Levi's comment about there being no need.

Relaxing, I set to work to find my morning elixir. I spy across the kitchen, seeing the glorious sight of a full pot already made. I approach and notice a mug, spoon, and sugar bowl has been set out with a note. It says, "For you. Enjoy your first cup and I'll join you in a few. Levi" I can't help the smile that breaks out across my face. He's so sweet and caring. He really does want to take care of me in every possible way.

I sit at the large center island with my coffee, enjoying the view, and wait for Levi to return. After a few minutes, I can feel someone hovering before entering the kitchen. I'm pretty sure it isn't Levi, leaving only one other person. Both men may be trained in stealth, yet, they have an incredible presence when they want it to be known.

"Dylan, you might as well come in."

Hedging, he says, "I was trying to not to intrude..."

"Oh, well, Levi isn't with me at the moment. Not sure where he is actually."

"He's in the garage," he says, his tone very matter-of-fact.

Now, I understand his uncharacteristic waffling. "So, that means you must be looking for me then."

"Yes."

"Something on your mind, Dylan?" I ask.

Looking everywhere except at me, he flounders, "Well, yeah...."

It seems I'll have to pull the words out of him. Slightly irritated, I sigh. "Just spit it out. You don't really strike me as the type to mince your words, or hold back for that matter."

Finding his nerve, he agrees, "No, you're right about that. Look, Lynn..."

I hold up my hand to stop him. "Dylan, you should know my name isn't Lynn. Well, it is, but it's not my first name. I go by Sam."

The muscle in his jaw ticks as his clamps his lips together. "I see." His tone is clipped.

Knowing how close he and Levi are, I try to explain. "I know it doesn't look good that I lied, but I have my reasons, ones I'd rather not go into right now. Levi knows some of it. I told him yesterday and he's accepted it, and my apology. I hope you can to."

Dylan has every right to be angry on Levi's behalf. I sincerely hope he can look past what I've done. But, honestly, the only person's forgiveness I truly care about is Levi's.

After taking a deep breath while considering me for a moment, he says, "Well, I guess that explains a few things. I'll admit I don't like it that you lied. However, I'm not here to judge you or your reasons. Whatever they are, they are your own. If Levi has accepted it, then I can too." Pausing, he comes to sit next to me. When he continues, he sounds sincere. "I like you. I really do. I think you're good for Levi. Seeing you two together reminds me of how he used to be before the accident. I haven't seen him this at ease in a really long time. Or, this connected to someone besides me and Miss Sarah. He doesn't let people in anymore. And you haven't even known each other for very long, which tells me whatever

143

is going on between you two is major. What you have together is a big deal."

"And, you worry I'm going to hurt him," I interject, now understanding his concern.

"Yes, actually I do. Levi is my brother in every way that matters. I want nothing except the best for him. And, from what I've seen between you two, I think that could be you. You might be able to give him everything he deserves, which is a lot. But, only if you intend on sticking around. He goes all in with everything, Sam, but he doesn't take risks with his heart. He's lost too much already."

"I know," I assure him. "I don't want to hurt him, Dylan. That's the last thing I want. But, things aren't so simple for me right now."

His lips thin with displeasure. "I get that. That's why I'm telling you. I won't see him get hurt. He doesn't need to lose anyone else, especially if it's by them walking away."

I mull over what he says, which isn't anything I haven't thought myself already. I know he's right and agree with him completely. Levi does deserve everything I can give him. He doesn't deserve me walking away. And if I wasn't in the situation I'm in, I wouldn't even consider not being with him. I've just found him and he's the only person I've ever wanted this way.

I'm sure my expression probably tells Dylan what he wants to know. There's no denying his words have gotten to me. I have no hope of hiding anything I'm feeling.

When he speaks again, he's very clear. "I can't pretend to know what's going on with you, but I can tell whatever it is, it's something big. This is something you have to deal with and soon. I'm just saying if your problem won't make it possible for you to stay here, or worse, to not come back, then you should consider ending things with Levi now. Before either of you gets any more involved. Although from what I can see, Levi is already in all the way. Just something you need to keep in mind." He looks at me pointedly, rising from the stool. No one would ever take Dylan Reed as only an easy-going charmer if they ever saw this side of him. Levi may be menacing by his sheer size, but Dylan is sly and wicked, and just as lethal.

With a last look over his shoulder, Dylan simply exits the kitchen, knowing he's made his point. The kick in the teeth is there was no need for it. I'm already in way too deep, deep enough that I'd rather have my heart ripped out when it does become time to leave. Unfortunately, I'm in even deeper with Richard. The question is can I make it out of both situations with myself in one piece and Levi's trust intact?

Staring into the bottom of my mug, I'm lost in my thoughts. I don't hear Levi come in until the screen door slams shut.

"Good mornin' darlin'," I look up to see a smile radiating on his face. This is the happiest and most relaxed I've ever seen him. It makes my heart ache again. Seeing my sad expression, he comes to my side, whispering, "Hey, hey, what's with the frown?"

Not able to tell him the truth, but hating to outright lie to him as well, I can only give him a superficial answer. "Oh, I'm fine. Coffee just doesn't seem to be setting well this morning."

His brow furrows. "Hmm, sorry about that. I tried to tone it down. I usually make it pretty strong, comes from years in the service. I hate for it to make you feel sick."

"I'll be okay," I assure him. "I probably just need something to eat."

He smiles while he brushes a strand of hair away from my face, kissing my cheek tenderly. "Well, then, what can I get you? How about the rest of that peach cobbler you brought me?"

I smile at his question. "Mmm, that sounds good, but it's for you."

"I'd rather share, but only with you." A naughty gleam sparks in his eyes.

I watch as he moves around the kitchen, gathering the cobbler and two spoons. He really is the finest specimen I've ever seen. He sits on the stool next to me and turns me toward him. He pulls me closer until his knees are caging my own.

He leans directly into my space and says, huskily, "I really like seeing my clothes on you, especially knowing there's probably nothing on underneath."

I can't help ducking my head and feel my face turn to fire. His finger lifts my chin gently. "Don't hide from me. You *never* have to hide from me."

His words have so many meanings to me. He's letting me know he wants me the way I am. Yet, more importantly, he's telling me he would never hurt me or put me in a position to be scared of him. I smile at him and he pecks me lightly on the lips. Settling himself back on his stool, he proceeds to scoop up a spoonful of gooey goodness.

As he lifts it to my mouth, he asks, "So, any plans for today?"

After swallowing, I answer, "I should really check in with Miss Sarah. I don't know if she needs me today."

"Already done," he informs me. "I called her earlier and she said she'll be fine without you."

I bristle a bit. "Oh, really? Taking charge are you? What if I wanted to go in to work? I hate thinking about Miss Sarah doing everything by herself."

Calmly, with his hands on my knees, Levi tells me, "Sam, that's entirely up to you. I'm not trying to control you. I just want to spend more time with you. I figured I would check with Miss Sarah to see if she needed you. I never want her to be without help either. If she said yes, then I could have spent the day with you at the store. Doesn't matter to me where we are as long as we're together. I'm just not ready to give you up yet."

His statement is so sweet and punches me right in the gut.

Feeling horrible at my outburst, I apologize, "I'm sorry." I've jumped on the defensive again even though Levi has given me no reason to do it. My knee-jerk reaction of taking charge of myself and my life is appearing at the worst possible times.

"No need to apologize," he says. Then, explains, "We're still getting used to each other. But, you need to know you never have to worry about me trying to make you do something you don't want to do. Okay?"

The tension in my shoulders eases. "Okay."

"So, since you have the day off, I have a suggestion." I can see his excitement brewing. He's practically bursting.

"Let's hear it," I tell him, chuckling.

Looking like that ten year old boy again, he reveals, "Thought we could go to the fair. I haven't been in years. It used to be one of my favorite things about this town. I'd like to show it to you."

Thinking about the rides, games, and all the junk food, I can't help grinning widely. "Sounds like fun." Then, I remember I am in desperate need of clean clothes. "But...I really can't go out like this," pointing to his shirt I'm wearing.

"Oh, hell no. No one gets to see you like this."

I might become upset at his demanding tone if he wasn't so adorable. I decide to tease him a bit. "Well, Dylan came through the kitchen," I say innocently.

Fiercely, he declares, "I'll burn out his eyes."

"Levi, stop," I laugh, not believing for a second Dylan has thought twice about me. "I'm sure he has no interest in me."

Growling, he argues, "Don't be so sure. He has to turn away droves of women. He had better not even think about you, if he wants to live, best friend or not. You're mine."

Every cell in my body shivers at his possessive tone. He doesn't sound like a controlling dictator. He is simply making a clear statement of fact that I belong to him, in the best possible way. I could bait him further and feign interest in Dylan, but I won't. Something tells me it wouldn't be a good idea. Besides, all I really want to do is agree with him anyway because no matter what happens, I am his. I can only hope that he still feels the same way later.

Stroking his cheek, I tell him, "Yes, Levi, only yours."

He sits with a slightly shocked expression on his face for a moment before his eyes dilate and his mouth is

148

on mine. His tongue plunges between my lips, stealing my breath. Then, he nips at my bottom lip and gives me a series of soft pecks. I smile openly at him. He looks like he's just won the lottery as he returns to his stool.

Struggling to regain his focus, he finally says, "Okay, your clothes. How about I drive you back to the store so you can get ready? I'll come back here to do the same, then pick you up and we can head to the fair."

I smile, loving how comfortable I feel. "Okay, that'll work."

After we've finished our coffee and the cobbler, which he feeds to me until I think I'll burst, and I'm dressed, Levi drops me outside the store. With a sweet kiss and a wave goodbye, he says he'll see me soon. I run upstairs to get ready, wanting to look my best for him. I already miss him. I don't know how I'll manage to leave when it's time.

24

Her

A few hours, I look in the mirror at my reflection. I resign myself to accepting what I see. I want to look perfect for him. Unfortunately, I'm limited with what I have. I've chosen one of my favorite summer dresses and the cute sandals that had fit easily in my backpack. My hair is up in a clip with soft tendrils framing my face. Without having much makeup on hand, I've kept my face simple with mascara and a little tinted lip balm. The excited flush to my skin provides me with color. Nothing else is really needed. Checking myself again, I feel flirty and ready for some fun.

A knock at the door tells me my chariot waits. I'm giddy with anticipation and have butterflies in my belly. I open my door to a clean smelling Levi. He's all muscle and raw power, looking wonderful in a black t-shirt and khaki cargo pants. I can't help my lingering stare as I take all of him in. Briefly, I debate about skipping our fun-filled afternoon and moving onto an even more fun-filled night. It seems he has the same idea from the heated expression in his eyes.

"You look incredible."

Shyly, I answer, "Thanks. You clean up pretty good yourself."

With another perusing look, Levi says, "Mmm, well, before I decide to lock this door and keep you holed up here for the day, let's get going. I'm in the mood for a little fun."

"You sure?" I tease with some sass and my hand on my hip. I know I could be playing with fire, but I can't stop myself. And, oh, what an adventure I would have.

Grabbing my wrist and pulling me to him, he locks his lips with mine, then growls with the best kind of heat, "Don't tempt me, Sam."

He breaks our kiss and practically stomps down the stairs with me in tow. A giggle escapes my throat at his frustration. I empathize with how he feels.

The carnival is in full swing when we finally arrive. The exhilaration from all the noise, smells, and animated people is contagious. Levi and I spend hours walking around, riding rides, and enjoying each other's company. I've had more fun than I can remember having in a long time. My cheeks ache from smiling widely and my sides burn from laughing.

I convince Levi to take the Ferris wheel one more time in deference to my aching feet. In truth, I just want to sit tucked against him. After rounding the circle half a dozen times, it finally slows to a stop. Levi kisses me softly on the cheek before he lifts the bar and steps onto the platform, extending his hand to me. Putting my hand in his, I gingerly step from the swinging bucket. I miss my footing slightly, wobbling on my feet, and become a little unbalanced. Levi's arm is instantly around my waist, keeping me upright. I expect him to pull away once I am set to rights, but he doesn't. He just pulls me in snugly against his side. I'm sure my skin is still flushed from his kiss even as innocent as it was, only now the heat deepens. I can't remember another time when everything felt so right. Whether he knows it or not, Levi can make me forget the world around me.

We pass by all the vendors selling their treats. I can't even consider eating any more I'm so stuffed. All the carnival game runners are shouting the odds of winning the games and their prizes loudly. I just smile and shake my head slightly, finding it foolish to waste money on something everyone knows is rigged for loss.

Levi must have felt my head movement. He is watching me with a smirk on his face. "What?" I question.

"I think you need a souvenir to remember our date."

I laugh with disbelief. "From one of those games? No, really I don't. There's no point in you wasting the money, especially when everyone knows no one wins at those things, at least not the good stuff."

His brows arches in challenge as he counters, "Oh, you have no faith in me. I'm wounded."

I protest, "Levi, don't be silly. Of course I have faith in you. That has nothing to do with it. The games are rigged, you know that. No need to waste your money."

Eyes twinkling, he says, "It's not a waste if I'm spending it on you."

The thought of him throwing money away on a silly game for me, especially just to prove a point, really shouldn't make me feel all warm inside. I have to admit that it does though. It's something so simple and ordinary, something so normal. It makes me happy. And I can't keep from smiling even more.

Grabbing my hand, he pulls me along to the typical bottle baseball pitching game. Levi strolls up to the counter, paying his money, and receives three balls. Three pitches later, he has only knocked down one of the bottles. I'm a little disappointed. To be honest, I expected him to knock them all down on the first try from his boasting. He looks over his shoulder and simply shrugs.

"I just need to warm up," he says.

Paying the money again, he ends the next round with only slightly better results. He knocks down two bottles from the pyramid. This result does earn him a small stuffed bear, but he turns it down.

"I'm going for the big one there," he indicates, pointing to the upper corner of the tent. Hanging there is a cotton candy colored pink bear. It's half the size of me.

Chuckling, like he's just been handed a gold mine with Levi, the operator says, "You're welcome to try, man. To win that one though, you'll have to do better than this. You've got to knock down *all* three sets of bottles in a row from a single turn."

Not wanting him to look foolish, I tug on Levi's arm. "Really, it's not necessary. I don't need the bear, Levi. Let's just go enjoy the rest of the carnival."

He looks over his shoulder, telling me seriously, "Yes, it is." Then, he winks before turning back to the man and says, "That's not a problem."

I look at the man. He's barely able to contain his greed. He thinks he's found the perfect sucker. I start to get really nervous as I notice Levi hasn't thrown the first ball yet. I watch him take a deep breath. A look of deep concentration pulls his brows together. Shifting his stance slightly, all the muscles of his shoulders and back bunch as he fires the ball. It hits the bottles with a crash, exploding, sending the first set in all directions. The operator is astonished, his expression changing instantly.

Levi lifts one shoulder saying, "Just lucky, I guess."

He fires the second ball with the same intensity and a duplicate result.

Levi, the picture of innocence on his face, comments, "Huh, what are the odds?" The man's face turns into a suspicious scowl.

I have to cover my twitching lips with my hand. It's difficult to suppress the bubbling giggle fighting to rise to the surface.

Levi sets up for the last ball. He pitches, the sound of the ball hitting the bottles like a crack of thunder. The third and final set scatters violently. The man's expression is murderous. He clearly didn't expect to be hustled on his own game. Ironic, considering that's exactly what he does with obviously weighted bottles.

"My lady's prize. Please," Levi demands, the tone of his voice daring the man to deny him.

Pulling a step ladder from under the counter, the man climbs up and pulls down the monstrous bear. He hands it to Levi, who turns and passes it to me. It's the most obnoxious thing I've ever seen. I look ridiculous holding it. And I love it. I am overcome with juvenile giddiness.

Batting my eyelashes at Levi, I coo, "My hero."

"Nah, I just like seeing you smile. Knowing it happened because of something I did makes it even better," he says, ducking his head slightly as if he's embarrassed.

My heart swells from his sincerity. Placing a hand on his shoulder, I rise up on my toes to kiss his cheek. I see a faint flush turn his ears pink.

"Thank you."

Moving away from the games, we cross the midway and are surrounded by food vendors of every sort. Levi buys a bag of rainbow cotton candy for us to share. We enjoy the sticky goodness while strolling through the mass of people. We walk in companionable silence for a while enjoying the sights and sounds of the festivities. I look up at Levi and grin. What a sight he is, having a bright, pink bear straddled across his shoulders like a toddler.

Suddenly, the back of my neck starts to prickle. I feel as if I'm being watched. My shoulders and back tense. I've become so comfortable being around Levi and in this town that I have forgotten to keep my guard up. I think I've made a costly mistake.

Levi must notice my change in posture. "You okay?"

Covering, I say sheepishly, "Yeah, I think all the sweet teas you've been making me drink has hit me. Finding a bathroom might be a good idea, if you don't mind."

He scans the area and tells me, "Of course. There's one right over there, darlin', end of the food tents. I'll just wait on the other side of this aisle for you, over by the stage." He adds with a wink, "Don't wander off on me."

I look to where he's pointing, seeing one at the end of the row. Smiling up at him and giving his hand a squeeze, I head in the direction he indicated.

As I'm walking away from the safety his presence provides me, the tingling feeling comes back stronger than before. Once I am about two-thirds of the way to the bathroom, I see the solid frame of a man and the back of his black trench coat swishing around the corner. My feet stop immediately. I am frozen in place. That frame seems familiar, reminding me of Richard's bodyguard, driver, and all-around go-to guy, Duncan. If who I saw is in fact Duncan, that means Richard is close to finding me, if he hasn't already. Panic seizes my chest like a tight fist. I feel like I can't breathe. I race to the bathroom and luckily find one unoccupied. I lock myself inside, taking deep, gulping breaths, which is a huge mistake.

I calm myself by knowing that I can't be seen right now. I am safe in the confines of this disgusting portable bathroom. I can't tell if I'm sweating because of an epic panic attack or the jumbo heavy-duty plastic oven I am hiding inside.

It takes me a few minutes before I realize Richard doesn't have the hold over me he once did. I am not his puppet anymore, or the naive, socialite prize that he covets. I'm also fairly certain I can bring him to his knees, at least figuratively by the suspicions I have of where he gets his money if I'm given the opportunity. There's a chance I could do it literally if I was able to get in a lucky shot, maybe. I'm positive I couldn't take on Duncan and I wouldn't even try. That man is a walking terror.

The one thing I do know is Duncan would never do anything to me without Richard being present. While I'm sure Duncan has done his share of Richard's dirty work, Richard would never order me to be harmed or....disposed of without him being there to witness it. He's likely too furious with me over leaving him. However, his anger leads him to be predictable in his behavior. And that predictability is his Achilles' heel. He would take too much pleasure in watching me suffer and seeing his brand of justice handed out, although never by his own hand.

I realize with great satisfaction I am not the same person I was several months ago. Before, I wouldn't have considered fighting back. The girl that came to Sugar, Kentucky was hell-bent on running and never stopping. I'm not that girl anymore. My gut doesn't churn any longer from the thought of staying in one place. I'm not constantly looking for an escape route or trying to keep myself at a distance from anyone I meet. I have done quite the opposite. I have the beginnings of roots, of a place to call home. I have started relationships. They are ones I cherish, friendships, and perhaps even something more, something lasting with Levi. I refuse to give them up. They are the first true and genuine connections I've made.

I strengthen myself with the knowledge that now I have something worth fighting for and keeping. I can feel my resolve cementing. I'm sure I have just stopped at the edge of the highest cliff on the pathway that is my now life. I only have to figure out when the right time is to take the leap and jump.

I open the portable bathroom's door and take a gulping breath of fresh air. I'm glad no one is waiting for me to exit. I feel like I have been baking in a rotisserie oven. I probably look about the same. Taking another deep breath, I smooth down my dress and adjust my hair. It's time to put my paranoia behind me and get back to my decadent date.

25

Her

As I step toward my intended reward, a hand firmly grips my arm. I yelp.

"Shh, we don't want to alarm anyone," says a strong, dominant male voice.

I don't recognize it, however, I'm sure I can guess its originating source. My time is up. Richard has made his move.

The voice speaks calmly. "Now, Miss Brooks, we need to talk. Please don't make a scene. We have a common enemy. You recognize the name Richard Whitman?"

"I do." Confusion floods my mind.

"May we speak for a moment?" He must sense my hesitation and urgency to return to Levi. "I won't take much of your time."

I turn toward him and take a step back. It allows me to extricate my arm from his grasp. Nodding to the opposite direction of where Levi is standing, I say, "Please, lead the way."

The man turns on his heel and escorts me between the campers the carnival workers use to sleep in while travelling. We are out of sight from everyone, but I don't feel uneasy. This man has a professional and analytical air about him. He isn't cold and distant like I've known Richard to be. And better still, he isn't Duncan. Plus, he took the lead with me at his back. Anyone Richard sent to collect me would have made sure they kept their eyes on me at all times.

When we've reached a spot away from all the noise, the man doesn't waste any time in getting to the point. "Miss Brooks, my name is Agent Wright. I work for the FBI."

Surprise fills me, however, I remain wary. "I'd say nice to meet you, but, honestly, I'm not sure at the moment. You'll have to forgive me."

He smirks slightly, saying, "That's understandable. I came to find you concerning Mr. Whitman."

"And exactly what can I help you with? I haven't seen him in months," I tell him, folding my arms protectively across my belly.

"Well, actually, we are aware of that. But, we know you have a connection with him."

Seeing there's no use in denying something he already knows, I agree, "I used to, yes."

Agent Wright's expression softens a little. "Based on our findings, we are certain you still do. Were you aware that Mr. Whitman is trying to find you?"

Sighing, I confess, "I knew he probably had been. I was hoping maybe he wasn't that interested anymore. Although, I didn't figure that was likely a possibility. How do you know he is?"

"Because we have been watching Mr. Whitman for quite some time. He's been on our high priority radar for about two years in fact." He watches me for my reaction.

Stunned, I respond only with "Oh." I realize two years ago was my college graduation and when Richard's interest in me heightened. It's also when he offered me the job, increasing his influence over me.

"I'm going to be honest with you, Miss Brooks." He pauses until he's certain he has my full attention. "Mr. Whitman is a very dangerous man. We've been building a case against him for racketeering, extortion, and blackmail. We're very close on completing our investigation. However, there are other, far worse transgressions we would rather link to him. A conviction on charges of kidnapping, suspected torture, and possibly murder, even by association, would put him away for a very long time. Unfortunately, we need more concrete evidence to guarantee a conviction of any kind. For more than a decade, Mr. Whitman has built an empire of crime and corruption. He's been extremely careful. Nothing has ever directly linked him with our suspicions until two years ago. Now, there are whispers and rumors swirling in Rapid City suggesting Mr. Whitman thinks he is untouchable because of the power he holds, along with the contacts he maintains. For these reasons, he recently hasn't taken his usual precautions and has gotten sloppy. "

I think back to the conversation I overheard between Richard and Duncan and how they mentioned my parents. Everything fits together.

I tell him my suspicion. "I know why, or I have my own hunch about it. It was my parents. The circumstances with them are personal. It's not just business with them. Before I left, it seemed like they were in trouble with Richard. I also got the impression they were going to run. I have no idea where they are now. I can't be sure if Richard did something to them or if they left and are hiding like me. Either way, there's one thing that is guaranteed. Richard does not forgive betrayal, ever."

Agent Wright's mouth pulls down in a frown. "Well, that sheds some light on it. If your parents are gone and Mr. Whitman is responsible for your parents' disappearances, then I'm sorry."

Snorting, I say, "Don't be. I don't mean to sound callous, but they aren't who I thought they were. Their home was just a different prison for me. If they left to save themselves, then that means they left me to fend for myself without a backwards glance. Regardless though, no matter how I feel about that, if Richard did do something to them, they didn't deserve it and he needs to face the consequences for it. What do you need from me?"

Candidly, he states, "We need information, Miss Brooks. More specifically, information that we believe is only kept in Mr. Whitman's possession, most likely on his personal computer."

"The obvious place would be in Richard's home office." I think about everything Agent Wright has told me, reaching the conclusion he intends. "So, you need me to go back and try to retrieve what you need." It's not a question, only a statement because I know what he wants.

"Yes."

With part of me still hoping I'm not as significant as he suggests, I ask, "Why me? I'm nobody."

"You're not nobody, Miss Brooks. Mr. Whitman has an interest in you. That makes you a valuable asset to us." His voice lowers, filling with frustration. "If I'm being honest with you, you would give us our best chance at taking him down. To gain the kind of access to him and his home that we need takes us months, if not years, to cultivate. You might be able to achieve it in a far shorter time."

I laugh a bit hysterically. "Oh, Agent Wright. You really are placing too much confidence in me, my value, and my abilities. Besides, there is a very real chance that Richard may not let me see the light of day for a very long time, or ever, if I return. The assumption he'll let me wander freely is borderline ludicrous."

Even though I was planning to do exactly what Agent Wright is asking of me, my stomach still tightens into a ball of dread. Going up against Richard isn't something to take lightly. In fact, I might have gone completely insane in thinking I can actually do it. I could very well be signing my own death warrant, literally, if any of what I now believe about Richard is true.

Sounding sympathetic, he says, "I understand this is a lot to ask. I can even understand you saying no. But, you have to know that Mr. Whitman will never stop looking for you if he has any notion you know something."

I sigh because I'm confident he's right. "I know he won't. That's why I was planning on going back anyway, to end this, to end him. If there is any way I can make him pay for the damage he's done, then I'll do it. At least you're giving me a better chance of getting away from him for good."

"And you will have that chance, Miss Brooks, I can assure you."

"How do you know that? You can't guarantee it." I snap. "I know Richard. Once I'm under his roof again, he won't give me any freedoms, especially at first. Me going in there could be useless."

"It won't be, I promise. You will have an opportunity to get out and get us the information." He looks so confident, almost cocky.

It infuriates me. With contempt, I spit out, "Don't make promises you can't deliver, Agent Wright."

"I'm not." The steel in his voice almost has me believing him. "I can't say when or how the opportunity will present itself, especially without compromising your situation, but it will. You just have to watch for it. Work as quickly as you can and be ready."

Warily, I ask, "And how am I supposed to gather the information you need? It's not like I can walk out of his office with his laptop."

Handing me a small black case, he says, "Use this jump drive to copy everything. You should only need a couple of minutes."

"Yeah, only a couple of minutes," I laugh cynically. "Easier said than done."

"Miss Brooks..."

Holding up my hand to stop him, I cut him off. "Please, if I'm considering going into the lion's den, you might as well call me Sam."

"Sam," he starts again, gently this time. "If you don't want to do this, you can walk away."

The hysteria tinges my voice again. "Want to do this? Ha. Hell no, I don't want to do this." Then calmer, more softly, "However, I can't walk away either." I look directly at Agent Wright, gathering my strength. "Richard Whitman has taken too much from me. He's taken too much from everyone who's ever shaken his hand. It stops now, one way or another. Now, if you'll excuse me, I'm pretty sure my date will be sending out a search party for me if I don't return in the next ninety seconds."

"Of course. Good luck and I'll be in touch." I take several steps to leave when Agent Wright quietly says my name, "Sam?"

I turn back.

"I am sorry about your parents," he says sincerely. He pauses. He looks me straight in the eye. "Thank you for doing this."

I simply give him a brisk nod and leave. I'm doing this for myself, to be rid of Richard, but I know somewhere deep inside me is the little girl who is desperate for her parents' love. Even if they don't deserve it, I have to try and save them, if they're still alive, or avenge them.

26

Her

I walk out from between the trailers to the row of carnival food. Noticing the stage and Levi waiting patiently by it, I walk toward him through an aisle of confections and treats. None of them can hold my attention compared to him. I smile at the thought of knowing how he tastes. My feet quicken their pace as does my heart at the sight of him. Suddenly, I need to be in his arms. I can't wait another moment. He is so beautiful. He's everything I've ever wanted, but didn't think existed. He's kind, decent, and strong, both inside and out, even if he doesn't know it. He's also fiercely loyal and protective. It's going to kill me to leave him.

I feel tears burning behind my eyes. I refuse to let them fall. I won't allow Richard to take away my time with Levi. I know now my moments with him are limited, even more than I originally thought. I won't waste a minute of it thinking about the task I have ahead of me or the time I'll need to be away from Levi. I pray it's only for a little while.

Lost in thought and moving slightly to the music, Levi doesn't notice me approaching. I'm given a rare moment of observing him unguarded. A small smile plays on his lips as he watches kids race around carrying bags of cotton candy, their parents laughing and chasing after them, and the sweet, older couples swaying gently on the dance floor. He really loves it here in this place. I am starting to see why.

The quaint town and its people with their warmth seep into your bones and heart, enveloping you with feelings of calm and goodness. If I could stay, I would. That thought sends a twinge to my heart, knowing I have to leave. I stubbornly push it aside. It doesn't have to be tonight and I fully intend on making the most of my time with Levi, however short it might be.

Levi turns his head and catches sight of me. The dazzling smile that crosses his face has me losing my breath. His feet immediately start in my direction and have him in front of me within four long strides. His expression is warm and open, showing me everything he has to offer.

"Hey," he says, grinning like he's turned into a teenage boy on a first date. Returning his smile, I respond, "Hi yourself. Sorry I took so long."

"No worries," he assures me. "Waiting for you is no hardship, as long as you return to me." I feel my smile dim just a bit, wondering if he'll still feel that way down the road.

As I'm thinking, a new song comes through the speakers. I recognize it as "Like I'm Gonna Lose You". The song is the perfect representation for our situation. Apparently, Levi agrees because he extends his hand to me. I take it and let him lead me onto the dance floor. He pulls me close while looking at me with pure affection in his eyes. I realize I've already fallen all the way in love with him.

Moving gently with the rhythm, our bodies fit perfectly together despite our height difference. I'm up on my toes as he molds himself around me. His arm is tight and securely encircles my waist. My hand is flat against his sculpted chest as his covers mine. There isn't a breath of space between us. Everything surrounding us has disappeared from my notice. It's only us and the music, the sad, sweet song just for us.

166

Levi leans in, placing a chaste kiss on my lips. It's sweet and filled with longing, or maybe that's just the way I feel. A shiver travels through me. The heat from his body feels like a drug to me. I'm as close as I can possibly get to him with decency since we are in public. It's simply not enough. I need more of him. It's probably not fair to him, but I can't deny myself any longer.

When the song is ending, it seems the perfect time to leave.

I look up at him nervously and whisper, "Take me home, Levi. Take me to bed."

The fire I see ignite in his eyes tells me my nerves have no place between us. I'm certain the only reason he's able to tamp down on his desire is because he is a complete gentleman.

He looks at me with openness and a little concern. His knuckles lightly trail across my cheek.

"We don't have to. We can wait." He pauses. "*I* can wait. You are worth waiting for, Sam. You're worth everything."

If I hadn't already fallen in love with him, I would have in this moment. I can only say the most honest word I have, "Please."

That one word is his undoing. His lips touch mine in a searing kiss this time, filled with passion and yearning. With an arm around my waist and his signature grin, he leans to my ear and says, "Darlin', you don't ever have to ask me twice."

We're off the dance floor and through the crowd in an instant, heading toward his truck, our bear in tow. At the edge of the field used for parking, Levi scoops his arm under my knees to carry me without ever breaking stride. I can't stop myself from giggling as he feathers kisses around my face. He slides me into the truck cab and rounds the front bumper, getting in himself. He pulls me tightly against him and devours my mouth. I'm helpless to do anything, except hang on to him and whimper. Several minutes later, he reluctantly pulls away and starts the truck, putting it into gear.

With blatant desire in his eyes, he grabs my hand and winks, "We need to leave before we fog up the windows."

My whole body shivers in anticipation. I know he feels it by the slight twitching at the corner of his mouth. It seems to take mere seconds before we are walking onto the porch of his house. He opens the door, stepping aside for me to enter. I go straight to the stairs to head to his bedroom. I make it up the first two steps when he gently grasps my arm and turns me to face him. His hands cup my face as his thumb brushes over my lips. They part on a breathy sigh. I ghost the tip of my tongue over the pad of his thumb and see his eyes go molten. I prepare for an onslaught of desire from him, but his kiss is just the opposite. It's so sweet and soft with only the slightest pressure. My knees go weak from the tenderness of his touch. He feels me sag against him and wraps an arm around me. We stay like this, simply holding on to each other for several minutes.

Finally, I gather myself, toeing off my sandals. I turn to head upstairs and take his hand. I lead Levi up to the place I have been longing to return to since this morning. Entering the room, I cross to the bed, positioning him right by the side. I push firmly on his shoulders to indicate my need for him to sit. He simply raises an eyebrow, but doesn't voice any question. I'm grateful because I'm not sure I could find the words to speak right now. With a second little push and a smile from me, he complies. I hold his jaw and kiss him, needing to taste him again. It's already been too long. His hands are on my hips when he starts to pull me toward him. I take his hands, removing them, before taking a step back. He growls low in his throat. I giggle. Then, I flush with anticipation at what I'm about to do.

I raise my hand and take my hair down from its clip. It falls around my shoulders, loose and in waves. I see Levi's breath catch. It bolsters my confidence. I already know he wants me. However, it's a powerful thing seeing the intense effect I have on him. It's identical to the one he has on me.

I reach for the buttons on my sundress, undoing them one by one. Never faltering, I look him straight in the eye and see a lustful haze take over his expression. His hands move to the edge of his bed, gripping tightly. His jaw is locked, pulsing. I can tell his control is slipping.

I undo the last button, which lands slightly below my navel. I slip the spaghetti straps from my shoulders, letting the dress fall to the floor. I hear an audible gasp, then a groan from Levi. I stand there in lace panties, soft waves of hair, and nothing else. I watch as Levi's hungry gaze travels over every inch of me. The air between us is charged with need. It's almost a physical touch and my body instantly floods with desire.

27

Him

I am struck completely stupid by the beautiful woman standing before me. Sam is the most incredible thing I have ever seen. Her porcelain skin glistens in the moonlight streaming in from the window. Flows of tawny hair brush against her body and make my fingers itch to touch the same places. Her eyes shine, looking like golden medallions.

A small smile curls her lips as she walks toward me, placing her hands on my shoulders. My arms instinctively wrap around her. I pull her close while one hand cups the back of her neck, bending her lips to mine. We crash together. Our tongues dance and duel to the same tempo as our sprinting hearts.

She tugs at the back of my shirt and whips it over my head. I hate to lose even a second of our connection. Her small, strong hands smooth over my skin. They leave a trail of goosebumps in their wake. I shift the pressure of my hand to angle her neck. It allows me to kiss down the column of creamy skin. Then, moving to her chest, I pause to place a tender kiss directly over her heart, savoring the rhythm beating there beneath my lips. I don't remain there long though because her perfect breasts call to me as they did the day before. As I move my mouth to them, I hear her whimper. She arches into me. Her silent begging shatters what little control I have left. I am a starved man and she has just become my last meal.

I clamp my mouth around her pebbled nipple, sucking deeply. My fingers bite into her hip. My other hand splays across her back, pulling her into the vee of my legs. Her moan is my permission to continue a slow, thorough worship of her body. She rocks up onto her toes. I lift her effortlessly and help her straddle my legs. She settles all the way down, bringing her heated core directly over my swollen cock. If all the blood hadn't previously rushed there, it would have now. I can feel myself grow impossibly larger, straining against the fabric of my pants. I have passed the point of comfort. My agony is torturous and completely exquisite.

Sam presses herself into me. Her breast crushes against my mouth allowing me to suck her even deeper. Her knees grip my hips like a vise. She is molding us together. She is so tiny, but surrounds me. She is everywhere, her body, her scent, her desire.

Her breathing is hard and fast. Low moans flow from her throat. I swirl my tongue around her tightened bud, then blow lightly. I can feel even more goosebumps spread over her skin. On her exhale, I suck again. She gasps.

"Oh god," she pants, "Levi, I need you."

She reaches for my pants button that is stuck between us. Her small hand makes short work of the task to free me. She's determined to reach her prize. I stop her with difficulty to set her on her feet. The whine she releases practically turns me into the animal I am trying to control. I lean down to quickly rid myself of my boots, cursing my habit of donning the intricately laced footwear.

Once finished, I stand to shed the rest of my clothing. Her gaze moves over me, hungrily, settling between my legs. She bites on the side of her lip. I can almost hear her lustful thoughts and remember her lush mouth wrapped around my length. I quickly consider my options of letting her take control or with me satisfying her in every way. My desire to make her feel good wins out. I can't be selfish with her. Or maybe I am because I have to have her taste on my tongue. I want to see her glistening with a shimmer of sweat as I lick every bit of frustration out of her. I want to hear her moan my name with need as I feast on her, never having my fill. She had her turn before, now it's mine.

I look at her, hiding nothing. Her eyes blaze as they meet mine. All flushed and wanton, she is incredibly hot. I pull her to me, lifting her. She plasters her body to mine. I turn us and lay her on the bed, settling myself between her thighs. The pressure pushes her down into the mattress. I ease up a bit not wanting to crush her. She immediately wraps her arms around me, claiming my weight, and practically purrs. The sound is delicious. I can feel her nails digging into my shoulder blades. It is a constant reminder that this is really happening and not my wild, sex- driven imagination.

I kiss her everywhere, reverently, all the way down her body. I pause at the light green lace which covers the place I want most to explore and claim as my own. Sam lifts her hips, allowing me to skim the fabric off down her silky legs. I force myself to go slow, savoring every second, when all I really want is to rip them off.

I run my hands along the inside of her legs to her inner thighs, spreading her apart. I can feel her watching me, but I can't take my eyes off the site that has claimed all of my attention. I doubt once I've tasted her I'll ever have my fill. She is already an addiction I don't ever want to overcome.

Pushing my shoulders against her, I stretch her legs wide. I see her fingers curl into the blanket, gripping tightly. Her breathing is shallow and tortured with anticipation. I want her like this always, on the verge

172

of losing her sanity. Leaning into her, I flick out my tongue, catching her gaze right before contact. Her eyes are sparking and wild, impossibly big. At the moment I lick into her folds, she bucks off the bed, crying out. I grab hold of her hips with both hands and pull her flush against my mouth, needing to devour her. As my tongue mimics the pumping motion I long to make with my cock, I feel her walls tighten around me. I quickly clamp down on her clit and suck hard. Her head thrashes wildly as she screams and shatters instantly. The site is wholly erotic and the best thing I've ever witnessed. I continue to suck and push two fingers into her to prolong her orgasm, stroking in and out. She moans for minutes afterward while her body starts to calm. I'm surprised I haven't erupted from her sensual sounds. They are enough to finish me off by themselves.

I ease my mouth and fingers off of her and crawl up her languid body. Her entire body is pink and glistening with sweat. I could take hours to lick every inch of her. However, in this moment I can think of nothing else except being inside her. I need her in the best possible way. I'm as hard as a steel rod and my balls are drawn up tight. Entering her might be all I need to finish me off.

Sam seems lost in her euphoria, but then, her hand reaches out, wrapping around my length. I stop breathing because it feels so unbelievable. She strokes me once, a devilish smirk on her face, and centers me right at her opening. I push in just the barest amount. We both groan from the exquisite sensation. My toes curl as I try to control the need to slam into her all the way. While I am wrestling with my personal dilemma, her fingers dig into my ass and pull me down. I am halfway inside her before my brain catches up. My body takes over, sliding all

173

the way home. I bury myself deeper than I thought possible.

"Oh god. Sam."

She moans deeply, sending a vibration straight to my cock. A growl leaves my throat. I hear her giggle. Looking up, I see a wicked glint shine in her eyes and then feel her walls tighten around me.

"Don't," I beg.

Vixen that she is, she does it again.

"Samantha!" I order, worrying instantly.

I've never used her given name because of what she told me. However, it becomes quickly apparent that in this moment I shouldn't be concerned. My demanding tone only seems to have strengthened her determination. Her core tightens its grip a third time, even harder than before. She is looking at me defiantly. The same look I first saw in the store that pulled me to her, the look that sends me over the edge.

"I can't hold back any longer, Sam," I warn.

Now, it's her turn to beg. "Don't hold back, Levi. Make me yours."

My need to claim her explodes. I wind my arm around her waist as my hips slam into her over and over again as far as I can go. Her defiant look is gone, replaced with one of bliss and need. She moans loudly. In the next second, she is catapulted over the edge again. I follow right behind her, roaring with my release. I am vaguely aware of my grip being so tight she will surely have bruises for days although it doesn't seem be an immediate concern to either of us.

As her body is still racked with little tremors and my breathing starts to steady, I lower myself onto her. She wraps her legs around me as I lay my head in the crook of her neck. I breathe in the scent of arousal, sex, and one that is completely Sam. I feel my eyes grow heavy as her hand strokes over my head. We stay like this for a long time, savoring the feeling of wholeness we have together.

28

Her

A soft moan in my ear wakes me from the best sleep I've had in ages. I blink my eyes open to the pitch black, taking a moment to remember where I am. I'm locked in Levi's embrace, his body tightly wrapped around mine. It's the middle of the night. I hear low rumbling outside of an approaching storm. I've never been a fan of thunderstorms. Right now though, I'm safe and secure in Levi's bed. I can't think of anything better than snuggling up to him as the claps echo through the sky.

The noise becomes louder with another roll of thunder. Levi moans again, becoming agitated. He groans in agony, "D".

He starts to move his head back and forth, obviously stuck in a dream. His hold on me tightens. "D!" he says with more urgency.

"Levi", I whisper softly, not wanting to startle him. He groans like he's in pain.

Suddenly, a huge crash sounds as the room is flooded with brilliant light from the storm. Levi's eyes fly open.

He grabs my upper arms roughly, tears flowing down his cheeks. "Dylan!"

He's frantic. He's sweating and anxious, his breathing labored. His eyes are completely unfocused. He doesn't even see me. It's as if he's looking right through me.

He wails. "Dylan."

I can feel tears of my own fall from the pain in his voice. I don't know what to do. Carefully, I brush my hand down his cheek.

"Shh, Levi. It's okay."

In the light from the storm, I can see his pupils are dilated. His heart rate is in a sprint. He continues to stare through me. I try again.

"Levi, it's just a dream. Everything is okay."

Finally, his breathing slows and his eyelids grow heavy again. Gently, he eases himself back down to the bed. The storm has moved over us quickly. It seems to have been a trigger because now, he's calm. He settles in beside me with his chin on my head. His breathing has mostly returned to normal. I don't think he even knows what occurred. It's like he was in a trance the whole time.

I stay awake for what seems like an eternity. I keep wondering if something else is going to happen. I'm not scared, only concerned. Levi obviously has a lot of things that he hasn't dealt with yet. I would stand by his side through it all, but given my current situation, it's not fair for me to stay. I have to deal with my own issues before I can be there for him. I know my time to leave has come too quickly. I can't put it off any longer.

At the first streams of sunlight coming in the windows, I gently extract myself from him. I gather up my clothes, dressing quietly. I make it out of his room and down the stairs without a sound. Grabbing my shoes, I exit through the front door, walking down the lane toward town. Every inch I take breaks my heart and almost my resolve.

With my arms wrapped around my middle, I stumble along, heading back the Miss Sarah's store. It's clear that my time in Sugar is up. Richard may or may not have found me yet, but I can no longer stay here. I finally need to put an end to my running.

I realize this means saying goodbye to not only Levi, but Miss Sarah too, and everything I've found here that I want. The thought has a sob breaking free from my lips. With no one around, I grieve for all that I'm giving up.

I make it to the store just as the sun is cresting the horizon. It's still early, although knowing Miss Sarah, she's up. Hoping I can make myself presentable before she sees me, I slip upstairs to my apartment to change. After brushing out my hair, rinsing my face, and putting on my established wardrobe of shorts and a tank top, I head to the small lounge for coffee. The moment I enter the small room, Miss Sarah looks up, smiling. Seeing me, her face falls. She is out of her chair instantly.

"Lynn, honey, what's the matter?"

Nearly choking on tears, I swallow. "Oh, Miss Sarah, I'm fine, really. But, I do need to tell you I haven't been truthful about who I am. My name isn't Lynn, not my first name anyway. It's Sam."

"Hmm," she considers for a moment. "I like that better. Now then, tell me what's going on to have you tied up in knots. Because I know you are not fine and haven't been since you first came to Sugar."

Surprised at her quick acceptance, I ask, "You aren't mad?"

Offering me a sweet smile of understanding, she says, "No, dear. I've known for quite some time that you had secrets. Secrets that were yours to keep or tell as you liked. It's not my place to judge or push. I figured when you were ready, IF you were ever ready, you'd tell me. I do have to ask though, does Levi know?"

Happy I am able to admit he does, I tell her, "Yes, ma'am."

"Then, that's all I care about." She pauses as if she's choosing her next words carefully. "When you have feelings for someone, you cannot keep things from them. They deserve to know."

With that statement, my stomach clinches and a tear slides down my face. I realize he's going to hate me. A floodgate opens at the thought. Miss Sarah gathers me up in her embrace.

"Shh. Now, now, Sam. Things can't be that bad."

"Oh, Miss Sarah," I wail. "Everything seems so impossible. I have some things I finally need to deal with. And I think Levi does too. I think he's having problems with coming home and the accident. I don't know how to help him or if I can. He's having dreams or nightmares, really. We're both such a mess. I don't know how we can be together."

I can't even tell her how truly horrible things are, not that I can speak through my sobs.

The bell above the store entrance rings indicating a customer. I pull away, wiping my cheeks with the back of my hand. Taking a deep breathe, I manage, "I'm okay. I'll be okay." I muster a small smile to try to convince Miss Sarah my words aren't hollow.

She pats my hand, using her usual all-knowing tone, "Everything will work out. You'll see." Pushing my hair behind my ear, she kisses my cheek, warmly, and leaves the room to tend to her patron.

Digging deep for strength, I try to put all my emotions back in a box. In order to achieve my goal, I have to be firm and resolute, concentrating on my task.

My emotions will only make things harder. Stuffing it all down, I lean against the counter, feeling empty.

I hear thunderous footsteps behind me and realize, hopelessly, I may not have to worry about what Richard might do to me. My breaking heart will most assuredly kill me first.

29

Him

She's gone. Sam left my bed, my house, me. Without a word. Not so much as a "thanks for the roll in the hay" or a "to hell with you". I thought she was different, that what we have is different. How could I be so wrong? After everything she said to me, all the things she told me, and all the ways she's opened up with me, I can't believe she would just walk out. Well, I'm not going to let her. If she thought I acted like a bear when we first met, it was nothing compared to how I feel now.

I throw off the covers and find the nearest pair of shorts. I couldn't care less about their state of cleanliness. I'm on a mission. Snagging a t-shirt from the dresser and my keys, I'm down the stairs, two at a time. My knee protests the quick movements, but my anger and adrenaline override its complaints.

Jumping in the truck, I peel out of the driveway, speeding down the road to town. Good thing there's no one out at the moment. I make it to the store in record time, not that it takes an eternity anyway. I throw myself out of the truck probably before the tires stop moving. I'm a bull with red in his line of sight.

Stomping my way to the back, I barricade the break room doorway with my body. Sam is standing at the counter with her back to me.

I snap, "You mind telling me why you left? And without the decency of any kind of goodbye?"

She turns around, but won't look at me. Softly, she mutters, "I'm sorry. Last night was wonderful, but...."

I cut her off, feeling hurt and bitter. "Wonderful, huh? It was so great that you felt like you should just up

181

and leave. Really, Sam? I thought we had something here or the start of something at least. I guess I was wrong."

I see anguish flash in her eyes. Without sniping back, she sadly agrees. "Yeah, I guess so." She walks toward me to exit. "Um, I need to get to work. If you'll excuse me."

Suddenly, I really look at her. I'm so stunned by what I see I simply move out of her way. She looks completely defeated, empty. She isn't fighting me. There's no sass or bite to her words. She's not pushing back. She's not acting like the Sam I've discovered. All I see is her retreating, physically and emotionally.

"Sam?" I call.

She doesn't hear me, or probably refuses to acknowledge me. She disappears through the aisles of the store. I'm still staring in the direction she left when a resounding smack stings across my bicep.

"Well, Mr. Levi Taylor, I hope you are proud of yourself! What on earth have you done to that girl?" Miss Sarah is livid.

"Me?" I sputter. Then with more confusion, "I, um, well, I'm not sure. I didn't think I did anything to her. I thought she did something to me. But, now I'm not exactly sure what's going on. Except that maybe I've been a jerk, again."

"At least we can agree on that at the moment!" I probably deserve every verbal lashing Miss Sarah wants to give me.

Trying to make sense of the situation, I plead, "Miss Sarah, what's going on?"

She sighs and admits, "Honestly, I don't know really. But, I will tell you that maybe you should do a bit more observing before you start growling and pounding your chest at people. Did you even bother to look at Sam when you came in? Or did you just start yelling?"

Surprised, I ask, "You know about her name?"

"Yes, and don't change the subject!" she snaps. "Answer my question."

"Well, no, I didn't pay attention. I was upset. I guess I just flew off the handle without thinking."

"Mm-hmm."

The times when Miss Sarah says the least are usually the times I feel the smallest. Right now, I feel about two inches tall and am willing to take any criticism she has. "What did I miss, Miss Sarah?"

"You missed that girl bawling her eyes out. She's been crying something fierce. Oh, she tried to cover it up, but I could still tell when I first saw her. You could have too if you're paying attention. Then, she practically dissolved into a puddle of tears in front of me, completely overcome with sorrow."

Hearing about Sam being distraught punches me in the gut. "Crying? Over what? She's the one who left me without a word."

"She wouldn't really tell me a lot," Miss Sarah explains. "She said she had some issues to deal with. Then, mentioned something about you having some nightmares?"

Ice cold dread spills down my spine. I don't remember having my nightmare last night. I always have before, or at least I think I've always remembered. It invariably plays in my head the following morning on a loop. It's the first thing that comes to my mind when I wake up, however, that didn't happen this morning. Then again, I was focused on other things when my eyes opened like the cold, empty space in my bed.

If I had the nightmare where I relive the accident while Sam was with me that would explain her leaving quickly. I terrified her. In my dreams, I feel like I come unglued. If she witnessed that, after everything she's been through, I can't imagine why she's still at this store or even this town knowing I'm here. I am the physical manifestation of her fear, a violent, lethal man who loses control and can hurt people. Understanding hits me.

My knees buckle and I crash into the chair behind me. I've scared and hurt the person that could potentially end up mattering to me the most in the world. I'm starting to love her. But, I've just given her the reason she needs to walk away from me.

Searching for a way to fix my mistake, I ask, "Miss Sarah, what do I do? I didn't mean to scare her."

In her confident tone, she says, "You go find her and explain. It's as simple as that. She'll forgive you."

On her last word, I am racing out of the room. I find Sam at the front of the store, which is thankfully empty.

"Sam," I plead.

Without looking at me, she whispers, "Just go away, Levi. Leave me alone."

I hear the ache in her voice and hold out hope it means I still have a chance to make this right.

Firmly, but gently, I tell her, "No, not until you hear me out."

"Please, don't make this harder than it has to be."

Laying my cards on the table, I say, "I have to explain what happened. If you still want me to leave after you hear what I've said, then I'll go."

184

Facing me with resignation clear on her face, she says, "Okay, but let's go upstairs."

I follow her up to her apartment above the store. My heart is pounding out of my chest the entire way. I feel like this could be the end with Sam if I'm not careful. I realize it's time for me to start facing my fears in order to let it all go. I have to deal with the loss of my parents, my guilt from the accident, the loss of my career, and most importantly, being the cause of Dylan losing his as well. It's eating me up from the inside out. And now, I'm terrified it's about to cost me the most significant person in my life.

Before she finishes closing the door, I begin. "I'm a disaster. I'm used to knowing how to handle any situation, to be prepared for any scenario. It's what I'm trained to do. But, right now, I feel like I'm barely keeping my head above water. I'm lost. I feel like I'm floating around without any kind of direction anymore. I'm not sure how to handle all the things that have happened in my life. My parents are gone, as is my job. And Dylan, well, I can't think of where to start to make things up to him."

"Levi, you and Dylan had an accident. I doubt he blames you. It wasn't your fault." There's conviction in her voice I wish I could believe.

"I'm not positive about that, but I need to figure it out in order to move on with my life. I understand that now. I'm so sorry I put you in a position to be frightened of me. I never meant for that to happen. If I had been dealing with all of this, it probably wouldn't have. And I can't tell you enough how horrible I feel. I'll do everything I can to keep you safe, including from myself." The last part pains me to think about even though I'll do it if it's needed.

Shaking her head, she says, "You can't do this for *me*. It won't work."

"I know, and I'm not," I assure her. "I am doing it for me, to make myself better. I'm doing it to get the life I want. A life I hope will have you in it. If you'll forgive me." I wait silently, feeling like a live wire has crawled under my skin.

Finally, she whispers, "I do forgive you, Levi. I understand." My relief is almost a living thing in the room.

"Oh, thank god." Crossing to her, I take her hands. "I know we have things to work out and that you're still unsure. We'll go slowly. Have dinner with me?"

I see her hesitate and realize I'm not above begging. "Please, Sam, just dinner, just us."

"Okay."

Thrilled she hasn't given up on us completely, I say, "Thank you. I'll pick you up later."

Still seeing the debate in her eyes, I kiss her forehead gently and leave before she can change her mind.

30

Her

As Levi walks out of the apartment, my stomach turns to stone. I've dug myself in deeper. I should have said no to dinner. I just couldn't. He looked so hopeful and sincere. It torments me for him to think why I left is in any way his fault. And honestly, I'm being completely selfish. I want more time with him. It's as simple as that. I'm not ready to give him up.

My gaze snags on the jump drive Agent Wright gave me. I realize with resignation I can't put off leaving. It has to be tonight. Given any other situation, I would have left already. I'd have slipped out before anyone noticed except I can't do that to Levi. I owe it to him to tell him face to face. I won't be a coward even if it means my insides will be ripped to shreds. He deserves better than that. He deserves someone who respects him enough not to sneak away, someone who loves him enough to face the devil.

I make my way back downstairs to spend the day organizing the front counter, restocking produce, and helping any customers that come into the store. It at least keeps me occupied for the day. Then, I return upstairs to pack up all my things, few as they are. By this time tomorrow, I'll be out of Sugar and hopefully, on my way to dealing with my own past.

Once I've completed gathering my meager belongings, I shower and dress for dinner. I slip into my other sundress and sandals, leaving my hair in flowing waves, just how Levi prefers. I want him to remember me how he likes me best, soft and fresh.

I realize I need to hide my backpack behind the couch to prevent Miss Sarah or Levi from seeing it in case either comes upstairs. I am determined to tell Levi in person I'm leaving because he deserves that respect. However, I know both of them would try to talk me out of it if they found out too soon. Even worse, I think they would probably succeed. Knowing this, I'd rather avoid having to give any kind of explanation if they saw a packed bag.

After putting the bag out of sight, I see the jump drive resting on the counter. I put it in my pocket, trusting that's the only place it will be secure. After looking around one last time, I walk downstairs to meet Levi in front of the store. A knot grows in my belly at the thought of this being one of the last times I might use these stairs.

I'm not left waiting long before Levi pulls up, smiling and looking eager. He also appears a bit unsure. He slides out of the truck, walking around the cab to open my door.

Brushing his lips over my cheek, he says, "You look beautiful."

"Thanks." The quiver moving over my skin is unstoppable. Even the barest touch from him leaves me breathless. That might be what I'll miss most while I'm away, other than his smile, the one that lights up his face.

I climb into the truck, trying to calm my nerves. I recognize now this idea is worse than I originally thought. I'm being selfish prolonging what I have to do, but I wanted one last moment with him. I should have ended things this morning when he was upset, or better yet, kept going when I walked away from his house. It would have been simpler then, although not easier. Dozens of times pop in my head for when it would have been a better time to end things than now.

The best idea would have been to never get involved. Then, I think of all the things I've learned about Levi I wouldn't have known. I think of all the things I've experienced being with him, friendship, laughter, and greatest of all, a love I have never known existed.

My heart twinges with pain.

Arriving at the restaurant, we're seated in a fairly private and secluded booth in the side corner. It's a quaint little place offering the usual American fare, typical of any country town. The lights are low. I say a silent prayer of thanks because I don't know how much longer I can keep myself from weeping. The window is across from me. I notice an impending storm off in the distance. The sky blinks every so often even though it's still too far away to hear the thunder. I consider the parallel between what is approaching outside and the storm I'm about to start inside. It seems fitting.

I look over the menu although I have absolutely no appetite. I'm not sure I can swallow water with how my throat is closing up. Any food I might manage to choke down will likely sit as concrete in my belly. When the waitress arrives, I order a garden salad. I hear him ask for the steak sandwich. After the food arrives, we sit searching our plates for answers that aren't there. I hope Levi isn't paying attention to me pushing lettuce around my plate. I see he has barely eaten any of his meal as well.

I decide there's no sense in prolonging the inevitable. If our evening is going to be about fear and unspoken words, I might as well put an end to things now.

Taking a gulp of water, I wash away the sawdust feeling in my throat. Then, I begin. "Um, I need to be honest with you, Levi." Honest, what a load of crap.

189

Thunder starts to roll through the clouds.

"Honest about what?" Wariness is plain on his face.

Considering maybe the truth would be best, or at least part of it, I say, "I can't stay here."

His expression is absolute shock. "What do you mean? I thought you liked it here, were getting settled here."

Sadly, I admit, "I do like it here, very much." More truth.

"Then why?" he asks.

I can hear the sorrow layering through his voice. I have to start building a wall around my heart before I change my mind.

"Because I never intended on staying. That wasn't the plan," I tell him. Truth again.

Looking for a way to fix the problem, he says, "Plans can change. Look at me. I didn't know if I was staying, but I found what I want here." He looks at me purposely then softly murmurs, "I thought you had too."

Knowing he's not going to make this easy by letting go, I have to do the one thing I will regret for the rest of my life. Hurt him.

"I did, except what I want isn't important right now." Lie.

"Oh, so I'm not important enough to matter?" He misunderstands my meaning. However, it works in my favor. It's a bull's eye, a direct hit. Mission accomplished and I feel horrible.

A sudden crash makes me jump in my seat.

"You do matter, more than you know." I can't stop myself from trying to make him see it has nothing to do with him, despite not being able to tell him why I have to leave.

190

Lightning illuminates Levi's face. His eyes turn to blue ice. He thinks I'm trying to pacify him, which multiplies his bitterness.

"Just not enough apparently, not to you." The angry Levi I've glimpsed before returns. I'll take every harsh word he dishes out because I'd rather have him furious with me than begging me to stay. I think that would break us both.

31

Him

Tonight was supposed to be my chance at redemption, my second chance at getting things right. I know I fucked up. I made the mistake of ignoring my problems and running from them, instead of facing them head on. Rather than taking control and overcoming my obstacles, I avoided them at every turn. I also decided there wasn't any point in wanting anything anymore because it took too much effort to make it happen. Then, I met Sam. She made me want.

I wanted everything she represented, a life filled with love and laughter, contentment and passion. I wanted all those things with her, just like my parents had. I wanted to take care of her. However, I failed to realize I'm no good at taking care of someone else when I'm still broken. I can't be what she deserves when I'm dragging ten tons of baggage behind me because it will keep pulling me down. And eventually, it'll drag her down too, destroying us both and what we have. I finally understand I can't let that happen. She is entitled to more. I vowed to myself and her to fix me. I thought it was enough, that she would stand by me knowing I mean every word. But, I guess it's not.

I'm sitting here at our table, staring at her. She won't look at me directly and is completely submissive. She won't give me any real explanation about what's going on with her. This is not the Sam I know.

I strive to control the raging beast inside me in order to get answers. Reaching across the table to her, I ask, "Sam? What are you not saying?"

For a second, surprise pops in her eyes like I've touched on something. Then, it's gone as quickly as it appeared. She straightens her spine as I've seen her do so many times before, preparing herself. "I'm saying this isn't going to work, Levi. We're too different, come from different worlds, and have too much baggage between us to make anything work." She pulls her hand away from mine, avoiding any contact with me.

I raise my voice to be heard over the pounding rain outside. "I don't get it. If this is about me, I apologized, told you I'm going to get help. I mean, I know I have a ways to go, but I don't think I'm a lost cause."

"Oh, Levi, you're not. You never have been. You only needed to find your direction again," she says.

I can't tell if she's trying to placate me or actually means it anymore. Everything she says is so confusing. I decide to focus on what I thought I knew. "I hoped maybe we were heading in the same direction, together."

Her voice is full of remorse when she responds. "I know, and I'm sorry. I just can't." There she goes again, talking in circles, giving me no concrete answers.

Bristling from the hurt, I start to lash out, trying to get her to react. "I see. Guess being an injured, lowly discharged Marine with no family or money to speak of isn't good enough. I thought you were different. That those things didn't matter to you."

Tears running down her cheeks, she protests, "They don't! You know that! Those things have never mattered to me. You're what's important."

"Ah, so important that you're leaving. I get it," I sneer because being a bastard is easier than feeling the pain. I'll feel like an ass later, but right now, all I can do is give her more reasons to walk away.

193

She stands from the table, twisting her napkin in her trembling hands. Her voice shakes as she says, "I have to leave. You don't understand. I can't stay with you right now." She turns and heads for the door, leaving me as quickly as her feet can carry her.

The storm is directly over top of us now. Lightning strikes in a far field setting the sky in a blaze of brilliance. The thunder booms overhead, rattling the windows of the restaurant. Rain is coming down in sheets.

I follow her outside.

Over the downpour, she's yelling at the top of her lungs. "Everything's such a mess!"

I have no idea if it's directed at me. I think she's still trying to convince herself that this is what she needs to do. If she would give me a chance, we could figure everything out together.

I call to her. "Make me understand, Sam," I beg. "Help me understand."

I see her shoulders shake even with the distance between us. She cries out, "I can't help you. I'm not strong enough. I can't be what you need."

Having no idea how to convince her, I tell her the only things I know to be true. "You are what I need, what I want. And you are strong enough, stronger than I am. But, I'm getting there. I *will* get there. Just don't make me do it alone, not without you. Please." I have no pride left to care that I'm begging. I'll do anything to make her stay, promise anything.

She's standing there in the torrential rain. Her dress is glued to her skin. Her lips are tinged with blue. Her chin is thrust forward, her shoulders back, and her spine is rigid. She is frozen, but not from the cold rain. She looks just as I remember when we first met in the store.

She screams at me over the crash of thunder, "You can't save me!!"

I stare at her as she turns and walks away from me. I have no idea what she means. How is any of this about me trying to save her? Is that what she thinks? She's right. I don't understand. However, I'm too lost in my grief to think about fitting the pieces together. I never thought she needed me to save her. But, I can't lose another person, especially one as important as her. I couldn't imagine needing anyone so much ever again. I'd closed myself off to make sure that I didn't have to go through the pain of losing someone else. And yet, somehow, Sam slipped her way into the cracks in my heart. She filled them and fused everything together with her strength and tenderness, with her sweet nature.

"Sam!" I yell, and then softer, "I'm trying to save myself." My words are lost in the drumming of the rain.

"Sam!" I scream one last time. The word is ripped from my throat. She doesn't hear me. She's already turned the corner down the block. My knees buckle and my shoulders hunch. I collapse in a heap on the pavement. A river of rainwater rushes around me down the street. I don't feel it. I'm exhausted from the fight, my fight. The one I don't think I can win alone. Not without her. I have tried over and over again. It seems never-ending. I've been wading through the muck, the shit of it all. I kept trying for so long to find something to grab onto to pull me out of this abyss. There was nothing before, nothing that worked. But, now there's her. I know she can't do the work for me. I have to do it. I have to come to terms with my demons. I have to be strong enough to forgive myself and let go of what I couldn't control. I realized too late she's become my anchor. She's also

195

became the balloon that can pull me to the surface before I drown from the weight.

Watching the spot where she disappeared, I'm sick knowing she's just walked out of my life.

32

Her

Every word that pours out of my mouth is a lie. I do want to help him, be what he needs. I am strong enough.

I know that now.

Hearing him plead is almost my undoing. He shouldn't have to beg me to stay.

I can hear Levi's roar over the downpour pounding on the pavement. It takes every ounce of strength in me not to turn around and sprint back into his arms where it feels safe. I quicken my pace instead of allowing my feet to stop moving. I've made it down the block. I have to get around the corner of the building, so I'm not tempted to look over my shoulder. There's a sudden wail swallowed by the wind. It's the kind of sound that seems more likely to come from an injured animal than a person. I can't imagine that sound coming from the solid force of the man I know. The man I love.

I turn the corner and hear it again. The sound almost stops me dead in my tracks. My heart shatters when I hear him sob my name. But, I can't turn around. If I see him, it will be my undoing and I have to stick to my plan. Our happiness and future together depend on me following through and facing my fear, stepping into the belly of the beast so to speak. I'm just hoping when I'm finished, Levi will understand and is able to forgive me.

I make it around the corner and move toward the market. I need to gather my few belongings quickly. I hope that Miss Sarah isn't around. I'm not sure I can bear to say goodbye to her or see the disapproving look she might wear on her face. As I approach my apartment entrance from the street, my eyes lock onto my greatest nightmare come true. I see Richard's solid black town car gleaming, parked across the street. He's found me, not that I'm surprised. I'm sure he's known where I've been for quite some time. It probably wasn't prudent for him to make his move until now. Knowing I'm a step ahead of him though allows me to put some steel into my spine.

I walk toward the car. There's really no point in getting anything from the apartment now. Everything in that space is a part of my life here in Sugar. It doesn't belong with me wherever I'll end up because there isn't any life with Richard or without Levi. Besides, I'm sure I won't be let out of Richard's sight anytime soon.

Duncan exits the vehicle to open the back door, holding an umbrella so big it should be an awning. God forbid Richard would get wet upon leaving the car. The drops would probably evaporate anyway since he seems to be the devil incarnate. He steps from the car with that air of authority and arrogance I hate so much. How could I not see what a truly despicable man he is?

"Samantha," he says in a tone dripping with condescension indicating I'm the equivalent to gum on the bottom of his shoe.

It's only one word, my name, but it's absolutely the only word I never want to hear pass through his lips again. Even though I'm already chilled and soaked through to the bone from the rain, the blood in my veins turns to ice. Walking toward him, I'm not sure I can do this although there's no turning back now. I think of Levi again. He's the reason I have to do this. We won't be free until it's over. I strengthen my resolve and square my shoulders. I'll see this through until the end with Richard, even if it means only one of us is left standing.

At the moment, I'm not certain which of us that will be, him or me.

Belatedly, I realize Richard must see something in my expression he doesn't like. His eyes spark. His hand shoots out the moment I'm close enough and cracks me across the cheek before I'm aware he's even moved. My head whips back to the right and my cheek burns. I'm sure the sound would echo through the street if it wasn't for the storm. My eye throbs, feeling as if it's going to explode out of my head. My eye waters, clouding my vision, however, I refuse to cry in front of him. He would view it as weakness and believe he had the upper hand. I won't give him the satisfaction.

His hand grips my chin as he moves his face close enough to mine I can smell his acid breath. I have no choice other than to look directly into his eyes.

"Make no mistake, Samantha," he seethes, "that is the least of what I will have done to you if you even think about trying to leave me again."

A streak of fear runs through me. I don't doubt him for one second. His hold on my jaw tightens painfully, punctuating his threat. He's definitely made his point. Then, he releases me roughly, grabbing my arm, and steers me toward the car door. I'm certain I'll have bruises in the morning, not that he cares.

"Get in the car." His voice is like venom.

I take one last glance back at the store that's come to feel like home, more of a home than I've ever known. I imagine for a moment I see Miss Sarah peering through the front glass. It must be the rain playing tricks on my vision. A pang of heartache settles deep in my chest as I think of the wonderful woman who took me in without question. I can only hope she'll look after Levi once she realizes I'm gone, or rather that he'll let her.

I slide into the car across the supple leather seats. The car reeks of Richard's money. I hate it. Everything about the man sitting next to me and what he stands for makes my skin crawl. I can't believe I ever found him even remotely attractive or relished in his attention. I can barely stomach being stuck in the general vicinity of him for any length of time now, much less a confined space. I find the possibility of being covered in fire ants a much more appealing prospect.

Richard is still standing in the space of the open door with his alligator leather covered foot on the frame of the car. I hear the low rumble of conversation outside the vehicle. He is no doubt giving instructions to Duncan. Even though I can't make out the words, my stomach clenches with dread. I'm sure Richard has plans for me, though I'd rather not know what they might be. Anything seems to be in the realm of possibility, which isn't good.

After a moment, he slides into his seat without looking at me. I can see the line of his jaw is tight. I am actually surprised at how well he is controlling his anger. He is known for restraint. However, I'd imagine once his fury has been released, the result is similar to the effect of a volcanic eruption. I stare straight ahead, not wanting to provoke him, plus I have nothing to say. I've just given up the one thing that means everything to me. Levi.

My throat clogs with emotion. I reach for a mineral water to try and wash away my grief. My throat is raw from crying and screaming in the rain. Holding the bottle gives my hands something to do as well. As I take a sip, I can feel Richard's eyes boring into me. I turn my head to see his gaze is cold as ice. He also has a feral smirk on his face. The combination makes me suck in a breath in fear. The possibilities of what it could mean are

200

terrible. The moment I part my lips to ask him what he intends on doing with me, I feel a heaviness travel through my arms and legs. My head feels fuzzy and my vision starts to blur. It hardly registers that he must have drugged the water because a fog quickly descends over my thoughts.

"I think you'll give me very little trouble now, Samantha, my dear." Richard's voice is muffled in my ears, however, I hear the malice lacing through his words. The endearment is dripping with disdain.

Too late, I realize I might have made the biggest mistake of my life, or what's left of it, by going with him. I hear his sinister chuckle. My stomach rolls with disgust as I see his eyes roam over me through the haze. In the next moment, everything turns to black.

33

Him

I have no idea how long I've been sitting on the curb. It could be five minutes or an hour. I'm drenched, waterlogged to the bone. Water is a river running down my head and arms. I don't feel it. My whole body is numb. I'm frozen in my grief.

I didn't cry at my parents' funeral despite the staggering emptiness I felt. I couldn't. I pushed it all down. But today, I can't keep the floodgates closed. Losing Sam crushes my spirit.

It's taken me close to nine months since the accident to convince myself I had a right to a decent life and maybe even a little love. I've been learning that sometimes things just happen you can't control. Now, the chance I finally believe I deserve is gone.

A light hand touches my shoulder. I'm not surprised. I knew by the scent in the air it was Miss Sarah before she even made contact.

With my head still hung, I mutter, "She left me."

Softly, she says, "She didn't want to, Levi. That girl loves you." The conviction in her voice has me looking at her as if I've never seen her before in my life.

Spewing rage and hurt, I seethe. "How do you know that? How can you say that?" I stand, not able to sit idle any longer. "If she loved me, she'd be here, right now! Obviously, I'm nothing to her."

Miss Sarah's own fury takes over as she yells, "You have no idea how wrong you are. I saw her. I saw her leave. It wasn't her ch…" Her voice stops suddenly. I see her eyes grow heavy as she sways on her feet. She is no longer stable as her knees buckle underneath her. I catch her as she falters, holding her up. Little as she is, it's not difficult.

"Miss Sarah! Oh my god! Miss Sarah!!" All of my anger vanishes being replaced with sheer panic.

I notice she's breathing and her pulse is strong. However, her skin is cold to the touch. I can see her face is drawn and pale even in the waning light.

"Levi," she murmurs.

Desperate not hear any final words from her, I say, "Shh, don't try to talk, Miss Sarah. I have to get you to the hospital."

Trying again, she whispers, "But, Levi, I have to.....you have to know....."

She doesn't get to finish whatever she was trying to tell me. Her eyes roll back in her head a moment before she's unconscious. Her body becomes a rag doll.

"Fuck!" I whisk Miss Sarah's slight body into my arms and scramble to my truck. Living in a small town has its disadvantages. Having no immediate emergency services available is one of them. I can get her to the hospital faster than waiting for an ambulance from the city because I will *not* lose one more person. I lean the seat back, laying her gently down, and buckle her in place. Rounding the truck, I dial Dylan's number.

Not bothering with greetings when he answers, I shout, "D! Hospital, now! It's Miss Sarah."

I hang up as I punch the gas, taking off with a hail of gravel. I break every speed limit there is the entire way. It's a good thing all the stoplights are green once I hit the city although I wouldn't care if they weren't. I'd fly through them anyway.

Reaching the hospital, I park directly outside the emergency room doors. In my urgency, I couldn't care

203

less if my truck is blocking the entrance and gets towed. I rush Miss Sarah into the ER and start barking at anyone who looks important. I'm frantic.

"Help me! You have to help her. *Now*!"

A short, brunette haired nurse quickly makes her way to me, ushering me through the doors. "Come through here, sir. Put her on that bed over there." She points to a small curtained area.

I place her where I'm directed, then simply stare at her. She's so small. I brush her hair away from her face and take her hand. Reaching for the chair in the corner, I sit with her tiny fingers in my grasp. Looking at them together, I remember when my little five year old hand would hold onto hers for dear life, just like I'm doing now. My head bows against our hands and my shoulders sag.

"Please, don't leave me," I beg. It's the second time tonight I've made this plea.

"Sir?"

I lift my head in question.

The young nurse stands inside the curtain, patiently. "I need to get any information you can give me. Are you family?" the nurse inquires.

"Yes. I'm all she has, except for her sister, Dottie, who's in Sugar." There's no reason for anyone to know I'm not blood. It wouldn't matter anyway. There is no way they are getting rid of me.

"Alright. Can you tell me what happened?"

Trying to make sense of everything, I tell her, "I don't know really. She seemed fine one minute. Then, she stopped mid-sentence and started to sway on her feet. Soon after, she passed out. I still felt her pulse. She was also breathing without difficulty."

"Okay. We'll see what we can find out." Next, she carefully tells me, "I'm going to need you to go back to the waiting room, so we can take care of her." I must give her a look indicating it would take an entire battalion to remove me because her eyes soften as does her voice. "Please. We can do our job faster."

Reluctantly, I agree. "Yeah, okay." I didn't want to leave, but knew they needed to take care of her. I would only be in the way in the claustrophobic space. Standing, I lean over to brush my lips across her forehead. "Love you, Miss Sarah. I'll see you soon."

Lumbering back through the double doors, I hear World War III about to take place.

"Someone better tell me what the hell I want to know!!" Dylan is about to send a poor candy stripper running from the room. He may be a charmer most days, but, he is a force to be reckoned with when someone he cares about is in trouble.

Feeling fatigued and hollow, I call to him. "Dylan."

His head whips around to me. He's by my side in three strides. "Levi, what is going on?" His concern comes through loud and clear.

All I can tell him is what I know, which isn't much. "I don't know. Miss Sarah collapsed in front of me. I don't know why. I immediately brought her here. That's really all I can tell you. The doctors are with her right now. They should know more soon." I hope.

Dylan looks around the room. I brace myself for the question he is about to ask.

"Where's Sam?" I'm surprised. I didn't realize he knew Sam's real name. As usual, he reads me like a book.

"Yeah, I know about her name," he says, sounding a little irritated. "She told me the day you two went to the fair. I figure whatever her reasons are stay between the two of you, unless you need my help with something. Now, where is she?"

I only have the strength to give him one word. "Gone."

He opens his mouth to get more information, but I give him the look he knows means I don't want to talk about it. I don't have it in me to think about that situation yet or maybe ever. I see his nostrils flare in agitation, whether it's at me or the situation, I can't be sure. It's probably both. After a moment, he gives a quick nod of acceptance.

Taking turns pacing throughout the room, we commiserate in silence. Two bad cups of coffee and almost an hour later, a doctor walks through the doors.

He comes over to us since Dylan and I are the only people in the waiting room. "You're here with the older woman?"

I stand as the doctor approaches, confirming his question. "Miss Sarah, yes. How is she?"

He pauses for a moment, obviously choosing his words. "Well, it's hard to say."

"Excuse me?!" Dylan barks before the doctor can utter another word.

"D! Knock it off. Let him talk," I thunder. My patience and control is slipping.

Clearly intimidated by us, the doctor stammers, "Y-yes, well, as I was saying. Overall, there doesn't seem to be anything major wrong with her. She is dehydrated and suffering from a mild case of exhaustion."

I hear the pause that's never a good sign.
"But?"

He continues, "But, she hasn't regained consciousness, yet. There doesn't seem to be any obvious reason why. Her vitals are stable and she's breathing on her own. All good signs. We just can't find any underlying cause. Did she bump her head?"

I think back to earlier in the evening when we were standing in the street. She never hit the ground because I caught her before she passed out. I tell him, "No, not that I'm aware. At least she didn't when she was with me."

"Okay. That's good." He seems relieved as he tells us, "We'll obviously need to keep her until she regains consciousness to monitor her."

"Yes, of course. We understand," I say.

Then, Dylan asks, "When can we see her?"

"She's being moved into a room. That should take about fifteen minutes. The nurse will escort you down when they're finished."

I hold out my hand to him, grateful he didn't have worse news. "Thank you, doctor."

He firmly shakes both our hands before returning to his work. As promised, the nurse takes us to the room where Miss Sarah is. All the monitors are beeping with flashing little lights. I haven't stepped foot in a hospital since I left rehabilitation for the accident. Judging by the look on Dylan's face neither has he.

They're all the same. The smell of the antiseptic is so strong it almost burns the inside of your nose. The walls and ceilings are plain and uniform. Floors that are buffed to a shine squeak under anyone's rubber-soled shoes. The silence of the place is deafening. I hate it. I never wanted to see the inside of a hospital again, but I refuse to leave Miss Sarah right now.

Standing shoulder to shoulder with Dylan, facing the unknown together again, he asks, "What do we do, Levi?"

He may not have known Miss Sarah all his life like I have, but, he's grown to love her just as much.

"I dunno, D. Someone's got to keep the store open. Miss Sarah will have a fit when she wakes up if she finds out people couldn't get what they needed." Dylan cuts me a fearful look. I see the questions floating through his head. I do my best to convince him and myself what I pray to be true by declaring, "She IS waking up." I won't accept anything less.

Scrubbing his hand down his face, Dylan says, "Okay, well, I'll go tend to the store. I'll have it open on time first thing in the morning." Now, it's my turn to look at him. I don't want him to feel like my connection with her is more important because it's not. As usual though, he knows what I need. "It's okay, Levi. You know I love her, too, but you need to be here. I get that. Besides, I want to stay busy. Sitting here, I'd be bat-shit crazy in about twelve minutes."

Feeling the weight of obligation, I insist, "Thanks, man. I owe you." Again. My running tab of paybacks is getting pretty long where Dylan is concerned.

With somber eyes, he simply responds, "Nah, you don't. For anything. Just keep me in the loop."

"You got it." Dylan wanders to Miss Sarah's bedside and kisses her cheek. "See you soon, pretty lady."

After a shake of my hand and pound on my shoulder, he heads out, leaving me to watch over the only other constant I have left in my life.

34

Her

I wake up with a throbbing headache. It feels as if two twenty pound sledgehammers are pulverizing the sides of my skull. To my surprise, that's the only thing I can find that's wrong with me. I'm still in the same clothes as I was the night before. I'm more than a little relieved about this. Upon a little more inspection, I see the bruises on my arms from where Richard grabbed me, but I expected that to happen. Other than that though, I see no real damage. Then again, Richard isn't known for handling any of the dirty work. He'll always be able to find someone else to do it.

I recognize the room I've woken up in. It's the guest suite in Richard's mansion where I've stayed previously, which tells me he's brought me back to Rapids City. It's the last place on earth I want to be, especially with him.

The bedroom is spacious and opulently decorated. There's a king size, four poster bed made of mahogany set in the center of the main wall. I have no doubt the sheets under the paisley down comforter are made from Egyptian cotton, having a thread count of over a thousand. The tray ceiling is twelve feet in the center with crystallized skylights. On a sunny day, the sunlight would reach every corner of the room. Seeing the skylights reminds me that this room is on the second floor. I cross to the windows, looking out over the expansive back lawn. I test the window and find it isn't locked. It opens easily without a sound. This, unfortunately, doesn't do me much good as a possible escape route, considering the back of the house is set more than two stories off the ground. There is no ledge

209

to climb out on to follow around to the front of the house. I also have no desire to break both of my legs by jumping from this height.

Closing the window and wool tapestry curtains, I turn to scan the room. I'm sure there is nothing of use to help me get out of my confined space. There's no point in trying the door. I know it's locked. I realize I'll have to wait for one of Richard's goons to come and fetch me, whenever that might be. I know I won't get away from them either considering they're all much larger than I am and trained to do who knows what. I can only hope at some point there will be a time I can create an opportunity for myself.

I know Richard won't keep me locked up in here forever. He doesn't want me hidden away, only contained. To him, I'm his property. He wants me on display. He'll, of course, want to give me a false sense of freedom, too, fully expecting me to be a good little captive. The little bit of freedom he will give me will be his downfall. Eventually, I know his arrogance will be to my advantage. He'll think he's made his point. He also believes I'm too scared and weak to consider leaving him again. He couldn't be more wrong. What he doesn't realize is I've changed in the months I've been away in Sugar. I've become stronger and more confident. I trust my own instincts now. I'm no longer the naive, fresh out of college and under-her-daddy's-thumb girl anymore. I've been able to take control of my own life. I refuse to willing hand it over to someone else. I know now I don't need anyone else to take care of me. However, I *want* someone to take care of me on my own terms. I want that someone to be Levi. I long for us to take care of each other.

Thinking of him brings an unbearable ache to my chest. I already miss him so much. I can't imagine the pain I'm putting him through by walking away from him. I hope he'll still want me once I deal with the situation I'm in and am able to return to him.

Forcing thoughts of him out of my head, I decide I might as well clean myself up. I know it's morning although I don't know the exact time. I assume it's still early because I suspect Richard will summon me for breakfast. I may be his "guest", but I know he'll assert his control and expect me to follow his demands. Appearances are important to him after all. He is nothing if not predictable. He has his schedules and routines he refuses to change. Remembering this raises my confidence about being able to formulate a plan to get away from him, permanently.

I make my way into the *en suite* bathroom to find everything I need stocked there though all of my personal belongings have been removed from the room. I strip quickly, refusing to think about for whom I wore this dress. Standing in the steaming shower, I allow myself a small moment to feel the weight of my predicament. If I'm not careful, it could break me into a million pieces. I can't let it. I have something to keep me going, the hope of a future with a man I could love forever, if he'll let me. I'll beg if I have to when I return. I need him that much.

After washing away everything from the previous day, I find clothes in the wardrobe that matches the furnishings. I choose black yoga pants, a plain lavender V-neck shirt, and canvas sneakers. At least I'm comfortable. I wouldn't have put it past Richard to give me linen pants and silk blouses with heels. As I finish tying the shoes, there is a solid rap on the door. It opens before I can utter a word. A linebacker sized man

211

enters. He is dark haired with brown eyes and an olive complexion. I can tell he's not nearly as tall as Levi, however he might be wider. He has a stockier build. Looking at his face, I see a scowl firmly in place.

Stepping into the room, he says, "Mr. Whitman expects you to join him for breakfast." The man lets his eyes roam over me in an open manner. I feel like throwing up.

I stand, crossing my arms in front of me. Irritated with the lack of decorum and privacy shown to me by this man, I seethe, "I'm pretty sure Mr. Whitman won't appreciate your bad manners, even if it is toward me. Or you eyeing me like I'm your next challenge."

"I doubt he'll take your word over mine," the man says smugly.

Sugary sweet, I tell him, "Oh, honey, don't bet on that. I guarantee you I know how to convince him better than you do."

I have no idea what this man knows about the situation I'm in. Given this, I have to use every possible advantage. I leave the disgusting insinuation hanging in the air. Even though I would never dream of using myself physically to get my way with Richard, I will use the suggestion to let this man think I will. I'm sure he understands the power of persuasion I would have if I followed through on my veiled remark.

I see a dilemma in his eyes before a shutter falls over his expression. Clearing his throat, his whole demeanor quickly changes. "Well, um, yes, if you'll follow me. I'll escort you to Mr. Whitman. My name is Rocco, by the way. I've been put in charge of your....protection."

"Meaning, you're my shadow," I say frankly as I saunter by him. "Where's Duncan?"

212

"Duncan tends to other business for Mr. Whitman now."

Ice spills down my spine from the thought of what Duncan would be doing for Richard. However, I'm relieved I don't have to deal with him. Based on this revelation, I have to assume Rocco is new to Richard's employ. I believe I have found my second loophole. This is a huge positive for me. I'm sure Rocco is already aware of Richard's expectations. He doesn't know what to expect with me though. He wasn't there when I was. This means I might have the opportunity to manipulate Rocco by using Richard's expectations against him.

Putting on my fake smile, I turn back, "It's nice to meet you, Rocco. I'm Sam, although I'm sure you already knew that."

We make our way to the center of the house. The dining room is directly across from Richard's office, his locked office. I enter and see Richard already seated. He's waiting for me. He rises, of course, presenting his excellent breeding. I want to gag because I know it's all for show. I can guess what kind of monster lies under the mask of sophistication he wears.

"Ah, Samantha," he says with condescension.

I cringe and resist the urge to wipe away the feeling of my skin crawling. I always hated him using my full given name. Now, it's worse since I've heard it come from Levi's lips. I'd rather pour acid in my ears than hear him say it again.

Richard continues, "So glad you are awake and well. Please join me. Sit beside me." His words express benevolence, but his tone is sour and cold.

I'd really prefer to sit at the farthest end from him. He, unfortunately, hasn't given me any choice in the matter. There is a place setting next to him already

213

filled with food. And while he made a courteous request, I know from experience the words are a demand. It would be foolish to poke the bear. I have to make Richard believe I am exactly what he wants me to be, a cooperative, submissive, docile captive. I have to play the role of my life. My only hope is to be better than any Academy award-winning actress.

Forcing my face to relax into a smile, I say, "Thank you, Richard. I am actually quite hungry."

He rounds behind my chair, pulling it out for me. I will myself not to groan in revulsion as he runs his fingertip along my jawline.

"Lovely." He returns to his seat then speaks in a business tone. "Now, we have much to discuss. First though, I have to apologize for last night. I think we were both a bit out of hand. You seem to have forgotten what proper behavior is. You've gone wild and become out of control." His jaw tenses at this statement, but he continues, "I apologize for my use of extreme tactics. I do so hate striking you and having to use other methods to keep you in line. It's so uncivilized, but it seemed necessary at the time. Now that you've returned, I'm sure we won't have to resort to such measures again." He raises his eyebrow in challenge.

Despite the war waging inside me, I have no choice other than to agree with him. "No, of course not, Richard. It won't be necessary."

"Good. So, we can work toward forgetting your ridiculous sabbatical and get things back to a normal routine around here." What he means is he wants me kept under lock and key and to know exactly what I'm doing every minute of the day.

"Yes, of course. It was foolish of me. I could use some normalcy and routine." My tone is a little too flippant.

I lower my eyes quickly and focus on pushing eggs around my plate. I have no appetite.

Richard eyes me shrewdly. His eyes narrow to thin slits. He is studying me. I realize this whole conversation has been a test, one I'm not sure if I passed or not. I mentally kick myself, understanding I have to be extremely careful from now on. I can't automatically act like the dutiful, submissive person he wants me to be. He won't believe it. Richard is not going to buy that I've changed so dramatically in a span of twelve hours simply because I've been forced to return especially since I wasn't this docile when I was here before. However, I also can't be the real me, the person I found while in Sugar. I feel like I'm walking on a tightrope between personalities and neither of them are actually me.

I watch as Richard goes back to methodically consuming his breakfast. He loads his fork with precision, eating everything in the same order until his plate is empty. It's creepy. After patting his mouth with his napkin, he feigns indifference. "Now, Samantha, I trust you will make yourself at home here again. The house is yours to roam. Unfortunately, I can't allow you to leave the confines of the house I'm afraid. I can't have you trying to slip away, not that you could. Rocco will be your....escort. He can always find me if you are in need of anything he can't provide." He doesn't bother to hide the undertone of menace in his voice when he emphasizes the word always.

I look at Rocco, who's standing the doorway to the dining room, a statue of defense. An odd expression passes over his face, something I can't decipher, then, it's gone.

Quietly, I say, "I see. An escort for the house. So, he'll be with me...." I know exactly what his intention is, but I want to be clear. I can't afford to have any gray areas where Richard is concerned. It's in my best interest to understand exactly what kind of situation I'm really dealing with before I can make any moves.

"Everywhere," Richard interjects. His tone leaves no room for argument.

Feeling a bit hysterical and trapped, I comment, "For his sake, I hope I can use the bathroom alone."

With a maniacal laugh, he says, "Of course. Don't be absurd. Now, if you'll excuse me, I have business to attend to." Standing, he strides out the room, leaving me alone with my shadow.

I hear the front door close. Finally, I'm able to take a deep breath since waking up in my prison. I slump back in the chair, aching with sadness. I miss Levi desperately. Leaving my plate untouched, I walk to my room with Rocco two feet behind me. I stop at my door and tell him I'm going to take a nap. In reality, I'm just going to cry until my eyes swell shut.

35

Her

Richard was right about getting into a routine. It's unavoidable when there's nowhere to go. I rise in the morning, shower and dress, because it's expected. I'm pretty sure there's no way Richard would allow me to stay in bed all day. I decide not to test the theory since I don't want Rocco in my room again. He's at least respected my privacy after the first incident.

I eat breakfast and dinner with Richard in the dining room every day. Or, rather, he eats while I push more food around counting the minutes until he's done. I usually confine myself to my room after Richard has left for the day, skipping lunch. In my cell, I either watch the clouds pass over the skylight, doze off and on because of the lack of rested sleep I'm getting, or play solitaire. Sometime about mid-afternoon, I'll wander into the lounge to watch game shows on television. I can't bear to watch soap operas because my life already has enough drama. I also stay away from movies since all the ones I like are sappy romances or action, both of which make me think of Levi. Every day is the same and it's mind-numbing.

Rocco is my constant, silent companion through it all. He follows me everywhere I go, just like Richard intended, and never says a word. Granted, I'm not really up for conversation at the moment anyway. At least with Rocco around I don't feel completely alone. He doesn't give me the creeps like Duncan did either, thankfully. He's simply a solid presence. I start to think my first impression of him was wrong. There have been a few times I've felt like he was observing me, waiting for me to do something. However, every time I look at him when I have the feeling, he's merely standing his post, staring straight ahead. Like a solider.

That's when it hits me. Rocco reminds me of Levi and Dylan. His demeanor is the same, strong, considerate, and protective. His carriage and bearing allude to military service. He is still obviously dangerous, but doesn't exude the same hostility and menace as Duncan.

Hanging on to my hunch, I wake up on my seventh day with Richard with renewed determination. I cannot sit and wait for the cavalry to arrive because there isn't one. I didn't want Levi involved and Agent Wright was clear about needing me to get the information in order for Richard to be put away for good. I'm it. I have to get myself out of this mess.

I stick to my usual routine in the morning, but decide it's probably a good idea to go down for lunch. In my time here, I've lost a few pounds I didn't have to spare. I can almost hear Miss Sarah clicking her tongue at me, suggesting I eat another helping of Miss Dottie's cobbler. Thinking about the gooey dessert has my stomach rumbling. At least I'm hungry.

Leaving my room, I catch Rocco's eye seeing a hint of surprise. He doesn't say anything though. I rummage through the kitchen, finding everything for a massive turkey and cheddar sandwich. Knowing I need something to wash it down, I make some sweet tea. Sitting at the island, I notice Rocco's eyebrows spring up slightly at the size of my meal. Other than feeling a twinge of heartache at my first sip of tea, I enjoy every mouthful.

Once I'm finished, I settle myself at the table in the lounge instead of retreating upstairs or turning on any shows. I pull the deck of cards out of my back pocket

I had brought down with me and proceed to play. Still, Rocco doesn't comment. I notice him watching me with interest. I can see him analyzing the changes in my routine.

I know I need to get him on my side or figure out how to be rid of him. It's time to engage.

"Rocco, come play rummy with me. I'm sick of playing solitaire."

"No," he says crisply.

Giving an exaggerated pout, I whine, "Oh, come on. Please."

His shoulders start to relax. "I shouldn't."

Well, it wasn't a 'no'. Progress. Time to push a little more.

"Look, I'm stuck here all day, bored practically to tears. I can't go anywhere and I'm tired of watching junk on t.v." I can see the hesitation. I need to use the figurative ace up my sleeve. "Besides, Richard said you are supposed to provide me with whatever I need. And I need entertainment."

The hesitation vanishes at the reference to doing his job and then a small smirk curls the corner of his lip. "Rummy is your idea of entertainment."

I shrug. "Hey, it's all I've got. You in?"

After a moment more, he says, "Yeah."

We spend the next two hours playing. I throw in a few little jabs when I have a particularly long run of wins. I haven't quite broken through his glacial exterior, but I sense he's beginning to thaw.

The next day I up my tactics. I start to wonder when the heck Rocco eats. He's a big guy, so he obviously does, but I have never seen him. At lunchtime, I make another huge sandwich, ham and Swiss cheese this time.

"Would you like one?" I mumble around the slice of ham I've stuffed in my mouth. Again, the hesitation slides through his eyes. Acting annoyed, I say, "Geez, Rocco, you have to be hungry. All the stuff is out. It's no trouble."

"Sure," he finally replies.

I want to high-five myself. Count on basic needs to win out.

After constructing his sandwich and cleaning up, I move our food to the end of the island where the stools are. Rocco sits and dives into his food. I pull out the packet of cards from my pocket, waving it in the air.

"Thought we could play and eat at the same time."

Swallowing, he says, "Yeah, that works."

Our afternoon is friendlier than the previous day. Rocco even manages to crack a smile or two, along with ribbing me a bit after a couple of quick hands turn in his favor.

On the third day of my experiment, I pull out all the stops. I go into the kitchen earlier than before to prepare the sandwiches for lunch. Grabbing the items I need from the refrigerator, I set to work. When I open the package of bacon to cook, curiosity is plain on Rocco's face. I assemble the sandwiches, the biggest yet, and set them by our perches.

I wait patiently until he takes the first bite, hoping for the reaction I want.

"Oh my....god." I can't help the smile that spreads across my face. Men and their food. "What is this?!" he mumbles with full cheeks.

"Just roast beef and provolone." I grin. He raises one eyebrow. Laughing, I continue, "With bacon and honey mustard, with a little horseradish on soft rye bread."

"I..... am in heaven," he groans loudly before taking another huge bite.

I'm thoroughly pleased. "Glad you like it. I guess we'll wait to play until after you've finished," I tease, also biting into my own lunch.

It's not long before we're both done and I'm picking up the cards. Time for more maneuvering.

"Thought we could play something different today? Rummy's gotten old," I tell him casually. "How about something more challenging?"

Reluctance draws his brows together. "What'd you have in mind?" he asks, sounding leery.

"Poker!" I say brightly.

Chuckling, his tension eases. "Sure. I'll warn you though. I'm pretty good."

I study him, rubbing my fingers across my chin. "We shall see."

Three hours later, my side hurts from laughing and my cheeks from smiling. I have unquestionably trounced Rocco in poker.

"You are a shark!" Rocco bellows, his words devoid of malice.

Demurely, I bat my eyelashes. "Sorry?"

Not buying my act for a second, he laughs, "HA! No, you're not."

I smile while announcing, "You're right." My expression becomes serious in the next moment, my voice softer. "I want to thank you, Rocco."

He stops and looks at me. "For what?"

I tell him honestly, "For making these last few days bearable. I've had fun hanging out with you, not that I can go anywhere. But, playing cards with you has taken my mind off the fact that I'm essentially trapped here."

221

"You're welcome." Rocco becomes quiet, thoughtful and then continues, "It certainly hasn't been a hardship. It's nice when you smile."

Touched by his kindness, I thank him. His are the nicest words anyone has said to me since I left Sugar and Levi.

Suddenly realizing how late it is, I say, "Um, I should probably clean this up since Richard will be home soon.

"Yeah, probably," he agrees.

After picking up the cards, I slide off the stool and head for the stairs. He doesn't follow me. Pausing, I turn. "Rocco?"

He looks up at me from his spot at the island. "Yeah?"

"I know it's a lot to ask, but could you tell Richard I'm not feeling well and I won't be down for dinner. I don't think I can stomach sitting with him tonight."

I probably shouldn't be quite so honest since I'm still not sure exactly where Rocco's loyalties lie, but, I can't help it. I'm tired of pretending. My gut tells me he's a good guy because each day I notice everything becomes business as usual when Richard returns. Yet, as far as I know, he's never mentioned our afternoons together. And I'm quite certain Richard would express his opinions on the subject.

With an easy expression, he tells me, "Sure, Sam, it's no problem. Go get some rest. I'll see to it he doesn't bother you tonight."

Giving a small, grateful smile, I turn back toward the stairs. I feel exhausted from...everything. I don't want to do this anymore. I'm sick of being scared and controlled. I want to go back to Sugar, where I knew who I was, who I loved, and who loved me. I want to go back to Levi, if he'll have me. I have to finish what I came here to do, soon, or I might never get the chance to leave.

I curl up in a ball on my bed without bothering to change. I let my head and heart fill with thoughts of Levi, his smile, his laugh. I drift off to sleep cocooned in memories and longing.

36

Her

Blinking my eyes open, the bedroom is full of sunlight. I have no idea what time it is although I'm positive

I've missed breakfast with Richard. I wonder why he hasn't come to get me, or sent Rocco to do it.

I sit straight up in bed. Rocco. He must have convinced Richard I was actually sick. But, why?

I pad silently out of my room. Rocco isn't standing at my door. Richard should have left already, but I hear voices downstairs. I tiptoe down the stairs, flattened against the wall. It's a familiar feeling. Coming to the corner, I'm only able to see Rocco, facing toward the stairs. Richard must be standing in the doorway to his office.

"You are required to Stay. With. Her. And watch her," Richard snarls, punctuating his words. "That is what I pay you for. Not to coddle her and act like a mother hen or to be a go-between for her with me."

"Yes, sir." Rocco's answer is precise.

"You will inform Samantha her presence is demanded at dinner!"

"Yes, sir." This time his tone sounds like he's not as willing to be compliant.

I hear feet walking away from the doorway, back into the office. Richard must be retrieving something he needs. Rocco sees me at the corner and I freeze, panic running through my veins. He gives me a minuscule head shake before looking away. I see Richard's suit jacket sleeve as he enters the foyer again, turning toward

224

the door. I press myself flush against the wall, barely breathing.

"I will return following the meetings with my associates and Duncan. See to it Samantha is present." Not waiting for a response, Richard storms out of the house.

Hearing the car pull away, Rocco turns to me. There is an odd expression on his face. Without saying a word, he walks to the office door, swinging it closed. Then, he crosses the foyer through the dining room and into the kitchen. Agent Wright's words ring in my head, "Be ready." I have an opportunity.

I slide off the bottom step and shuffle to the office door. I never heard the lock engage. I try the handle. Bingo! The door never latched. I look toward the kitchen. Rocco is nowhere to be seen. I don't have time to think about what he's doing or why. I pull out the jump drive from my pocket. I've been carrying it with me since the night I had dinner with Levi. Having it on me was the safest place for it. If the drive had been found, it meant I was in a much direr situation. Likely I would be close to death, or would want to be.

Heart pounding in my chest, I sprint across the office to the desk. Richard's computer is open and logged on. He's such a cocky bastard. I knew it would be his downfall. With fumbling hands, I connect the drive and select the 'copy all' option. The dialog box displays the file transfer animation with the clock showing three minutes until completion. I glance at the door. Nothing.

I open drawers, looking for anything additional that might be useful, like the ledgers. I doubt I'll find them though. What I do find has my heart racing. Opening the second drawer on the right, there's a .38 caliber revolver. I've handled a gun a few times, but I'm nowhere near comfortable with them. Debating for a moment, I grab it and tuck into the back waistband of my pants. I figure I might be able to create my own exit if needed because I can't stay here any longer.

The computer dings, signaling the transfer is complete. I click the exit button, closing the dialog box, and pull the drive from the port. Stuffing it in my pocket, I hear a car round into the driveway out front. Terror clamps on to me. I bolt out of the office, making sure the door latches behind me. Flying around the corner into the stairwell, I catch the sound of the front door opening. My heart is beating out of my chest. I put both hands over my mouth to cover the sound of my panting. Keys jingle as the door to Richard's office opens again. Only one person has the key. Richard came back.

Peeking around the corner, I see the entrance of the house standing open. Rocco is still MIA. The reality of freedom being only a dozen feet away grips me. I take a step in that direction. My gaze snags on Richard's office door. It's open. I see a glimpse of him rummaging in his desk, looking for something. The cool metal of the gun hits my back, reminding me of the fear I've felt over the last few months.

My feet move toward the office. I grip the handle of the revolver with my left hand while pushing the door open with my foot. Leveling the gun directly at Richard, I sneer, "Looking for this."

For a moment, Richard stands completely still. Alarm ghosts across his face, but only for a second. Then, his expression turns smug.

"Oh, Samantha dear. Really? We both know you don't have the nerve to pull the trigger."

Walking with deliberate steps farther into the room, I snarl, "Can you honestly be so sure?"

"Yes, you are as weak as your parents." His arrogance is astounding.

The mention of my parents has me deflating for a moment. The gun lowers slightly. I remind myself that this man's entire existence is built on lies and manipulations.

Raising the gun back to an even level, I straighten my spine. "I'm nothing like my parents. And I may have been weak before, but I'm certainly not now. I'm going to bury you Richard, one way or another. It's your choice of how." He can't deny the confidence heard in my words.

Richard's expression changes although not the way I expect. The corners of his lips turn up to a gruesome smile as I hear footsteps behind me and the click of a gun. Ice cold dread spreads through my limbs. The realization that maybe this wasn't supposed to be my opportunity for escape settles in the pit of my stomach like lead.

Richard's expression is absolutely gleeful. "Ah, Rocco, just in time."

I slowly ease to the side in order to look behind me while trying not to turn my back on Richard. My eyes widen as I recognize Rocco's gun isn't pointed at me.

Suddenly, everything is a chaotic blur. I glimpse Richard's eyes narrowing as his arm moves under his jacket. Metal glints in the sunlight from the window. Rocco's hand pushes me to the floor as the sound of gunfire explodes around me. My head feels like I'm underwater. All the sounds are muffled. Then, Rocco takes a knee beside me, grunting. He fires once more before everything is silent.

I lie there too scared to move, shaking. My arms cover my head as tears stream down my face. I think I'm in shock. Strong hands grip my shoulders.

"No, no, no!" I scramble away from whoever is trying to restrain me, too fearful it's Richard.

Rocco murmurs, "Shh, shh. It's okay. Sam. It's over."

I look wide-eyed at him. He's holding up his hands in surrender.

"Over?" I croak.

Answering softly, he says, "Over. Mr. Whitman is dead."

Stunned, I ask, "Y-you shot him?" It's a foolish question since I know I didn't do it. However, my brain is having a difficult time making sense of what happened.

Rocco speaks clearly and says, "I did." Standing, he extends his hand to help me up. I take it to steady me. My legs feel like jelly.

Warily, I say, "But, you work for him."

"Well, not exactly," he hedges.

Gathering my wits again, I look around the room. My eyes land on Rocco's shirt sleeve. "Rocco!" I gasp. "You're bleeding!"

He shrugs his opposite shoulder. "Yeah. Mr. Whitman shot me." He's so nonchalant about it, like it happens every day.

"Oh my god! You have to get to the hospital!"

Putting his hand on my arm, he tries to stop my panic. "Sam, it's okay. It's just a graze. I'll get it checked out once I know you're safe."

Suddenly, I remember an important part of what Rocco said moments before now. "Wait a minute. You said you didn't work for Richard."

Right then, Rocco's phone buzzes. He puts the phone to his ear, giving short answers to whoever is on the other end of the line.

"No, the situation is contained."

"Yes, she's here."

"No, she's fine."

"Yes, we'll wait."

Finally, he disconnects the call, turning his attention back to me.

Refusing to be stalled any longer, I demand, "Rocco, who do you work for?"

"Me, Miss Brooks." A familiar, authoritative, male voice comes from the doorway. Agent Wright strides into the office.

I look between the two men in confusion. Then, all at once, the pieces click into place.

My eyes narrow on Agent Wright as my blood boils in anger. "My opportunity? You couldn't tell me Rocco was on my side?"

Without an ounce of remorse, he explains, "No, actually I couldn't. You needed to think Rocco was loyal to Mr. Whitman or else it wouldn't have been believable. Your reactions had to be real, not staged. It would have put you in danger."

"I was already in danger," I snap hysterically.

Rocco steps forward, touching my arm again. "Sam, I wouldn't have let anything happen to you. I swear." My venom recedes at the sincerity and apology I see in his eyes.

Instantly, another thought occurs to me. "Rocco, if you were already working for Richard, why did you need me?"

Agent Wright responds for him. "Agent Parker, I mean, Rocco, has been undercover with Mr. Whitman for

229

almost two years. He's been moving up in his organization gradually. We knew things were coming to a head when Rocco was brought into the residence for security purposes. That position used to be held by another individual, but it seemed he was moving up in the command chain, leaving Mr. Whitman to find a suitable replacement."

I know exactly who he's referring to, unfortunately. "That would have been Duncan. Before, he was the only other person I ever saw here at the house. He's always been Richard's right-hand man. You said he's moved up?"

Acknowledging that I'm correct, Agent Wright says, "Yes, Duncan Merchant. Apparently, he has been given a more hands-on role in the business. Exactly what that entails, we're not entirely sure. He's actually more like a phantom. We have very little information on him."

That feeling of dread returns as I consider what Duncan's promotion could mean. I hope my misgivings can be proven wrong.

"But, since Richard is dead, it seems like that shouldn't really matter. I mean, it was Richard's business and he's not around to run it. It's finished, right?"

Giving the response I want to hear least, he tells me, "Unfortunately, that's not necessarily true."

A slow trickle of fear filters down my spine. I put my hands in my pockets to keep them from shaking. My fingers feel something there. I remember the jump drive. Pulling it out, I hand it to Agent Wright.

"I guess you might still need this then. I copied everything from Richard's computer, but I have no idea if all of his business stuff was on it. I have a feeling it wasn't."

"Why do you say that?" he asks, intrigued.

I explain my suspicions. "Well, when I first...I guess you could say, *worked* for Richard, I used to make copies of things. After a while, I noticed some of the copies I was making were ledger pages. Nothing on them made any sense to me, but I had a feeling they were important. Especially since the number of pages I copied seemed to increase pretty quickly. And when I was copying the information off his computer, I looked through his entire desk for anything else that might be important. I never saw any ledger books. So, where are they? He has to keep them somewhere or with someone he trusts."

"Who do you know that he trusts enough to have complete access to everything about his organization and dealings?" I can see Agent Wright already knows the answer to his own question. He's simply verifying his information.

I tell him with certainty, "Only one person. Duncan."

He sighs heavily, signifying the problem might have increased tenfold. "Then, it seems Mr. Whitman's business might not die off quickly or easily."

With worry in my voice, I mutter, "I don't think I like the sound of that."

Sounding confident, but weary, Rocco, explains, "We knew this was a possibility when the investigation started. A business or organization, really, such as Mr. Whitman's doesn't get to be as profitable as his is without having his hand in many, many pots. It also doesn't happen by only one person doing the work. Now, granted, there is no doubt Mr. Whitman has been the man in charge of it all. But, I'd bet my career on him having safeguards in place for everything to continue without a hiccup especially on the chance of something happening to a major player, including himself."

"So, what does this mean for me?" I had hoped I would be finished with my impromptu civic duty.

Candidly, Agent Wright says, "Nothing really. As far as we can tell, you were significant to Mr. Whitman alone, no one else."

His words are like a punch in the gut even though I know he doesn't mean the words how they sound. I thought I was significant to someone else, to Levi. I hope I still can be.

I think about his words again. Hope blossoms as I ask, "Does this mean I can leave? You don't need me for anything else?"

Telling me what I've longed to hear since the night of the carnival, he says, "It appears you were able to accomplish the task we wanted. Other than being asked for any information you have about Mr. Merchant at a later time and possibly identifying him, under protection of course, I don't see any reason why you can't be free to go."

My lips break into a wide smile. "Thank you."

"No, thank you, Miss Brooks," he responds with sincerity. "I hope you can find some peace now. Agent Parker, why don't you see if there's anywhere she needs to go, then find the nearest hospital for your arm?"

Shrugging his shoulder with indifference, Rocco says, "It's just a scratch. It'll keep." Then, grinning at me, "Sam? Need a lift?"

Agent Wright tells Rocco, "Agent, you'll wrap that arm before proceeding anywhere else or I'll escort you to the emergency room myself." His tone leaves no question he means it.

Looking between them, I feel like I'm watching a power tug-of-war.

"Understood" is the only response Rocco gives.

I hesitate before answering Rocco because of the tension in the air. "Um, sure, if you don't mind." Then, I offer, "I can help you with your arm before we go."

"Thanks. There should be a first aid kit in the car out front," he says, pointing in the direction of the driveway.

"Okay."

Walking out of Richard's house, I feel the weight of the world lift off my shoulders. I don't have to walk around in fear anymore, wondering when the boogeyman is going to get me. I do, however, have two more people to deal with before I can truly be free.

Determined to banish all the ghosts from my life, I ask, "Rocco, is it okay if we make one stop along the way?"

Smiling, he answers, "Wherever you need to go. Point the way."

After cleaning and wrapping his arm, we climb into the car. I give him the address. I think about taking deep breaths to soothe my nerves, but, honestly, I'm the calmest I've ever been. I wish Levi could see what I'm about to do. He'd be so proud. His voice rings in my head, "You've always been strong." And, now, I'm going to prove it.

37

Him

The hospital has been my home for days. So many days, I've lost count. I stare at the walls, waiting helplessly until my vision blurs. The food here is crap, not that I have any appetite. The coffee is worse. I've hardly slept and I feel like my sanity is hanging by a thread. God, what I wouldn't give for a fucking decent cup of coffee and my own bed. But, I refuse to leave Miss Sarah alone.

I've stayed here the majority of the time at her bedside while Dylan's been running the store. A few times, he came in to trade places, saying I needed to focus on something and get away from this place for a bit. He's probably right, but I think he mostly needed to see Miss Sarah. I can't blame him for that. There's no one else like her and anyone who has met her, loves her instantly.

The upside to not sleeping is I don't have to deal with the nightmares. I still feel like I'm trying to walk through quicksand, especially with everything's that has happened. However, I don't mind the break from waking up in a cold sweat.

The downside is I'm suffering through a completely different hell. I miss Sam so much my soul aches. I'm hollow. I don't understand how she couldn't give us another try.

This afternoon I'm at the store, trying to work myself into exhaustion. Physically it's working. Mentally, not so much. My mind keeps looping through all the time I spent with Sam. I get stuck on our last night together. Her words echo in my head. I still can't make any sense of them. She acted like she couldn't handle dealing with everything I'm going through, at first.

Then, she said I couldn't save her before walking away. I feel like I'm missing a piece to the puzzle, but my brain is too addled to grasp it.

Suddenly, my phone rings. It's Dylan.

I answer with a lump in my throat and my heart pounding. "Yeah?"

"Levi! You need to get back here, now. Miss Sarah is waking up." I can feel Dylan's excitement and relief through the phone line.

Breaking into the first smile I've had in over a week, I yell, "On my way!"

Locking the store, I high-tail it back to the hospital, much like I did the night Miss Sarah collapsed, except with a much more positive outlook.

I barrel into her room, stopping in my tracks right inside the doorway. I know Dylan said she was waking up, but until I actually saw it, I couldn't let myself believe it. Sitting propped up in her bed, she still looks incredibly small, but her cheeks have some color to them again. Her eyes shine brightly as she looks at me, smiling. All of my fears and despair crash down around me. Unable to hold it in, I stumble to her bed, weeping and grasp her hand as I sink onto the bed beside her. I feel her hand brush over my head to soothe me just like when I was five years old with a skinned knee.

"Oh my sweet boy. Shh."

An eternity later, I raise my head. "You're okay."

Even though it wasn't a question, she answers, "Yes, Levi, I'm okay." She scans the room briefly and then looks at me with confusion. "Where's Sam?"

I wish I didn't have to tell her although I can't hide the truth from her even if she doesn't remember.

"You don't remember? She's gone. She left the night you collapsed."

She sucks in a breath as she recalls what happened. Her hand covers her mouth in horror. "Oh, no. Levi, you have to go after her!"

"Why? She didn't want me." Bitterness seeps from my words.

Sternly, she says, "No, that's not true. I remember. I was coming to tell you that I saw her from the store window. She didn't leave on her own. Sam got into a car with a man."

I'm too stunned to say anything.

"What do you mean she didn't leave on her own?" Dylan asks.

Miss Sarah looks at me with sorrow before telling me what I don't want to hear. "I couldn't hear what was being said because of the storm. It didn't seem like they were having a friendly conversation. He seemed very forceful with her."

My blood starts to boil at the thought of someone hurting Sam.

Nervously, Miss Sarah looks at me. I can tell I'm not going to like the next words she says. "Levi, he struck her then made her get in the car."

The room is suddenly too small. I'm enraged knowing someone put their hands on her, especially in anger.

There is lava flowing through my veins. I look at Dylan. He has a similar expression on his face.

Through gritted teeth, he grunts, "Just say the word, Levi. What're we doin'?"

Forcing myself to stay calm, I rethink everything about that night. Now, Sam's words finally make sense. She knew what, or who, was coming. Yet, she never said a word about it. I remember all the things she did tell me about her parents and them being involved with the wrong person. Apparently, their mistakes did land right at her feet. And she accepted it, accepted the burden of two people who didn't deserve her loyalty or sacrifice. Sam willingly put herself in danger and walked into the belly of the beast, alone.

My respect for her swells, as does my fear. If she was coerced into leaving Sugar, it means everything she told me that night was a lie. I need more information and I only know one place to start, her parents.

Planning my course of action, I look at Dylan. "I need you to stay with Miss Sarah. I gotta go back to the house to look some stuff up about her parents and get what I need. I going to get answers and they should have them."

"Done. Let me know if you need me for anything else."

Thankful for his support, I say, "I will."

"Levi, bring Sam home safely," Miss Sarah pleads. Her eyes are near tears.

Sam. Home. To Sugar. Yes, that's exactly what I'm doing. And she's never leaving me again. I don't care what I have to do to convince her to stay.

I quickly kiss Miss Sarah on the forehead and clasp Dylan's hand. "Thanks, D."

He responds with the only thing we both know to be true. "We're family, brother, through everything. Now, go find your woman."

I make the return trip to the house in minimal time. Vaulting onto the front porch in two steps, I surge to the desk in the living room. My entire body radiates electricity from the adrenaline flowing through me. I boot up my computer and start searching under the name

237

Brooks' for Rapid City. After impatiently weeding through dozens of listings, I come across one for Carl and Janice that has a connection with a Samantha Lynn. Switching to the site for the Rapid City newspaper, I set an inquiry for the names. A result is returned quickly. I pull up a picture linked with a graduation announcement. Golden hazel eyes are staring back at me from the screen. It's Sam and her parents. Jackpot!

Once I find their address, I grab the 9mm pistol from my dad's gun case, shoving it in my waistband. I don't know what I'll run into, but I definitely want to be prepared to protect myself and Sam. I snatch the truck keys off the entry table and stalk out the door.

I almost feel sorry for the fool who thought he could take the love of my life from me. Almost. After I'm done dealing with him, I'll find out I'm correct about Sam lying to me when she said she didn't want to be with me. And when I do, I'm going to tan her hide, right after I kiss the fight right out of her.

38

Her

Rocco pulls the car up the drive and cuts the engine. I look around, not seeing any other vehicles. I'm disappointed. I was hoping there was a chance my parents would be here to confront them. I guess either Richard dealt with them or they went into hiding like I did. No matter which it is I can't say I'm bothered by either outcome. Both leave me feeling ambivalent.

Breaking me out of my thoughts, Rocco asks, "You want me to come in with you?"

Feeling safer than I have in a long time, I'm not worried about going in the house alone. "No, I'm good. Doesn't seem like anyone's here anyway. I'll just be a minute." I really have no idea why I'm going into the house. If my parents aren't here, there's nothing I need from inside. I just feel like I need to see the place one last time in order to let go of everything.

Giving Rocco a small smile, I get out of the car and head to the door. I punch in the code then press enter for the lock to disengage. The door sweeps open noiselessly. I step over the threshold of the place I thought was home and stop short.

"Samantha Lynn!" My mother's high-pitched voice rings through the house. Both of them look at me wide- eyed. They are clearly surprised to see me.

Holding the door handle in a death-grip, I narrow my eyes. "Mother. Daddy." Every lie they've ever told me winds through my mind. I ask, bitterly, "What are you doing here?"

Acting offended, my mother grouses, "Well, is that any way to greet your parents after all this time?"

239

She plasters a fake smile on her face and begins to make her way over to me, arms outstretched for an embrace. "Sweetheart, we've been so worried..."

Her voice trails off as her feet slow to a halt. I hear a low rumble directly behind me.

"Sam? Everything okay here?" Bless Rocco. If I wasn't so irate and nauseated by my mother's lies, I could kiss him for not listening to me.

Bunching the fingers on my left hand open and closed, I mutter, "Yeah." Then, to my mother, I spit out, "Worried? Huh, what a joke. Enough with the lies, Mother."

The picture of innocence, she asks, "Samantha Lynn, whatever do you mean by that?"

I've finally reached my limit. The act causes me to combust. "Don't call me that!! And as for what do I mean? I mean, you two left me to fend for myself against a monster. Do you know what kind of a man Richard is? Ha! Of course you know or you wouldn't have tried to run! You tried to ruin my life all because of *your* mistakes and stupidity. The only thing you were interested in was saving your own sorry asses!"

Looking like his face might explode, my father bellows, "Do *not* raise your voice and curse at us, young lady! We raised you better than that." Apparently, he thinks now is a good time to try and assert some authority. He couldn't have picked a worse time.

"GO TO HELL, Daddy!" My chest is heaving. The silence in the room is volatile. Feeling the weight of their sins and rejection, I practically sob, "You made me the solution to your problem. How could you? You're my parents. I'm supposed to be your whole world."

240

After letting out all of the fury, my shoulders sag with disappointment. It's the only thing left.

I feel a light touch on my shoulder. It reminds me I am not alone, not anymore. I have people who will protect me, accept me, and care about me without expecting anything. They will love me just as I am. I can make my own family from those people. And I have someone to love in return, if he'll let me.

Rolling my shoulders back, I do what I came here to do.

"Mother, Daddy. I'd like to introduce you to Agent Rocco Parker. He's with the FBI. I think he's very interested in speaking with you about Richard and your dealings with him." Then, turning, I say, "Rocco, they're all yours. I'm going to get out of here, if you don't mind. There's nothing here that I need. However, there is someone who deserves an explanation and an apology from me."

With concern written on his face, he asks, "You sure you're going to be alright? I can still give you a ride anywhere you need to go."

Smiling at his thoughtfulness, I reassure him, "Yeah, I'll be fine. If you could call me a cab, I'll meet it at the end of the driveway." Gripping his arm and rising on my toes, I kiss his cheek. "Thanks for everything, Rocco." I see the faintest blush turn the tips of his ears pink.

Before I leave, he looks at me seriously, vowing, "Anytime you need anything, you call me, Sam. I'll be there."

"Thanks." Sighing, I turn to my parents. "If I were you two, I would make Rocco my new best friend, but that's just my suggestion. You can take it or leave it. I don't really care. By the way, Richard is dead." My mother gasps at the statement and the blood drains from my father's face. Continuing, I say, "I know for certain he won't be bothering me anymore. As for the relationship we have or whatever you want to call it, I think it's best if we forget each other exists. I don't expect to be hearing from you ever again. I'm moving on with my life. *My* life, controlled by me alone."

My parents have contradictory expressions. My father's jaw is locked, his lips pinched, and his nostrils flaring slightly. My mother, however, actually looks sad and remorseful although I can't be sure it's for the right reason. Neither one affects me. I'm just...done.

Briefly glancing between them one final time, I say, "Goodbye" and step out the door. I walk down the driveway without a look back.

The cab picks me up within five minutes of leaving my past behind me. I direct the driver to drop me at the bus station. I could have taken the cab all the way to Sugar, but it seems fitting to use the bus since it's my choice this time, not a necessity. Last time, I was running away from my life. This time, however, I'm running toward it. Hopefully, it's waiting for me in Sugar because Levi is everything I ever dreamed of wanting.

39

Him

My boots thump on the front porch as the screen door slams shut behind me. I have no plan in mind for how I'm going to deal with Sam's parents, but I *will* get answers. I look up and come to a complete halt because what I see can't be real. I must be dreaming.

There, at the end of the walkway, is Sam. She is a vision, the best mirage I've ever seen. She looks just as she did the first time I spoke to her at the store checkout, determined, sad, and scared. I swallow hard and feel like I can't breathe.

"Sam?" I croak.

With her voice shaking, words rush out of her. "I know you may not want me here, but I couldn't stay away. Not until you understood why I left. I needed to tell you it wasn't you. I never wanted to leave you, Levi. I had to. I had to face the things I was running from in order to be free. I couldn't be with you with my past hanging over my head. It wasn't fair to us, to you. You deserve to be with someone who's with you completely without any reservations. I'm sorry I lied, so sorry. But, if I told you what was going on, you would have tried to keep me from leaving. Or, you would have wanted to help and I couldn't risk you getting hurt. If anything had happened to you because of my past, well, I couldn't have lived with that. I know you're probably angry with me, and I don't blame you. You have every right to be. I just hope you can forgive me, even if we can't be together." Tears are streaming down her face by the time she's done.

"And?" Still in shock from seeing her, I have no clue what I'm asking her. I can only manage to force the one word out of my throat.

"And, I know I was wrong. You asked me to trust you. You never gave me any reason not to. I just couldn't tell you about this. It wasn't that I didn't trust you, because I do, in every way. I couldn't tell you because I had to do this for me. I had to prove to myself I'm strong enough and that I'm not anything like my parents. You deserve that, to have someone as strong as you are who'll stand by your side through everything. And I will, if you'll have me, because I love you."

My entire world shifts and redefines itself with those three words. She loves me.

My feet still haven't moved because I need to know one last thing. "It's all done then? Everything you had to do?"

A disheartened look crosses her face as she answers, "Yes, it's finished."

Gruffly, I nod, "Good."

She stuffs her tiny fists into her pockets. "Okay, well, I should leave you alone then. Take care of yourself, Levi" she says as she turns to leave.

Wait, what? She's leaving?

Rushing down the steps, I call, "Sam!"

Glancing over her shoulder with hope in her eyes, she asks, "Yeah?"

I stop three feet in front of her. "Where are you going?"

She looks around with confusion and bites her bottom lip. "Um, I said everything I came here to say. I figured it was time for me to go. I thought you didn't want me."

244

I can't help looking at her as if she's lost her mind. "Not want you? You just told me you loved me."

She hesitates before replying softly, "Well, yes, but you didn't say it back."

I suddenly realize I'm the one causing the confusion. If I stay stuck in neutral, I'm going to screw up my chances with this woman for a second time.

Mentally, kicking myself in the ass, I tell her, "Because I'm an idiot, clearly." The corner of her mouth turns up into a small smile. I breathe deeply then make a simple request. "Tell me again. Please."

When she faces me, her eyes are sparkling with gold. She is beaming with the brilliance of a thousand suns as she whispers the sweetest words I've ever heard. "I love you, Levi."

Falling on my good knee, I bury my face in her belly. My arms lock around her waist. I'm terrified of letting go. My shoulders shake as relief heaves out of me and I weep uncontrollably. I have no pride left. If I had lost this woman forever, I would be nothing, except a shell.

Her fingers tunnel through my hair as she comforts me. "Shh, shh. Oh, Levi. It's going to be okay."

I know it will be okay now that she's with me. But, I have to hear from her that she's willing to stay. "Promise me. Promise me you're not going to leave me."

Without a single moment of hesitation, she pledges herself to me. "I promise."

Her arms grip my shoulders as she lays her cheek on top of my head. I listen to the steady heartbeat of the woman I love, savoring this moment. I will remember it always. She is here with me. She is strong and caring, and makes me want to be better, for myself and for her.

Finally, I stand and cup her cheeks with both my hands. I kiss her lips reverently then lean my forehead against hers. "I love you, Sam."

She hiccups softly, "You do?"

Smiling, I tell her what I believe and then make my own vow to her. "I think I have loved you since that first day in the store. I promise, Sam, I promise to be everything you deserve. To never let you question for one second if you are loved or wanted. I promise to be strong. Together."

Agreeing, she says, "Together, always."

I shower her with kisses, leaving her lips for last. Taking my time when I get there, I pour everything I feel for her into the kiss until I sense her knees go weak. I burn with satisfaction at knowing I'm responsible for that and commit to making it happen at every opportunity for the rest of our days.

Epilogue

Him

The sun is starting to peek above the mountains in my beautiful Kentucky town. I feel like I've been hit by a truck. I have a crick in my neck, a charley-horse in my side, and my arm is asleep from Sam leaning on it all night. I'm uncomfortable as hell, but I wouldn't trade this moment for anything in the world. Other than the fact that I'd rather be in my own bed, making love to the woman of my dreams.

After Sam returned home and practically had to be pried from my grasp, we talked about everything that had happened. I'm not sorry to admit I'm glad Richard Whitman is gone. However, my heart broke when Sam found out Miss Sarah had collapsed shortly after seeing her leave with Richard. She sobbed uncontrollably. She insisted we come to the hospital to see her. She swore it was her fault. I know how that kind of bullshit story a person tells themselves can turn out. It took some convincing, but I think she finally believes me when I tell her it's not. No matter the case though, Sam made us come directly here to sit by Miss Sarah's bedside, refusing to leave.

She's told the nurses they'll have to physically throw us both out to be rid of us. I do love her sass, though I think the staff might have actually considered removing her bodily, if it wasn't for me. Even though I haven't said a word, I think my presence is a sufficient deterrent to keep them from completing the task. I don't mind being the brawn to her brains.

So, here we've been, sleeping on this horrible couch in a cramped hospital room. Me with my feet

247

propped on a coffee table while Sam is curled against me. I'm in heaven.

The only thing that makes the day better is Miss Sarah being released. The doctors are still vague in their diagnosis for her, saying with her age, her collapsing was a result of stress and exhaustion. It was her body's way of telling her to start taking it easy and enjoy life without so much stress. I have my own theory that it was caused by a broken heart when Sam left. Having no children of her own, I saw Miss Sarah take to Sam more than anyone I've ever known. Yes, she's a mother hen to all who know her, but with Sam it was different, more personal. When she left, Miss Sarah's heart broke from having lost a child. That kind of loss is unimaginable. I know a similar feeling from when I lost my parents.

Thankfully, Miss Sarah is now on the mend although it's the doctor's advice that she has even more help at the store. I suppose we'll have to fight with her about that. She's not likely to let other people run her store. I'm hoping if Sam and I can maintain a united front, we can convince her to listen.

Sam stirs next to me, yawning and stretching.

"Hey," she says with a smile.

I brush my lips over hers softly as I cup her cheek. "Good mornin' darlin'."

Looking uncertain, she asks shyly, "Sleep well?"

"Slept fine. You don't have to worry," I assure her.

When we had a moment to talk after she came back, I told Sam I had set an appointment to see a therapist to help deal with my guilt and nightmares. I know it won't be smooth sailing all the time, but I'm hopeful for good results. I think once I start talking about all my crap, it'll be easier to unload and finally let it go. I might always feel somewhat responsible for the accident because of all that it cost Dylan. I'm starting to realize though everything happened the way it was supposed to for me to get where I am. I just have to keep moving forward.

Sam looks over at Miss Sarah. She whispers, "Do you think she's awake?"

"Of course, I'm awake, you silly girl," Miss Sarah says. "I run a business that opens with the rooster's crow."

Sam glances up at me indicating it's time to say something to Miss Sarah about taking it easy. I clear my throat to begin.

"Yeah, about that, Miss Sarah. You know, the doctor says..."

"I know perfectly well what the doctor says, Levi," she reprimands sternly. "And that's why I've come to a decision."

"A decision?" both Sam and I question at the same time.

Frankly, she says, "Yes, a decision, but it depends on you, Sam." Miss Sarah's face glows with a mischievous smirk.

"Me? What about me?" Sam sputters.

Pulling her face into a frown, Miss Sarah looks down her nose at Sam. "Well, I need to know if you are staying in Sugar for good this time."

Blushing and then looking at me, she beams, "Yes, I'm staying. For always."

"Okay, then. I think it's time for someone else to run the store," she states firmly.

Sam moves to the edge of the couch, giving Miss Sarah her full attention.

"You're giving up the store? But, Miss Sarah, who can run the store as well as you?"

Smiling widely, she glances between the two of us. "Why, you, of course, my sweet girl."

Stunned, Sam stares wide-eyed at Miss Sarah. "Me?" she parrots.

"Yes, you and Levi, although I'm putting the store in your name. I mean I'll expect to put my two cents in from time to time, but I'm sure you two can handle things just fine." There is a satisfied smile on Miss Sarah's face.

"My name?" Sam repeats. "I don't know what to say."

She gazes up at me to find the right answer. There is only one.

I tell her, "You simply say yes, darlin'."

Beaming, she skips across the room to hug Miss Sarah, saying, "Yes! Thank you."

"It's absolutely my pleasure, Sam," she chuckles. "I know you'll do a wonderful job."

Overjoyed for my girl, I watch as my self-made family binds together. I'm stuck with them and I couldn't be happier.

Dylan enters the room in the midst of the celebration. Taking in the hugging and tears on both the women's faces, he misreads the situation. Sounding worried, he questions, "Hey, hey, what's going on?"

Putting him at ease, I inform him about what's happening. "It's good news, man. Don't worry. Miss Sarah is turning over the store to Sam."

"And to you!" Sam exclaims.

Winking at her, I tease, "I'm just here for the heavy lifting." Sam blushes as her eyes travel down over my chest and arms. I do so love that blush.

Relaxing, Dylan smiles. "Well, congratulations! Sam, I have no doubt you'll do great."

"Thanks, Dylan. That means a lot coming from you," Sam replies.

Suddenly, the door crashes into Dylan's shoulder, nearly knocking him off his feet. "Son of a b....," Dylan stops himself just short of finishing his expletive.

Flying through the opening rushes a slender, raven haired beauty. She doesn't appear to notice if anyone is in her way. She also seems like she'll simply mow them down if they are.

"Aunt Sarah!" she wails.

"Jasmine?" Surprise clear on Miss Sarah's face and in her voice.

Dylan, Sam, and I simply stare at each other. Sam slides out of Miss Sarah's embrace and comes back to sit with me, tucking in close. I have no idea who this woman is. However, she obviously knows Miss Sarah, and vice versa.

Miss Sarah continues, "Jasmine, what are you doing here?"

The girl cries out in disbelief, "You're in the hospital! Where else should I be?"

"How did you find out I was here?" she asks calmly.

As if the answer should be obvious, the girl admits, "Well, Grandma Dottie, of course."

"Hmm, of course," she agrees then says, "I just didn't expect you to show up here."

Slightly annoyed, the girl huffs, "Aunt Sarah, you're in the hospital."

"Yes, dear. I know." It's apparent from Miss Sarah's mocking tone that she's used to dealing with the girl's attitude and isn't bothered by it at all.

Suddenly remembering they have an audience, Miss Sarah looks over to us. She makes a round of introductions.

"Jasmine, I'm sorry. I've been rude. Everyone, this is my great-niece Jasmine Bishop, Dottie's granddaughter. Jasmine, this is Levi Taylor, Joan and Roger Taylor's son, his girlfriend, Sam Brooks, and his best friend, Dylan Reed."

Jasmine looks at each of us. She regards us with an air of superiority. Her eyes land on Dylan last and her lip practically curls into a sneer. I've never seen a woman have such a reaction to him. This girl is an ice princess.

Having recovered from his near face-plant on the tile floor, Dylan interjects, "You know it's often polite to say excuse me when you run into someone. Maybe even offer an apology." He stands glowering at her with his arms crossed over his chest.

Completely, unfazed by the chill in his tone, Jasmine narrows her eyes at him. "Excuse me?"

"So, you do know the words," he says. Sarcasm drips from every word.

Bristling, she replies, "I don't know who you are exactly, but I'm here to see my aunt. You'll have to forgive me if your feelings are not my priority."

Obviously offended, he spits out, "No, I don't think will. You haven't even apologized yet." Dylan is beyond exasperated.

Sounding like a petulant child, she snaps, "And why should I?" Jasmine's tone is snippy and rude. "I mean, really, you shouldn't be standing in front of a closed door." With that, she thoroughly dismisses Dylan by turning her back to him and talks softly with Miss Sarah.

Dylan glances at me, looking frustrated, awed, and bewildered. Finally, he throws up his hands and stalks out of the room.

Sam and I have watched the entire scene unfold in front of us in rapt fascination. I've never seen Dylan Reed riled up by a woman, any woman. He's usually all easy-going charm and Southern manners. However, this woman seems to have pushed every button he has and without any remorse.

All I can do is smile and shake my head because I know my best friend. He will most certainly take this woman's disdain for him as a challenge. And that means my brother is in for one hell of a roller coaster ride.

Miss Dottie's Peach Cobbler Recipe
(created & taste-tested by the fabulous, Jamie)

Filling:
5-6 cups peaches peeled and sliced (fresh or frozen)
¼ cup brandy or peach brandy (water can be used if you want to omit alcohol)
1-1.5 cups sugar (depending on how sweet you like it)
3 T. cornstarch 2 T. cold water
¼ t. nutmeg
1 t. cinnamon
1 t. lemon zest (optional) Pinch of salt

Crust:
6 T. butter, chilled
2 T. shortening or lard, chilled
1 cup all-purpose flour plus extra for rolling the dough
½ t. salt
¼ cup ice water

Freeze the butter and shortening (or lard) for 15 minutes. Cut into small pieces. In a medium mixing bowl combine flour and salt. Using a pastry cutter or fork, cut in shortening or lard and butter until pieces are the size of small peas. Sprinkle with 1 tablespoon of ice water and mix. Repeat with 1 tablespoon of water at a time until the mixture can hold together when squeezed. Form the dough into a disk, put it in a freezer bag, and freeze for 30 minutes.

In a large pan over medium heat combine peaches, brandy, sugar, nutmeg, and cinnamon. Combine cornstarch and 2 T. of cold water to make a slurry. Add slurry to the peaches and cook for 5 minutes. Remove from heat and let cool slightly.

Meanwhile, remove the dough from the freezer, flour your work surface, and roll the crust out to ¼" thick.

Cut ½" wide strips if doing a lattice top.

Grease a 2 qt. casserole dish or a 9" x 9" pan, add peach mixture, top with crust (you can sprinkle course sugar and cinnamon on the top) and bake at 375 degrees for 40-50 minutes. When the crust is golden remove the cobbler from the oven and let cool 45-60 minutes.

Note from the Author

This story is obviously fiction. I have the romance and happy ending to make everyone feel good. However, I know it touches on some difficult topics and I wanted to talk a little bit about that. I have always admired anyone who has served in our military. It takes an incredible person to decide to serve our country and sacrifice for others to maintain our freedom. I can't begin to know what it's like to go to war and come home changed, to put your life in someone else's hands while holding theirs in yours, to lose friends so quickly, or to be injured simply doing your job.

I talk about my character sustaining an injury that costs him his career and allude to him experiencing PTSD along with depression. I know this is a reality for so many. These are difficult issues, which is putting it mildly. Unfortunately, I can't spend two thousand pages showing how my character tries to deal with everything. Besides, I could barely scratch the surface in that amount of space. Instead, I tell a story that makes it all nice and pretty even though that's not the reality. The reality is often dark and ugly. I wish it wasn't.

I understand that nothing is as simple as it appears when written in a book. I know that people don't move past the things they experience in a matter of days, weeks, or even months. Sometimes, they never get over them. I wish it were as simple as just choosing to let go of all the bad stuff. However, it's never that easy.

I wish that those who choose to serve didn't have to come back home changed forever, whether it's physically, emotionally, or mentally. The sacrifice they make and the price they pay are exorbitantly high.

So, even though it doesn't begin to cover the depth of my gratitude, I wanted to say, "THANK YOU". And let it be known that the sacrifice and dedication is appreciated. Using characters that I so often think of as heroes and warriors is my way, small as it is, of paying tribute to them and honoring them. I pray they all find their own happy endings.

With sincere gratitude,
Emily

Acknowledgements

I have to admit as a reader I never used to pay attention to the Acknowledgements pages in books. I just sort of skipped right over them. Then, the more I read, I started to wonder why the pages were there. As I began to write my own stuff, I read through some from my favorite authors' pages. They show a real side to authors and all the craziness we go through to complete a book. And sometimes it isn't pretty, but it can be extremely funny. They also show how the finished product is a collaboration of so many different people who help us authors get to where we want to be. Those people deserve thanks and recognition. That discovery has solidified my belief on the importance of Acknowledgement pages. The people who help me and keep me sane deserve to be recognized. So, even though my clan is small at the moment, I know I would be lost without them! Here goes.

First, I have to thank my thesaurus. I would be lost without it and probably still staring at the computer screen using the same one hundred words! I also have to thank the comma for which there is a love/hate relationship. I love it. My assistant/editor hates it.

Next, I have to thank my cheering squad. They are friends and family who have given me so much love and support from the moment I said, "I'm writing a book." Thank you from the bottom of my heart to Laura, Kim, Diana, Susan, Jamie, Marjory, Val, Robin, and Gay. If I left anyone out, I apologize, but know that any time anyone said, "Way to go!" it meant the world to me and kept me believing in myself. An extra special thanks goes to Jamie for taking on the challenge of creating "Miss Dottie's peach cobbler recipe". I have no doubt the taste testing was a hardship!

Then, there is the new person on my team, Karlie Hyder. I am truly amazed by her and her talent. She whips together my covers so beautifully and never complains when I feel like I am constantly saying, "Can you fix this one little thing?" She is always so sweet and just smiles, saying, "Of course." My words on the page wouldn't look any good without her efforts. Thank you! I hope to keep you incredibly busy!

And next, I have to thank Maegan. She is so valuable to me that she gets her own individual paragraph. Thank you for being my person. You help me whenever I need it. You take on any task I give you. You calm my fears, motivate me, keep me sane, and smack me in the back of the head (figuratively, usually) when I need it. I honestly don't think I could do this without you. I definitely know it wouldn't be as much fun.

Finally, I have to thank my husband and my children. The house never looks the way I want it to, laundry is often in baskets, and dinners are many times easy things to fix, but I never hear a complaint. I know I've said, "In a minute" or "Hold on" too many times to count over the last months because I couldn't stop in the middle of my thought. Or gone to bed extremely late and gotten up grumpy due to writing because I wanted make sure I didn't lose the scene in my head. And yet, I still get, "Thanks Mom", "You're the best", "I love you", and support that fills my heart. I appreciate (more than you know) you allowing me the time to accomplish a dream.

Emily

About the Author

Emily Gray is an author of contemporary romance and romantic suspense. Her debut novel, *The Marine*, is part of her Heroes & Warriors series, focusing on flawed, but passionate men and women, who find love when it is least expected.

She lives in Florida with her husband, four out of five of her children, and the biggest baby of all, her dog, Bear. When she's not immersed in the lives of her characters, she's trying to maintain some balance while juggling the hectic schedules of her family.

For updates on upcoming releases and other information, you can visit her at www.emilygray.org or www.facebook.com/authoremilygray. Follow her page at www.facebook.com/emilygrayauthor. If you enjoyed *The Marine*, please consider writing a review at https://www.goodreads.com/emilygray.

Thanks for reading and look for Ace & Cat's book, *The Fighter.*

Made in the USA
Columbia, SC
23 June 2019